A Summer of Dandelions

MEADOW HILLS

A Summer of Dandelions

CAREFREE

One Carefree Day

One Day Too Late

Something Bright and Burning

A Summer of Dandelions

WHITNEY AMAZEEN

*For my cousin, Haley.
You're my real-life Miss Meadow.*

There isn't one question that will keep you up longer at night than the question, "What if I didn't give up?"

Captain Deshauna Barber, Miss USA 2016

Playlist

Dandelions —Ruth B
Sunflower, Vol. 6 —Harry Styles
Records —The Ivy
Invisible String —Taylor Swift
Chartreuse —Capital Cities
golden hour —JVKE
Absolutely —Ra Ra Riot
Feather —Sabrina Carpenter
Bloom —Matilda Mann
Amerika —Young the Giant
Sweet Nothing —Taylor Swift

A Summer of Dandelions

Chapter One

ADDISON

THIS APPOINTMENT IS PURELY PRECAUTIONARY.

I really don't believe myself to be pregnant, since the huge mistake of sleeping with my then-boyfriend only happened twice, with protection. My menstrual cycle isn't late. I'm symptom free. But still, I need to make sure, because of all the rules a Miss Meadow contestant must follow, I refuse to let this be the one that gets me eliminated.

To qualify, every candidate must be:

1. A permanent resident in the town of Meadow Hills, Maine, for at least three years prior to entering, and remain a resident through the pageant.

2. Between 18 and 26 years old.

3. Unmarried and must never have been married or had a marriage annulled/divorced.

4. Sponsored by a local business exclusive to Meadow Hills.

Those rules are all fine and dandy. I don't plan on

breaking any of them within the next year and a half. The one I'm currently sweating about—as I sit in the exam room with my nails crunched between my teeth—is number five:

Contestants must never have birthed a child or been a parent/guardian to any adults or minors, and cannot currently be pregnant.

I knew I should have never broken my wait-till-marriage pact.

I imagine sending a text to my roommate, Bronwyn. Saying something along the lines of, *Hypothetically speaking, would you still let me live with you if Asher got me pregnant?* Knowing her, she'd probably tell me no in all three languages she's fluent in. But then again, we need each other so we can afford to share our crappy apartment without having to pay a high price for rent.

I tap my hands on the plastic bed in the doctors office, swinging my feet as I sit perched on the very edge. The suspense is killing me. I mean, both of the tests I took at home were negative. But there's still that part of me that's terrified they were wrong, especially since the start of the pageant is only four months away.

Those two times with my ex, and now all this. The possibility of not being able to compete for the Miss Meadow title. My dream. *Gran's* dream.

"Addison Ellsworth?"

My head snaps up when I hear the nurse call my name. He peeks his head through before entering my room and offers me a reserved, sad smile. "Your pregnancy test came back negative."

I pump both fists in the air, whooping loudly. A chorus of victory sings in my chest. "Really? You promise?"

He backs away, releasing a surprised laugh. "Yes. It was highly unlikely you'd produce a positive test, given your current contraception."

I nod. "This may seem backwards, but I want my IUD taken out. I won't be needing it anymore, starting today."

"Oh." He blinks at my bluntness. "Of course. I'll tell the doctor and we'll get that taken care of for you."

"I'm going to be the next Miss Meadow," I continue, my words spilling out of me. "Which means I can't get pregnant, or everything I've worked for will be for nothing. So, I guess I'll just have to avoid, uh, intercourse from here on out. Which is what I want to do."

He offers me a tight nod and inches backward toward the door. "Got it."

"It's my last year to win. Next year I'll be twenty-seven. That's a year too old."

"Mhm." He clears his throat. "Like I said, I'll get the doctor, Miss Ellsworth."

He disappears, leaving me pacing the room with joy, still wound up from my unrequested monologue.

Nothing, *nothing* will stop me from winning this year. It's all I want in the world. It's everything I've worked for. It was my grandma's dying wish.

And there's no way I'll let her down.

Once I'm safely and securely de-birth-controlled, I drive home. 'Home' is really just the loose term I use for the room I rent from Bronwyn. I'm not allowed to loiter in her common areas, including the living room or kitchen.

A pre-packaged parfait is waiting for me in the fridge,

and it gets scanned straight into my food-tracking app. I try not to make noise as I retrieve a spoon from the chipped cabinet drawer, so Bronwyn doesn't yell at me, and speed-walk to my room.

My unmade bed, which literally takes up my entire bedroom, is my favorite sight in the whole world. I jump onto it like I'm cannonballing into a swimming pool. While I eat my parfait, I watch videos of past Miss Meadow winners on my laptop. It's my favorite way to prepare for the pageant, and it's also a great distraction from the fact that Asher has probably already moved on in the month we've been broken up. He's probably found someone chill, unlike me. Someone who's willing to go with the flow and keep "putting out."

I reach between my mattress for the booklet that lives there, fingering the worn cover once I'm holding it in front of me. *Hymns of Praise.* The gold lettering is so familiar to me, it brings me right back to my childhood, standing next to Gran at church while we sang the songs in this book. I'd try to make my voice sound light and feathery like hers, instead of scratchy and off-key. I remember resisting the urge to pull my wedgie, because Gran never did things like that at church. "Stand up straight. Sing your praise to the Lord," she'd say, a bright smile crinkling her eyes.

She'd slip the hymn book out of her purse and into my hand at every service, and I'd play with the folds on the corners of the paper cover, just like I am now. Sometimes, when I miss Gran, or I'm feeling sad, I take it out and read some of the hymns, remembering the way her voice sounded when she'd sung them. It's the closest thing I have to a hug.

I say a quick prayer, asking God for this to be the year I finally win the pageant, and for strength to not have another slip-up like Asher.

When it's time for work, I quickly get dressed and brush my teeth. I'm about to rush out the door but stop in my tracks when I notice Bronwyn glaring at me from the couch in the living room. She stands up, tilting her head sideways. "Why did you go to the doctor to have a pregnancy test done?"

"How do you even know—"

"This was on the floor. It must have fallen out of your purse." She thrusts a pack of papers at me. The title of the front page reads, *Understanding Your Negative Pregnancy Test.*

I close my eyes. Great. "I just wanted to make sure. But it was negative, see? No big deal."

She narrows her gaze at me. "Are you and Asher being safe?"

"We broke up a month ago." As I say it, I realize she's probably wondering why I didn't tell her sooner. And the answer is because I didn't know how to bring it up. Bronwyn and I like to stay surface-level, never treading deep enough into our "friendship" to require a life jacket. Besides, crying over break-ups is something I save to do with my best friend, Romilly.

After a long pause, Bronwyn clears her throat. "Got it. Sorry."

I tug down the sleeve of my cardigan. "It's fine. I have to go to work. See you later."

When I pass her to finally reach the door, she says

almost too quietly to hear, "Don't forget, rent is due next week."

If anyone were to check my search history, they'd see how many jobs I've applied for in the past hour, and they'd probably laugh at my desperation. But if you were a server who slapped a customer at a fine-dining establishment, wouldn't you want to avoid showing your face there again?

Before I start the car to head to work, I read the most recent email application I sent last night. I scan my attached resume—pink, of course—and cross my fingers that this nanny job will call me because it's the highest paying position I've found so far. It's perfect for me, since I used to nanny in high school and my long-term goal is to work with kids someday.

Asher calls me on my way to work. I press ignore so fast, I almost regret it, because I have to admit, I'm curious why he's contacting me for the first time in a month, but not curious enough to answer. Asher can bite me. Actually, he can't. Currently, I want him nowhere near my bitable body parts, or in my general vicinity.

I try not to think about the six months I wasted with him when I know perfectly well dating is a bad idea in my situation. The last thing I need is a man to distract me from becoming the next Miss Meadow. Yes, he was a fun way to pass the time, but it was a risk allowing myself to get close to him. Dating leads to falling in love, or in our case, to *sex*. Dating also leads to marriage and babies, both of which are impossible for me right now because of the pageant.

I know this, and yet, I still found myself wanting to see him, eating foods with him that aren't part of my regimen. I let him sway my core values and beliefs because it felt good to be the center of someone's attention for once. As the host for Miss Meadow, he's always been around, and we've gotten closer year after year. First, as friends, and inevitably, we became more. But getting on birth control made me feel sick, and squashing my waiting-till-marriage hopes for him—someone who never truly valued me—left me feeling foolish and regretful.

But when I finally got it through to him that I wanted to stop sleeping together after only two times, and go back to the pact I started with Romilly, he winced at me. "There are other girls in the world," he said. "You can't possibly think I plan on marrying you, Addison. You're pretty and all, but you're really nothing special." Hearing that was like a punch to the gut. It's one thing to have a sinking fear you've never told anyone else, but it's another to have someone voice it as truth.

When I get to the packed parking lot of Rosemary Banquet, I pull my brown, curly hair into a high ponytail, apply a layer of lipstick, and dust some blush and high-lighter on my cheekbones to add contrast to my dark skin. I'm right on time for today's nine-hour shift. Unfortu-nately, I'll have to face my co-workers today. The memory of last night flashes through my mind. The way the two men at one of my tables kept making jokes about Lyle, one of our regulars, unfolding and refolding his linen napkin for the duration of his meal.

Nobody makes fun of Lyle. Not on my watch. I don't care if those new customers were unaware of his sensory issues. It wasn't cool. So, I slapped one of them, and it shut them both up real quick. But now I have to face the consequences.

I enter the tall white building and blink as my eyes adjust to the warm glow of the intricate chandeliers hanging from the ceiling. Even after working here for a year, my mouth waters when the smell of the exquisitely prepared food hits my nose. Weaving through the white linen table-clothed settings, I exchange smiles and waves with my co-workers on my way to the kitchen where I clock in.

My manager, Lillian, is back there with a frown and crossed arms. Standing next to her is a stranger so handsome my jaw practically becomes unhinged. Though he's dressed in slacks and a button-down, something about him looks unkept. Maybe it's the fine stubble surrounding his mouth and jaw, or the dark shadows beneath his hazel eyes. He and Lillian are engaged in a serious conversation from the look of it, their voices in hushed tones I can't discern. They go back and forth for a while. I glue my eyes to the stranger's face as he balls a fist into his messy, dark hair, and for the briefest moment, our eyes meet. I stare at him for a moment too long, and then heat creeps up my neck. My gaze darts away immediately.

When they're done talking, he leaves through the back door. I try to come out of my daze as I finally clock in, my nerves in a jitter.

"Addison?" Lillian is at my side, her mouth down-turned. "Sweetie, let's talk in my office."

I frown. "Um, okay?"

I follow her past the kitchen to the tiny office near the

back exit. I've been in here countless times. The first time was a year ago for my interview, and the second time was to go over some onboarding information once Lillian hired me. I spend the end of every shift in here, tipping out at the end of the night. But for some reason, seeing her back in her leather office chair behind her oak desk brings back all the memories of when I first started here. I take a seat in the chair on the other side of her desk.

She sighs, running her fingers through her blond hair. Then she turns on her essential oil diffuser, as if it will help her avoid whatever's on her mind. Once the scent of peppermint fills the room, she blurts, "Honey, we have to talk about yesterday."

It's the sentence I've been dreading, but I know she's right. I nod grimly. "I'm so sorry. I don't know what came over me. I just couldn't handle them making fun of Lyle like that!"

Her smile is tight. "I get it. And I know it probably struck something in you because of your brother." I flinch at that, but she continues. "But they almost sought legal action because of what you did."

My eyes round into saucers. "Are you serious?"

She calms my rising voice with a hand. "Don't worry. I talked them down from the lawsuit they threatened to file by offering them free appetizers for a year. But this could have been bad. Really bad."

"I get it." I take a steadying breath. My insides are swirling like a merry-go-round. "I'll be more careful from now on. This won't happen again."

Lillian bites her lip. "Actually, Sweetie . . . you're being let go."

"Excuse me?" My brain struggles to catch up with her sentence.

"Our new owner was in a few minutes ago and he made the call himself. Told me he can't have someone like you as a liability being part of the staff." Lillian studies her desk, unable to look at me. "I tried to defend you, but he wasn't having it. Sorry."

So that handsome stranger was the new owner? Wow. As gorgeous as he was, knowing he'd come in and just have me outright fired like this kind of makes me miss the blunt gruffness of Frank, the old owner. He was intimidating, but always liked the way I worked when he'd come observe. He might have at least given me a chance to explain, even if he never could remember my name, or the fact that he'd met me the last time he came in. And the times before that.

I blink away my stupor and get up from my seat. "No, it's . . . alright I guess. I'll be fine. I understand."

I think she says something else, but I don't catch it because I'm rushing out of the restaurant I've worked at for the past year, back to my car where I can cry in peace, if necessary. I shut the door to my red Kia Rio and cover my face with my hands.

All those long days spent with my co-workers. All the times Lillian and I couldn't wait to talk about the most recent episode of the K-Drama we're both watching. Me getting to know her. Her getting to know me. The astronomical tips I'd receive from nearly every table I'd wait on. The *regulars*. Lyle.

It's all over now. A sob bursts through my chest. And then I start the car and drive. I don't listen to music the entire way, which is a new low for me. I'd like to consider myself fairly optimistic, but today has felt like one big suck-fest from the moment I woke up.

I park in my assigned spot outside the apartment fifteen minutes later. I'm not ready to go inside yet, so I open my phone and scroll through my notifications. I see the missed call from Asher, along with several messages from him.

ASHER

Is there something you need to tell me?

ME

Yes, actually. I hope you step in dog poop on your way home and track it all throughout your apartment.

ASHER

Wow. I meant do you have something to tell me about being pregnant? Bronwyn said I should ask you.

That traitor. I knew I shouldn't have given her his phone number when we started dating in case of an unlikely emergency!

ME

No Asher. Not pregnant, just fired. Now leave me alone.

ASHER

I know you're still all hung up on me, but I swear, if you're trying to trap me with a baby . . .

I stare at the message, cheeks burning. He really thinks I'd do that? I mean, yeah it hurt when he dumped me. But the idea that I'd be so torn up over losing him that I'd have to trap him? It's embarrassing. I'm not sitting around moping after him, and I need him to know it.

Before I can stop myself, I'm already typing the response.

ME

> Actually, I'm already seeing someone else. I think he might be the one . . . I've never felt like this before.

ASHER

> Lol. Sure.

> If it's that serious, he'd be the perfect topic for your preliminary interview with me. Can't wait to meet him.

My stomach drops.
Great.

ME

> Yes. Yes, you will. Can't wait to introduce you.

Chapter Two

PERRY

NO MATTER how many times I've heard it, I can never really prepare myself for Dad's booming voice on the other end of a call.

"You better get yourself over there, Perry, before I have to."

There's no use explaining that I'm already in my car, halfway to Violet Villa Square, where my restaurant, Rosemary Banquet, stands. I've been on my way since the customer notified me, stating that yesterday, one of my employees *slapped* him. Apparently, he's not going to seek legal action, but just wanted me, the new owner, to know what kind of employees are working at my restaurant.

I stay silent as Dad continues to berate me on the other end of the phone, because defending myself will do much more harm than good.

"This is what's wrong with your generation," he continues. I can practically quote him at this point, but I smartly keep my lips closed. "You're all lazy. None of you want to work anymore. You just let customers leave unhappy. You let someone leave an establishment I built from the ground up—a restaurant I've entrusted to you—after being slapped in the face. Unbelievable."

"I'm almost there, Dad. Believe me, I'll take care of it."

"Oh, I know you will. Otherwise, you'll be going from restaurant owner to server quicker than I can snap my fingers."

I sigh. "I'm sure there's a good explanation for what happened."

A pause. I imagine steam coming out of his ears as he rears up to bark back at me again. "If you so much as accept a single excuse from any of the staff, I'll come down there myself and clean the place out. How am I supposed to retire knowing you'll be running my business like this? You get rid of the employee who harassed my customers, and you leave, Perry. Understand?"

I nod, and then remember he can't see me. "Yes."

I hang up the phone as I park in the parking lot. I send the manager, Lillian, a quick text that I'm here before going inside.

My dad has been training me to take over for him these past six months, mostly back-end stuff. I haven't had the chance to meet much of the staff yet, except Lillian, so I have no idea who's responsible for this mess. From what I know of her so far, Lillian is a sweet girl and a great business person. It surprises me that something like this happened under her watch.

She's already at the entrance when I walk in. "She didn't mean it," she says before I can even get a word out. "Addy is one of our best servers, and she's never done anything like this before." She fiddles with the end of her blond braid.

I walk with her to the back as I answer her. "While I'm sure that's true, she's being let go. It's already decided."

Her eyes round, but I swallow down my pity. My dad was clear. I can't accept any excuses.

"Can she at least finish today's shift?"

I shake my head. "Sorry, but that's probably not appropriate." Poor girl. She probably has no idea she's about to get fired. The thought makes me ball a fist in my hair.

I feel someone's gaze burning into me from afar, and I glance up to find a woman in a serving uniform who looks like she's in her twenties. Her face is so stunning, I get distracted for a moment. She has golden bronze skin and full pink lips. Her dark hair is pulled up into a ponytail, and the way she's looking at me reminds me of a child seeing a new animal at the zoo for the first time.

The eye contact makes her blush, and she quickly looks away.

I clear my throat, trying to remember what I was just saying to Lillian. "She'll have to leave immediately, and she isn't eligible for rehire."

Lillian's eyes gloss over, but she nods. "If I could just explain—"

"That's not necessary." It pains me to cut off her sentence like that, but I also can't let my dad be right about me. As much as I try not to let the insults like soft boy, weakling, or spineless affect me, they really do. And I hate that.

I go over some termination details with her before I

exit out the back door. Lillian's disappointment practically embeds itself inside me.

It seems like no matter what I do, I'm disappointing someone.

❧

For a five-foot-one Russian fifty-year-old, Yvette can be quite terrifying. Her latest scowl makes me shrink back as she shoots it in my direction. "I thought I made myself clear when I said that I quit." Her naturally pink complexion is made more intense by all the increased blood flow to her face. In her defense, she has every right to be angry. It's been two-weeks since she first notified me she'll no longer be a live-in nanny to my four children—two sets of twins—which gives her every right to pack her bags and dip out while she still can.

And she has. Packed her bags, that is. But with a restaurant to manage that just took up my entire morning, I haven't had enough time to hire a replacement for Yvette.

"Yes, of course you were clear," I say. My hands come together in a praying position. "But I haven't found a replacement yet, and I really need the help. Please, Yvette."

She curses in Russian. Her blouse is torn, half hanging from her torso, and a colorful pattern of children's hand-prints covers her jeans in acrylic paint. I'm pretty sure she didn't buy them like that. "You need help, alright. I've never met such terrible kids in my life."

Ouch. No matter how many times I've heard that one, it still seems to hurt the same every time. I reach out toward Yvette, but instead of touching her shoulder, I fist the empty air. "Please, try to understand. They've lost their mother. It's only been a year."

Some of the ferocity on her face dims. "That's right. I'm sorry for your loss."

I don't bother correcting her, telling her Jill isn't dead, just gone. Off with some other guy, because our life together didn't meet her expectations. But I keep those details to myself, because I really need her pity right now, and I'm definitely not too proud to take it.

"Yet, it changes nothing," she continues. "I am leaving now, and you must accept it."

The nanny I desperately need right now picks up the duffel bag at her feet. She rolls her larger suitcase in her other hand and ignores my weak attempts at hearing me out as she crosses the foyer to the front door. Her sneakers make a wet, squishing sound the entire way.

She slams the door shut behind her.

Wonderful.

"Daddy?"

I glance down at my side to find Izzy staring up at me with her large, curious brown eyes. "Is she leaving because we put her shoes in the potty?"

I purse my lips. "I think that might have something to do with it, honey."

"Or maybe it's because we touched her with our paint hands after she said no."

"Always so observant, Izzy. See, what I don't get is why you don't think of these things *before* they happen. This kind of stuff isn't going to fly when you start kindergarten, you know."

She giggles and runs away, probably to find her twin sister, Moxie, so they can laugh about it together.

The only silver lining here is that Yvette lasted three weeks—a few days longer than the others usually do. That's progress.

I groan and spin around, taking in my house and the damage that's been done while I was gone. There are several acrylic paint handprints on the white walls in the living room, and even some on the leather sofa. Breakfast from this morning is still on the table, mostly untouched. There's a pile of leaves and twigs on the ground by the back door.

And now I hear the younger twins, Enzo and Abel, crying in the next room.

"Here we go," I mutter, running to their room. Abel has Enzo's nose pinched between two fingers while he wails. I'm guessing it's because Abel's favorite toy train is locked in his grasp. "Knock it off, both of you. Right now." Prying them apart, I take a deep breath. "I don't care if you're in the terrible twos. I don't need this right now." I swear under my breath, but apparently Abel hears me, because he laughs at my serious tone and repeats the phrase right back to me. Enzo joins right in with a gleeful smile.

I close my eyes. I really need to get a grip on all my swearing before this gets out of hand. But more importantly, I need to find a new nanny for these kids, and fast. I'm blessed to be able to do most of my work at home, but with these four to attend to, the amount of work I'm able to get done is pretty much nonexistent without a nanny.

I take out my phone to review some applications, but freeze when I see the email at the top of my inbox.

Dear Mr. Whitmore,

I hope this email finds you well. This is a reminder about the meeting you requested with our agency. As we stated before, our availability is extremely limited, so any rescheduling would put you on the calendar for next year. Please get back to us if you wish to confirm your appointment for June 5th.

Regards,

Donna Caldwell, Marriage Coordinator

United We Band

Fantastic. I completely forgot about them. But thanks to the stipulation in my mother's will, there's no way I can wait another year to get matched with a potential wife, so I can't reschedule. I close my eyes, pinching the bridge of my nose. I've still been having anxious flashbacks from the way my dad banged on the front door last month after someone left a one-star Yelp review for the restaurant.

My dad is so old-school, he hardly ever texts me and likes to do most of his dealings in person. Despite our relationship being pretty strained, he has no issues showing up unannounced when he needs to get a point across to me.

"You have a lot of nerve," he stated when I answered the door.

Big surprise. "What did I do this time, Dad?"

He shoved his phone in my face with the review on

display. "Have you been keeping up with the business? It's like you don't have a head sometimes, Perry. This is exactly why I should have given Rebecca everything. You're lazy and entitled."

"Dad, they gave us a bad review. It's not the end of the world. It happens." I sighed. It had been a particularly stressful week, and instead of just nodding and shutting my mouth like I normally do when I'm getting berated like a toddler, I let out the words I couldn't hold in.

My father narrowed his dark eyebrows, streaked with harsh gray, making me regret what I just uttered. "I didn't let you take over the restaurant so you could be this careless. And I know you love living in this house, but I'm glad Rebecca gets to have it when I move. You get the business; she gets the house. It's going to work out well. I can finally retire in peace knowing I'll never have to spend another winter in Maine, and knowing this place is going to have a proper *married* couple living in it."

His words were like alarm bells in my mind. *The deadline. It was here already.*

I struggled to speak. "I still have time though, Dad. Technically, I have until the end of the year to get married before Rebecca can claim ownership of my house."

Dad shrugged. "Since that isn't happening, it's time for you to pack up, son. The sooner you start, the less stressful it will be. You don't want to leave yourself only a month to move out."

The note of finality in his tone made me panic. *No. It can't already be time yet. It can't.* "You're going to make me and my four children move out of *my* childhood home so

Rebecca and her husband can live here . . . because she's married and I'm not?"

"When your mother and I set up the will and trust, Perry, we chose the terms for good reasons. I'm not about to contest your mother's will over your hurt feelings. At least you and Rebecca have been given your first disbursements. But if you're not married by the time I leave the state, the house goes to her since she *is* married. The terms are final. So, it's time to start the moving process, son. Six months isn't as long as you think it is." As he started to turn to walk away, panic clawed its way up my neck. I would rather die than lose my house. Especially to Rebecca.

"Dad, I'm engaged!"

He stopped in his tracks and turned around. I expected him to look angry at the way I yelled those words, but his bushy brows relaxed slightly, and even the curve of his mouth appeared less tense. "Excuse me?"

"I've been seeing someone for a while now, and I think —uh—I *know*, she's the one."

"Why haven't I heard about her?"

I want to laugh, but I don't. It's not like we have the type of relationship where we share personal details with each other. I can't remember the last time my dad talked to me about something other than work, no matter how many times I've wished we were closer. "I wanted to make sure she was the one first. I-I wanted to get engaged before introducing you since I know how you feel about . . . girl-friends."

My dad stared at me for a long moment, and then he did something I've only witnessed a handful of times.

He smiled.

"About time, my boy." He clapped a hand on my back.

I staggered forward against the slap, disguising my stumble as shifting my weight from one foot to the next. But I couldn't deny hearing the warmth in his voice directed at *me* filled an emptiness I'd been trying to ignore since my mother passed away. "Thanks."

He pointed at me. "I want to meet her. I need to make sure she's nothing like the last one. I can sniff out a gold digger a mile away."

I nodded—smiled, even—despite the reminder of the painful memories of Jill. "Of course."

My dad regarded me like maybe he's been wrong all this time about me being as useful as a goldfish. "I'll be in touch. We'll plan something soon. The three of us."

As soon as he left, I thrust both of my hands through my hair.

How am I going to get out of this one?

I spent the rest of the day researching how to find a fiancée as quickly as possible, and came across United We Band, an international marriage broker. Apparently, there's an entire community of misguided souls like myself who need to get hitched asap. I made an appointment sometime in April to get matched at their next availability.

But that was a month ago.

Now, staring at the email from Donna, it's hitting me that this whole thing might take longer than I thought. There's a chance my dad will find out I lied, and any possible ounce of his approval I might've had will be nonexistent. Or worse, I won't find a wife by December, and I'll lose the house to Rebecca.

Still, I *have* to make it to the appointment, which

means I need to fly out to the agency in Chicago in two weeks.

And I need to find a nanny, like, today. I check the applications that have come through so far.

There's only one. Some girl with a pink resume. It's a nice touch, but I don't even bother looking it over and forward it to my assistant, Kiera. I type, Can you vet this applicant as much as possible and if all is well, get her hired and moved in by tomorrow or the next day, latest?

There's no time left to waste and there's still so much to go over with her regarding the kids before I leave for my meeting with United We Band. Two weeks hardly seems like enough time to get a new nanny comfortable enough with my kids for me to leave the state.

Time, it seems, has never been my friend. There wasn't enough time—or money—to marry Jill when she first got pregnant, since I wasn't old enough to receive my first trust disbursement. There was never time for us to spend together once the first set of twins were born. Two years passed too quickly after that, leading to the second set of twins. I ran out of time to fix things between us before she disappeared, leaving me alone with all four kids and a mere explanation of 'I don't want to be a parent anymore. It's not for me.'

She wasn't supposed to leave. She was the one I was supposed to marry.

The only thing that seemed to work out for me was learning to pray. I desperately wanted Jill to come back, which didn't happen, so I found myself turning to God and asking for peace to get through it all. And it worked. He gave me patience to make it through the long days. He gave me a sound mind when I felt like I was going to lash out at everyone around me. I found myself leaning on Him through all the times I watched loving mothers with their own children out in public.

And best of all, He gave me enough rest through the chaos of raising four small children that I was able to make it through business school. Because finishing school and taking over Dad's fine-dining establishment has already earned me more money than I need to support the kids on my own.

After Jill left, my father graciously let me and the kids move into my childhood home after the previous tenants left, as long as I paid him rent. It's the house my parents lived in before Mom died, and it holds more fond memories of her than I'd admit to a stranger.

This house means more to me than anything.

The only problem? I straight up lied about having a living, breathing fiancée—not very Christian of me—and Rebecca is perfectly eligible to receive the house.

I probably shouldn't have panicked and told Dad I'm engaged, but at least it bought me some time to get hitched before he moves. Otherwise, I'm not inheriting a shingle on this roof.

Fine. Whatever. I've done the whole love thing, and it wasn't all it was cracked up to be. A *practical* marriage, I can do. And if it fulfills the terms of the will so I can get what I want?

Ball and chain, here I come.

Chapter Three

BRONWYN IS DOING yoga in the living room when I get home. She doesn't even glance in my direction as I go straight to my room—like we've discussed after past interruptions of mine. Once I've halted her concentration, she apparently can't get back into the yoga mindset and has to resume on a different day. But today, I don't care.

I slam my bedroom door behind me, surely irritating her beyond belief. Then I take out my phone.

I need to talk to Romilly. She's been my best friend since my first time competing for Miss Meadow eight years ago. She won the pageant that year, twice more, and then again last year, but has been kind enough to never brag or rub it in my face. I'm pretty sure she would stop competing to give me a better chance of winning if it weren't for all the charities close to her heart she wants to win the funds for, like feeding the homeless and saving stray dogs.

I send her a message.

ME

I just got fired

ROMILLY

What? Why?!?

ME

For slapping a customer. Long story.

ROMILLY

Uhhhh

ROMILLY

I'm going to need the story, Adds. NOW

ME

I'll call you soon.

Oh yeah, and I told Asher I already moved on with someone else, but that someone else doesn't exist and he wants to meet this invisible, fake boyfriend during my preliminary interview. HELP!

I'm about to tap her photo and call her, but my bedroom door bangs open. Bronwyn glares at me from the doorway like I'm vermin. "What's wrong with you? You know I need silence during yoga."

I roll my eyes. "Now's not a good time. I just got fired."

"Seriously?" Her eyebrows fly to her hairline. She moves toward me, and for a split second, I think she might hug me. But she holds out her hand expectantly. "Do you at least have the rent money?"

"Huh?"

"I told you rent is due next week."

"Yes, I have the rent money. But that's the least of my worries right now." What I don't tell her is that without a job, I have no idea how I'm going to pay the pageant entry fee, or afford dresses and all the other hidden, necessary costs associated with becoming Miss Meadow.

"But if you just got fired, I'm assuming you won't be paying rent next month. That doesn't work for me."

"You can't just kick me out, Bronwyn." My stomach churns. "It doesn't work that way."

She crosses her arms. "It does when I'm the only one on the lease."

"I'll get a new job. No biggie."

"Maybe, but I'm not supporting you while you look for one. Sorry." She laughs without humor. "And as mean as this might sound, I'd really rather have a less bouncy, optimistic, and messy roommate from here on out. It's almost like this was meant to be." Her blue eyes are unflinching and ice cold. There's not a single strand of her dark hair coming out of her neat yoga bun. There never is.

Sometimes, Bronwyn says things she doesn't mean. I'm used to her prickly personality, her affinity for avoiding displays of any compassion she might feel every once in a while. I search her face for signs of this rare compassion. A knot appears in my throat when I find nothing.

"I'm leaving now. If I were you, I'd start your job search." She moves toward the door, lingering for a moment before she closes it.

I plant my face in my pillow once I'm alone. *God, what am I going to do now?* My pulse hammers in my ears as I take deep breaths.

I could call my mom. I know she'd be willing to let me live with her in Vermont. But the Miss Meadow pageant begins mid-September, and it's already the end of May.

That's only four months away and I have to be a resident of Meadow Hills, Maine, to compete.

As if in a daze, I retrieve Gran's hymn book from under the mattress. I flip through the onionskin pages until I land on a verse that catches my eye.

"Trust in the Lord with all your heart and lean not on your own understanding; in all your ways submit to Him, and He will make your paths straight."
    –Proverbs 3:5-6

I'm about to bang my head against the wall in frustration when my phone rings. I fully expect it to be Romilly, begging to hear how I got fired from Rosemary Banquet, but it's a number I don't recognize.

I lift the phone to my ear. "Hello?"

"Hi, may I speak with Addison Ellsworth? This is Kiera Fang." I have no idea who that is, but Kiera's voice is so warm and friendly that I don't hang up.

"This is Addison."

"Wonderful," she says. "I'm calling because after reviewing your application and resume, we've determined you're a top candidate and would love to meet with you to see if you're a good fit before we offer you the nanny position you applied for. Mr. Whitmore will be thrilled to have you on board. If you're interested, we'd love to meet with you tomorrow evening."

I blink as my brain struggles to catch up and realize which job she's talking about. The only nanny position I applied for is here in Meadow Hills, on the super nice side of town. According to the listing, it pays triple what I was making as a server and offers full benefits and living quarters.

I got the job? I get to be a nanny and have a whole new place to live, away from Bronwyn and the peeling drywall surrounding us? No more crazy rules about tiptoeing during yoga and only using the blender between three and four o'clock, and not bringing anything purple into the living room because apparently, it's bad luck?

This sounds way too good to be true. There has to be a catch, but I'm in no position to be picky. Besides, I've nannied in high school and my degree is in childhood development. If being a waitress didn't pay so well and I didn't love my coworkers so much, I would have gotten a job working with kids already. Ultimately, this will be a smart move for my career, and it will help me afford the pageant. There's absolutely no reason for me to say no. "I accept!" *Too loud, Addison. Too eager. Tone it down.* "What time would you like to meet?"

"We'd love to have you at Mr. Whitmore's home tomorrow evening at six. Is that a suitable time for you?"

"Um . . ." I swallow, my heart practically thudding into my throat. "Six is perfect, Kiera."

The next day, I organize my stuff. If all goes well tonight, I might be moving. And as an averagely messy person, I'll need the head start to get all my belongings in order. Plus, it feels good to arrange everything into the packing cubes I purchased on a whim last month.

When most of my stuff is jammed into suitcases and

duffel bags, I sit on my bed and thumb through the photos in my camera roll. Even though we've been broken up for a month, I haven't been able to delete all the pictures of Asher and I. As I scroll through them, my chest tightens. The hardest part about dating a friend who isn't the one is losing the friendship part after things end. I can't help but remember all the times Asher would whisper jokes to me and only me during the pageant. How I'd look forward to seeing him every time a new season started. The first time we met up outside the pageant and went to the arcade. How it became our tradition every weekend until he finally kissed me in the photo booth.

I stare at the picture on my phone that I took of the photo booth picture and hit 'delete' before I can talk myself out of it. It doesn't hurt nearly as bad as I thought it would. In fact, I feel lighter inside than I have in a while.

With a smirk, I filter my photos by Asher's face and select all the photos of us from our six months of dating. I delete them all.

It's hard to imagine what this season is going to be like. The Miss Meadow pageant is like my town's version of The Bachelor, without the dating part. But it's televised on the local channel, and nearly half our 17,000 members of the town tune in each year to watch how the pageant contestants are portrayed. They dial in over the phone to vote for their favorite contestant, which doesn't do much to sway the judges' votes, but does boost engagement.

When Asher and I started dating, it was at the end of last season. He kissed me on the cheek when I was elimi-nated, right there on the stage, with the cameras rolling and everything. The audience went wild, and after, I got letters in the mail from people around town, saying how cute Asher and I were together, and they couldn't wait to see us as a couple next year.

There's really no way to avoid our break-up being highlighted since he's the host. I just hope it doesn't mess things up for me with the judges.

When it's time to leave for my meeting with Kiera and what was his name—Mr. Whitmore? I get in the car and connect my phone via Bluetooth. I haven't talked to my parents in months, but I'm really craving my mom's voice right now.

She answers after a few rings. There's a rustling on the other line before she speaks, like she's cleaning or something. "Hi, honey!"

"Hey, Mom."

A beat of silence. My mother and I have never been close, but there's still a part of me that's always been desperate for a connection with her.

"Asher broke up with me," I say.

"Asher . . ." she draws out his name. "Is he the one who works for the pageant? I didn't realize you two started dating."

"I told you about it seven months ago, when he first asked me out, remember?" I shake my head. "Anyway, it's over. And it's probably for the best."

"Well, good then." It's all she says. I can't help but feel unsatisfied. I let the silence between us hang in the air, so she'll feel inclined to fill it for once.

"Your dad's at work, but would you like to say hello to Finn?" She finally asks.

"Oh. Um, sure." It's not that I don't want to talk to my

brother. It's that he doesn't speak, not really. I never know how my interactions with him will turn out. There have been times he's laughed after hearing my voice, and others, he's gotten upset by the sound and ended up in a screaming fit. He's had Autism and other developmental delays my whole life, so it isn't that I'm not used to it. It's more that tantrums coming from a thirty-year-old man hit a lot differently than they do coming from a child. I feel bad when I know what I might be leaving my parents with after I hang up.

When the sound of his hums fill my car, I murmur, "Hey, Finn. It's Addison."

More humming.

"I miss you," I tell him. "I'll have to come visit soon, okay? I hear you got a new computer. Congratulations."

"Computer," he says.

Hearing his voice, knowing that he's listening makes me smile. "Yeah. I'm really happy for you."

Mom takes the phone back. "You got him all excited, Addy. Good job."

"No problem." A cluster of elegant, timeless cabins comes into view, signaling to me that I'm almost at my destination. "I'll talk to you soon, Mom. I just got to—uh—work." No use explaining to her my work situation. She probably won't remember, anyway.

"Okay, honey. Be safe. Love you."

"Love you, too."

I press the button on my steering wheel to hang up the phone and squint through the bright summer light out the windshield. My GPS says I've arrived, so I pull into the stone driveway on my right.

Mr. Whitmore lives in a three-story house in Orange-wood Estates, one of the wealthiest communities in Meadow Hills. His home reminds me of the Lighthouse Inn, where the pageant is always held here in town. It's glorious; crafted of gray stone and dark wood, and surrounded by tall pines.

I walk up the wide steps to the front door. When I knock, a forty-something woman answers. She's dressed in a gray skirt suit that matches her eyeshadow, and her eyes and mouth have friendly smile lines surrounding them. When we shake hands, I'm pleasantly surprised by her tight grip. "Miss Ellsworth, it's a pleasure to meet you. I'm Kiera Fang."

Ah. So this is Kiera.

"You can just call me Addison." I peek around her into the foyer, which leads to a giant stone fireplace in the center of the living area.

"Please, come in," she says, noting my curiosity. She moves aside so I can enter. "I'll happily take your bag."

I hand her my purse. I'm guessing she'd take my coat as well if it were a cool season, but in this warm summer, I'm wearing nothing more than a yellow sundress.

Kiera leads me into the house, and it takes some genuine effort on my part not to squeal and clap. I can't believe whoever lives here would hire *me*. My last nanny job was my sophomore year of high school. I hardly feel worthy to be here.

"Down here you'll find the kitchen and bar, dining area, powder room and living room." Kiera motions around the open floor. The stone fireplace I saw from the entryway is double sided, separating the living room from the dining room. "There's a wine cellar down that far hall, as well." She smiles, clearly enjoying watching me take it all in. "The children's rooms are on the second floor, but they're all in bed, so unfortunately you won't be able to meet them tonight."

I raise my eyebrows. All in bed at six? "Do they typically go to sleep so early?"

"No. But last night, one of them had a night terror and woke up the others." Kiera winces. "Apparently, the four of them were up *very* early this morning. But if you'll follow me upstairs to the third floor, I'll show you Mr. Whitmore's office and the wing where you'll be staying."

The wing? All I can do is nod. I don't trust myself to speak at the moment, because I'll probably turn into a babbling, incoherent child. We glide up the stairs, pausing on the second-floor landing so she can silently point to the hall containing the kids' rooms. Hung along the landing wall are professional photographs of each of them. At first glance, they all look close in age and very much alike, but I don't have enough time to study them further because Kiera leads me to the third-floor next.

"Up here you'll find the east and west wings. On the east side, we have Mr. Whitmore's office and bedroom, the latter of which is obviously off-limits. But you'll find that he'll most likely call you to his office regularly for updates on the children, especially Abel. He's . . . um, well, he's a bit of a wildcard." She laughs lightly, like wind chimes, easing any worries her statement might have given me. Then she leads me down the opposite hallway. "And the west wing contains your living quarters. I hope you'll find them accommodating. Please make yourself comfortable while I fetch Mr. Whitmore. Let us know if you have any requests or concerns once he's here."

I nod, still standing in front of the closed door while she goes to the east wing. I turn to open the door. *My door.* The thought is startling.

I open it, revealing a small sitting room with two vintage chairs perched in front of another fireplace. The chairs remind me of something Gran would have in her house and seeing them makes me feel immediately at home. Something about the faded blue pattern on the fabric and the light wood legs and arms. There's a tea table between them with a key on top, probably to this house. An archway off the side of the room opens up to a bedroom holding a queen-size bed with a cushy, green comforter tucked neatly under the mattress. Two white end tables stand on either side, and a matching dresser is on the wall to the right of the bed. There's a connecting bathroom on the left that makes my stomach swim with excitement. I've never had a connecting bathroom before, and this one has a shower with gold and black accents, nothing like the one at Bronwyn's with the pattern of missing tiles.

It's too perfect. I've never been anywhere so nice, except during pageants. Suspicion bubbles in my stomach. It doesn't make any sense why this position isn't already filled. Words Gran used to tell me on more than one occasion play in my mind—*If it seems too good to be true, then it just might be.*

"Addison, right?"

The deep male voice startles me, making me spin around to face the door. Kiera is there, and next to her is a man in a white shirt and navy jeans. Maybe that's why it takes me a moment to recognize the messy dark hair, the thick brows and handsome, stubbled face that I laid eyes on yesterday.

I frown. And then replace it with a smile. If there's one thing pageants have taught me, it's smiling even when there's been a horrible, hideous mistake.

"It's nice to meet you." He crosses the room to shake my hand. My heart rate increases with each step he takes.

"Mr. W-Whitmore?" The words fall out of my mouth.

"Please, call me Perry."

I swallow, my suspicions confirmed. Though I never met the new owner of Rosemary Banquet, I heard Lillian say his name once when he took over. Perry. And I'm almost positive this man is the same one who was at the restaurant with Lillian. But it seems like he doesn't remember me. Otherwise, I doubt he'd still be smiling, his eyes regarding me with nothing but professional benevolence.

I shake his hand firmly, like my dad taught me to at a young age. "Nice to meet you. I'm Addison." Now that he's closer, I notice his eyes are hazel. I stare into them for a moment too long.

If there's going to be a moment for him to realize I'm the same employee he had fired yesterday, it's now. But he dips his head down, not breaking eye contact. "Nice to meet you. I can't wait for you to start. Would it be too much to ask you to have your things here by tomorrow?" His words come out in a slight rush, his cheeks turning pink. It would be cute if he weren't such a cold-hearted, employee-firing jerk.

There's no way I can take this job. I haven't even

started yet, and I already hate him for making Lillian let me go. He and his fancy, pretentious mansion can have a nice life.

I imagine giving him a piece of my mind. Driving back home and telling Romilly everything on the way back to Bronwyn's.

Oh, no. *Bronwyn.* Just thinking about going back there after being presented with a place like *this* to live . . . and if I turn down this job, I'll be saying no to plenty of money to support myself through the pageant. I won't even have to pay rent here, either.

I keep my smile frozen on my face as I contemplate my options. This is a pretty sweet deal, despite Perry being the one who's offering it to me. Maybe I can somehow ignore my disdain for him in order to make this work.

No, not maybe.

I have to make this work.

"It's not too much at all," I tell Perry. Behind him, Kiera beams. "I'll bring my stuff tomorrow. There's not much of it, so it should be easy."

"Fantastic. I'll be pretty busy with work when you arrive, so let's go over a couple of ground rules. No matter how convincing my kids might get, don't give them sugar after four o'clock. Trust me, it's better this way."

I nod, still in a daze. "Limit the sugar. Got it."

"There's plenty of wine in the cellar," he continues, "but please, try to limit any drinking to after the kids go to bed."

"Wait, seriously? That's an actual rule?"

He smiles faintly. "You'd be surprised how many nannies have had trouble following it."

His comment makes me wonder how many nannies he's had in general, but I'm worried it might be rude to ask. "Anything else?"

"Yes. I want you to feel comfortable here. This will be your home as much as it is mine and my children's. That means you can help yourself to anything you'd like. Feel free to have guests over on the weekends, and you're also welcome to change up any decorations in here that aren't your style." He gestures around my new room.

"I can't imagine changing a single thing in here. It's perfect." The words kind of just slip out. But I can tell they mean something to Perry, because he blushes.

"Thanks. I had some of my mother's old things brought here from storage when I moved in. But I'm not exactly one for interior decor."

"Well, she has great taste."

Perry stares at his shoes, a small smile gracing his mouth. "So, if all those rules work for you, then me and the kids will see you in the morning."

"Sounds like a plan." *A horrible, impulsive plan. But a plan, nonetheless.* "See you in the morning."

Chapter Four

THE NEXT MORNING is a disaster the moment it begins.

Abel goes missing for the better part of the morning, and it takes me longer than it should to find him hiding in the oven. *The oven.*

Sometimes, I think maybe I shouldn't be allowed to be a dad. I'm clearly failing these kids. Even now, Moxie is almost in tears as I struggle to brush her dark hair into a "princess twist." It's stick-straight, which should mean it's easy to detangle, right? Wrong. The poor thing is currently cringing as she sits on the bathroom countertop while I hold her head still with one hand and comb through her knotted strands with the other. Her red-faced reflection is visible to the both of us. Finally, she screams at the top of her lungs.

It's times like this that I really wish I had a partner, or just someone to give me a breather from all this chaos. Maybe then, I'd know how it feels to tread water from time to time instead of constantly drowning.

"Just hold still, Mox." I continue to separate her knots with the comb.

"Stop it! Ow!" She pulls her head away from me.

I sigh. "Fine. Go play. It will be fine." I kiss her forehead, lift her off the counter, and set her on the tile floor. She runs off like a wind-up car toy with its wheels already spinning mid-air.

"Kiera?" I call down the stairs from the second floor. "Have you heard anything from Addison yet this morning? What's her ETA?" I try not to let my voice convey the desperation I'm feeling, but who am I kidding? I am desperate for help. There's no point trying to hide it.

Kiera's smooth voice floats up the staircase. "She's on her way, Mr. Whitmore. She's expecting to arrive in about thirty minutes."

Crap. That's sooner than I expected. I know I should be thrilled, because the sooner she gets here to manage these kids, the better for me. I haven't answered a single phone call, sent a single email since my last nanny, Yvette, walked out the door. But I wanted to at least make the kids presentable and take some time to show Addison that the new task she's about to take on won't be, well, completely miserable. My kids do have a good side. It's just hard for others to see sometimes.

When I get downstairs, Enzo is eating his scrambled eggs out of a potted plant with a fork.

I cover my face with my hands. I'm doomed. She's going to quit on the spot, just like most of the others have.

I scoop up Enzo and move him to the kitchen island. The barstools are too high for him to get down from, so at least I won't have to worry about him escaping to ingest any more soil and compost with his breakfast.

The girl twins are in their room, engaged in some sort of pretend play—thank God—so that only leaves Abel to find. Again.

I spend at least twenty minutes searching for him, my panic rising when he's not even in the oven this time. When the doorbell rings and Kiera appears downstairs to answer it, I still haven't found him.

And, still wearing the clothes I slept in, I'm not dressed for the day yet. My new nanny is here for her first day, and there are fresh orange juice stains on my white shirt. This is a new low for me.

Blood rushes to my face when Kiera guides Addison inside and she takes in my gray sweatpants and rumpled white T-shirt—yellow splashes and all. My tousled hair is completely unprofessional, and I know she notices. I see the way her eyes take it all in, lingering. It's humiliating.

"Good morning, Addison," I say, trying my best to sound upbeat so she won't run out the door. Compared to me, she looks like a literal supermodel. Her clothes are clean, and her hair is up in a polished ponytail with the ends hanging down her back in defined ringlets. There's a shimmer on her cheekbones that looks like she put it there herself. Everything about her screams beauty. I can only hope she's ready to get her hands dirty.

"Good morning, Mr. Whitmore." She shakes her head quickly. "I mean, Perry."

"Don't worry. I respond to both, technically."

She appears to be fighting a smile. "So, where are these mystery kids of yours? I can't wait to meet them."

Yes. Where indeed are they? I try to keep my voice neutral. "Let's go find them. I know where one of them is, at least." I rub the back of my neck as I gesture for her to follow me to the kitchen. Kiera disappears to the coat closet to hang up Addison's bag.

I want to cry in relief when I see Enzo still seated at the bar. He frowns deeply when I approach with Addison, pointing at her. "Who that?"

"This is—"

But she cuts me off, skipping past me to Enzo. "Hey there, buddy! My name's Addison. You can call me Addy if you want." Her voice sounds animated. Sweet. Enzo's shoulders loosen. His face becomes unpinched.

"I eating scrambled eggs," he states, pointing at them. "See?"

Addison examines them like they're a rare gemstone. "Oooh. I love scrambled eggs. Do you know what animal gives us eggs, Enzo?"

"A chicken. Bock, bock, bock!"

They continue to go back and forth, talking about animals, colors, and all kinds of fun conversation pieces I never would have thought of. Then we leave Enzo to finish his breakfast and she meets Moxie and Izzy in their shared bedroom. When she sees they're playing with dolls, she brightens, dropping to her knees to join them. "Can I be this one?"

"Hmm. No, but you can be this one," says Izzy, holding out a doll with hair resembling a troll. It's wearing pants, mismatched shoes, and no shirt.

Addison beams. "Ahh, she's so pretty. Thanks, Iz."

Iz? They're already on a nickname basis?

Moxie is less talkative, probably still wounded from Operation Hair with me not too long ago. But when she observes Izzy playing with Addison for a few minutes, she brings her doll back into the game, giving her a few lines that Addison playfully responds to.

An unfamiliar sensation spreads through me as I watch her engage with them. I'm not sure what it is, but for some reason, it makes me want to gain distance. Perspective. She's kind of just thrown herself into playing with my kids much better than I ever have, and it's happening so fast.

"I'll be right back," I murmur. "There's still one more kid, and as soon as I find him, you can meet him too."

She giggles like I'm joking. "Okay." Then, turning back to the girls, makes her doll say something about lipstick.

As I retreat upstairs, I catch Izzy saying, "Abel always goes missing. He's a very bad boy."

I hang my head. She definitely repeated that after hearing me say it a few times. And coming from her, I realize just how bad it sounds. It's like a punch to the gut.

I enter my office on the third-floor. I've caught Abel hiding in here a few times. Sometimes in the giant desk drawer, and other times behind the curtains or the tall snake plant by the window. One of the biggest downsides to having a large house is keeping track of all the places I can lose my kids in it.

Abel isn't in any of his regular hiding spots. I throw myself into my leather office chair and cover my eyes with the heels of my hands.

As happy as I am to have a new nanny, I can't help but feel guilty that I didn't at least look at Addison's resume before I hired her. Kiera did, of course. I'm grateful she runs background checks on all my employees, but still. As their father, it's my responsibility to make sure the person my kids will be spending all their time with is good enough. And after watching her interact with three out of four of my kids, Addison seems too good to be true.

I turn on the laptop on my desk. Scrolling through dozens of unread emails, I finally find the opened one from Addison titled RE: NANNY JOB APPLICATION.

For the second time, I open the attachment—her pink resume. It has her name, her address, and her age, twenty-six. Only two years younger than me. It also says she's been competing in the Miss Meadow pageant for eight years. I should have guessed. She has the face worthy of a beauty pageant. I glance at her work history next, noting her previous nannying experience, and freeze when I see the most recent job she has listed.

SERVER AT ROSEMARY BANQUET. APRIL 8, 2023-MAY 21, 2024.

Wait a minute...

I'm certain it's no coincidence that her last day was yesterday. She must be the problem employee I released. What did Lillian call her when she was trying to vouch for her? For the life of me, I can't remember her using the employee's name. I was too busy trying not to let my emotions get in the way. I do remember Lillian saying something about the employee normally being a kind and hard worker, that this was out of character for her.

The problem is, I don't care right now.

If Addison is the same employee who physically assaulted a customer at my five-star establishment, then I don't want her anywhere near my children. I can't imagine what she'll do once she realizes how difficult my kids can be. Someone who's capable of snapping like that in a professional restaurant setting can't possibly have enough patience for kids. Especially mine.

I shoot out of my chair and exit the office. I need to question her *right now*. If she's who I think she is, then I hope she hasn't started unpacking her things yet, because I'll have her out of here before she can even make it to her new room.

I must look as crazed as I feel because when Kiera sees me, her eyes widen a fraction. "Is everything all right, Mr. Whitmore?"

"Where is Addison?"

She frowns. "Right outside with the children, sir." She points across the house to the kitchen. Through the window above the sink, I see Addison soaking wet, her hair coming out of her ponytail and sticking to her face.

Oh no.

I dart to the yard, swinging the back door open. A sound meets my ears, stopping me in my tracks. Laughter. Addison's laughter. And the kids are laughing, too.

There's an inflatable pool in the center of my grassy backyard. Colorful pieces of rubber decorate the lawn, and all four of my children are soaking wet as well, wearing oversized T-shirts as they run around throwing water balloons at each other. It takes me a moment to register what's going on. They're okay, and Abel is here, too.

I move closer until I'm standing right in front of Addison.

"Perry!" My name escapes her lips as a giggle. Her

pink shirt clings to her torso in ways that make a hot blush creep over me.

I clear my throat. "What's going on out here?"

"We play water balloons, Daddy," Abel shouts when he sees me. He lobs one in my direction, sending it exploding on the ground halfway between us. Laughing, he tugs on Addison's hand. "More, please."

She tousles his wet blond hair. "Of course, little guy. Come on." Hand-in-hand, they walk to the inflatable pool, and I follow behind them like a dumbstruck dog.

Inside the pool is an impressive bounty of water balloons floating on the surface. It looks like a colorful, squishy ball pit.

Addison hands a yellow water balloon to Abel. He takes it and runs after Moxie.

I walk closer to her when she turns back to me. There are water droplets stuck to her eyelashes, making them look thicker and darker than before. "Where did all this come from?"

A little V appears between her delicate brows. "It was all in your upstairs hall closet. I came up with the idea when Izzy showed me where you guys keep the rest of the toys." She studies her shoes. "I hope that's okay . . ."

"You came up with this idea for the kids?"

She meets my gaze again. With the sun shining on her face, her brown eyes look like butterscotch candies. "I thought it would be fun."

"I think . . . you thought right."

She hesitates. "Then why do you look upset?"

It's my turn to pause. I try to recollect my frustration from a moment ago, but all my thoughts have fizzled away like steam. I'm not sure if it's because she's so beautiful, or because of how happy she just made my kids when I've seen them do nothing but cry and cause trouble since their mom left last year. "I'm not upset," I finally say. "I'm just surprised at how quickly they warmed up to you. Especially Abel."

A faint smile appears on her lips. She jerks her chin in his direction. "You mean my new bestie? He's awesome!" She sounds genuinely excited. Not at all sarcastic or like she's just trying to be polite.

I don't know how to respond, and thankfully, I don't have to, because she walks away, across the yard to where the girls are attempting to juggle water balloons and failing.

Do not check her out, Perry.

I try to tear my eyes away, but her blue leggings are hugging her body, just like her shirt is. My body goes rigid in response.

This is the last thing I need. It's bad enough that this girl might be the same employee I just fired. It's even worse that she's too attractive to keep my eyes off of. One thing is clear though—I can't fire her from this job, not when she's this good with my kids. I really hope she has a decent excuse for attacking that customer. And I really, really hope I can find a way to stop ogling her, especially since I'm supposed to be getting married as soon as possible.

Chapter Five

ADDISON

I CAN FEEL Perry still watching me as I walk toward the twin girls—who I keep mixing up, even though they look completely different. The smaller one has brown eyes and fine, blond hair. The other is taller, with eyes like the sky and has a brunette bob with bangs.

"I still can't tell you two apart," I tell them in a silly voice that makes them laugh.

The brunette one spins around while yelling, "My name is Moxieeeee! Like the soda."

The other one sighs dramatically, but I note the way her cheeks lift. "And my name is Izzy. Actually, my whole name is Isadora Mary Whitmore," she points to her sister, "and her whole name is Maxine Nicoletta Whitmore, but it was hard to say when we were little, so she says her name is Moxie because it's her most favorite drink ever."

I pick up a pink water balloon from the ground. "How old are you?"

"We're both five, but I'm older than Moxie," Izzy informs me. "Our birthday was not that very long ago. And we're starting kindergarten very soon."

"That's awesome. Kindergarten is a lot of fun. You'll like it."

Moxie tugs on my shirt. "Is it nap time yet?"

"It can be." I drop the yellow water balloon I was about to toss at Enzo and pat her head. "Let's go inside and eat lunch first, though."

Something I remember from my time nannying while I was in high school is that most kids are picky eaters. But I cracked the code once, and I'll never forget it. The girls follow me as I scoop up Enzo and Abel—one boy in each arm—and head inside. Perry seems to have disappeared, which is inconvenient, because I need to ask him if any of his kids have food allergies. I set the boys on the couch and find the remote perched on the fireplace mantle.

I quickly find a video on YouTube of a bunch of kids making slime so I can sneak away for a minute. And it does the trick. All four of them are mesmerized, watching the TV like they've never seen anything like it. *What on earth does Perry normally have them watch?* Maybe they're a no-screens family.

Before they can ask questions, I dart up the stairs to floor three, where Perry's office is. I'm following a hunch here, assuming this is where I can find him. I knock on the door before opening it a crack, and peek inside. My hunch was right. Perry is sitting in a leather office chair at an expensive-looking oak desk in the center of the room. His spine straightens when he sees me standing in the door-way. "Everything alright? Did somebody get hurt?" His chair rolls back loudly on the wood floor like he's about to get up and rush downstairs.

I want to laugh. He looks so worried, with his thick brows all pinched together. The expression makes him look older than he probably is. I can't help but wonder what kind of problems he has to deal with as a parent that I don't. What happens on the day-to-day here that would cause him to expect trouble already?

"Someone might get hurt if you don't tell me whether or not your kids have food allergies." I let the slow smile spread across my lips so he knows I'm joking. And to my surprise, the tension leaves his shoulders. He drops his head down in a quiet laugh. It's cute. Or at least, it would be if he wasn't the unkind human who fired me from Rosemary Banquet. "But on a serious note," I add, "I, myself, am deathly allergic to pineapple."

"Thanks for sharing your kryptonite." He stands from his chair. "My kids aren't allergic to anything, but I should probably come down so I can show you what they normally eat." He rubs his hand down the front of his face. "I'm sorry. This is probably a really stressful first day for you. You haven't had proper instruction, and you haven't even had a chance to unpack. I've just been so busy up here, and you kind of just jumped right in." As he laughs, I observe how his smile is one of those soft ones that makes the eyes go sweeter.

I shake my head. "This isn't my first rodeo. I know what to do with kids. Why don't you just give me your phone number so I can text you if I have any more questions?"

He pauses a moment before nodding slowly. "Okay."

Taking out his phone, he hands it to me so I can enter my contact information, and I hand mine over to him so he can do the same.

Once we're done, we exchange phones and I stand there, unsure of what to say next. There's an awkward beat of silence before Perry's gaze slides down from my face to my damp shirt. "You're still all wet," he murmurs. "Aren't you cold?"

The way he says it, so kindly and quietly, sounds like it's a secret he's telling me. Goosebumps form on my arms, as if in response to his question. "It's fine. I'll rinse off and change when the kids go down for a nap."

His Adam's apple bobs as he swallows. "All right. In the meantime, I'll turn down the AC for you."

"Either way." I shrug. I don't know why I'm still standing here. That video I put on for the kids won't entertain them forever, and the sooner I go back downstairs, the sooner I'll remember why I'm not supposed to like Perry.

I spin on my heel and walk away before he can say anything else. Back in the living room, all four kids are somehow still in front of the TV. I snap a picture of them because they really are adorable. They each have a mix of the same features without any of them really having the same face. Moxie has Perry's dark hair, but her blue eyes are probably from her mom. Izzy has blond hair, but Perry's eyes. Abel must be an exact replica of his mom, a blond, blue-eyed baby. And Enzo is Perry's twin.

I send Perry the picture of the four of them on the couch, and write underneath:

> Do you starve them of electronics or
> something?

Shaking my head in amusement, I go to the kitchen and open the fridge. It's fully stocked with mostly fresh fruits, meats and vegetables. Even the pantry—which is the size of my old bedroom at Bronwyn's—is full of healthy whole grains and organic foods. Hardly anything is processed, which is great. It's the kind of eating I would do if I could afford it. Which now that I live here, I guess I can. The thought sends a rush of endorphins through my body.

My phone buzzes. It's a text from Perry.

> Of course not. They've seen Sesame
> Street a few times. But I try not to let
> them watch too much TV.

I snort. Typical. Perry can't be that much older than me, and my generation watched plenty of TV. We're also the ones who seem to think of our kids plus electronics as a taboo activity.

ME

> Um, how old are you? We turned out
> fine, didn't we? *rebel emoji*

PERRY

> I'm 28. And depends on your definition of
> fine.

You, Perry. You are exactly my definition of fine.
But instead of conveying my thoughts, I don't type

back, not trusting myself. When I set my phone on the countertop, I realize I'm smiling. Quickly, I force it to disappear from my face. Over my shoulder, I call toward the living room, "Who wants to help make lunch?"

Just as I expect, all four pairs of feet come running in my direction. Their voices soon follow. A combination of *me*'s and *I do*'s surround me.

I hand Moxie a loaf of bread from the pantry. "Your job is to lay out two slices of bread for each person, okay?"

She nods, her teeth visible from her grin.

I give Izzy the mustard, Enzo the package of sliced turkey, and Abel a pack of cheese. I tell them, "Put one slice, or squirt, on every piece of bread Moxie sets out. You guys got this. Ready, go!"

They get to work immediately, and I giggle as I watch them crowd around the small table next to the island to make their own lunch. Enzo and Abel struggle to follow my directions, as expected, but I don't interfere as they make a mess with the sandwich ingredients. I know it probably seems like child labor or something, but it's a trick my mom taught me when my brother, Finn, was young. Kids, even the pickiest of eaters, can't resist tasting something they created themselves.

And she was right. The kids have no problem eating their turkey sandwiches in their little chairs at their miniature table. Even Abel, who is apparently a secret terror or something, is digging in. I snap another pic and send it to Perry.

ME

Lunch time!

PERRY

Wow. I'm officially keeping you.

His response makes me blush. I know he's joking, but still. Guys like him can't just say things like that and expect it not to have an effect.

ME

Haha, I doubt their mother would appreciate that.

I can't help but wonder if Perry and the children's mother are together. She hasn't been mentioned by Kiera or Perry yet, so I'm assuming not, but I'd rather play things safe, just in case.

I tuck my phone into the waistband of my leggings. The kids are starting to play with the food now, a sure sign that they're done eating.

I clear the table despite their cute, squeaky-voiced protests. "It's nap time," I whisper. Abel starts wailing, so I scoop him up and carry him while the rest follow me upstairs.

It only takes twenty minutes to put each set of twins down, and once I'm done, I go to the third-floor, where my new bedroom awaits me. I'm surprised to find my bags already in the seating area, parked next to the fireplace. I smile, imagining Kiera bringing them up here for me. Leaving the door wide-open—in case one of the kids wakes up and decides to look for me—I roll my bags through the archway where my bed and dresser are waiting.

I plop the largest suitcase onto my bed and open it up.

My toiletry bag and a change of clothes are soon in hand before I head into the connected bathroom.

There's a larger-than-average shower and a separate bathtub, and though I'm tempted to take a bath, I don't know how long the kids will sleep, so a speedy shower is probably smarter.

I get in and turn on the hot water. The shower walls are a coarse, black texture that feels good to run my fingertips along. My warped reflection stares back at me in the gold handle as I gently scrub my hair and skin. It's one of the fastest showers I've ever taken, but the last thing I want is for one of the kids to catch me up here, naked.

When I'm done, I almost panic because I forgot to bring a towel from my bag, but quickly find one in the cabinet under the bathroom sink. There's a whole stack of them—fluffy, white towels, folded professionally. It reminds me of being in a hotel.

I wrap one towel around my body and use another to scrunch some of the moisture out of my dripping hair.

While I dry off, I can't help but admire my bedroom. It's tastefully decorated, with a sage green duvet cover draped over the bed. Thick, ivory curtains hang high over the windows, and the plush green rug under my feet makes me feel warm and cozy. The room is giving off academia vibes, with a sprinkle of cottagecore because of the fireplace and honey-oak accents, including the bed frame. I run my finger over the smooth bedding and grin. Part of me wonders if Perry hired someone to decorate this place with his mother's things, or if it was the kids' mother. And then my thoughts travel to the possibilities of what could have happened between Perry and his former partner. Are they still together and she's just away on business or something? Or . . . is he a single dad? But I push the thoughts away as quickly as they come.

"Addison?"

I stiffen when Perry's voice floats into the room. Before I can respond, he's filling up the entryway while I stare at him from across the room, still in my towel.

Chapter Six

MY WORDS CATCH in my throat as I gawk at her.

Hair wet and dripping. That towel barely covering those long, toned legs. The dip below her collarbone where her towel keeps sliding down. And those big brown doe eyes, searching my face for answers. Holy . . .

"I'm so sorry," I finally ground out. My voice sounds deep and husky to my own ears. I silently pray she doesn't notice. "I didn't realize you'd be—" I gesture to her barely covered nakedness and clear my throat. *Wrap it up, Perry.* "I'll be in my office. Can you meet me in there when you're dressed?"

She nods, still stunned into silence.

I rip my gaze away from her and stumble down the hall to the wing containing my office. I think I black out a little, because the next moment, I'm at my desk and pinching the bridge of my nose, trying not to think about Addison in a towel, like a fool.

The perfect distraction arrives in the form of a text from my dad.

> **DAD**
>
> I want to have dinner with you and your fiancée in about two weeks. What day works?

Practically choking on my panic, I try to take deep breaths, try to force the anxiety away, but it's no use. I have no one to show him, no fiancée at all, currently. I imagine the way he'd look at me if I came clean, like I'm the disappointment he always thought I was. But if I somehow found a way to bring a woman to dinner, I bet he'd be proud of me for once. Or at the very least, temporarily satisfied.

I have no idea how this works—this matchmaking thing I'm about to embark on. Can I just meet someone at United We Band and bring her home with me to play the part? All I can do is hope.

I text him back.

> **ME**
>
> How about Saturday?

> **DAD**
>
> I'll be there at 7, after you have the kids in bed.

Of course. Some grandpa he is. For how adamant he is about them being raised to his standards, you'd think he'd actually want to see them once in a while.

I don't know how much time passes before Addison comes into my office dressed in a flowy, white sundress.

Her curly hair is still dripping wet, and the vanilla scent of her bodywash permeates my nostrils.

The sight of her like this isn't much better than the towel.

She stops walking once she's standing in front of my desk and bounces on her heels, smiling just enough for one of her dimples to pop out. "You wanted to see me?"

My stomach clenches, because it's finally time to address what happened between her and that customer. If I'd known before I hired her she was the same employee I fired, I wouldn't be standing here with her right now. But it's only been a day, and it's already more than clear that my kids love her. No other nanny has made such a positive impression. And I don't have anyone else.

"I want to talk to you about your resume, Addison."

There's a long beat of silence before she smirks. "You finally put it together, didn't you?"

"That I fired you?" A seed of relief germinates in my gut. At least she already knows, and I won't have to spring my sudden revelation on her because she's up to speed. Of course she is. I close my eyes, laughing a little. "Yes." When I open my eyes, she's biting her lip. She's probably nervous, and she has every right to be. "Apparently, you slapped one of my customers?"

I wait for her to try to deny it, but Addison crosses her arms, staring me dead-on. "Yep. I did." The challenge in her tone is unmistakable. Surprising.

"Why?"

She shakes her head. "He deserved it. He was making fun of Lyle—I mean, one of our regulars who happens to have sensory issues. It was messed up."

My eyebrows knit themselves together. "Sensory issues?"

"Yes. Lyle told me himself that he's on the spectrum."

I stare at her. I can't believe what I'm hearing. Her reasoning isn't at all what I was expecting. I thought that maybe she knew the guy she slapped, that he made a pass at her perhaps, or kept sending his food back to be funny.

Knowing she lost her job because she stood up for someone else . . . it makes me look at her with fresh eyes. Should she have slapped that guy? No. Definitely not. But regardless, I can't help but feel a sense of respect for her and for the way she's taking ownership of her actions right now. If I didn't need her to be my nanny so badly, I might even make arrangements for her to have her old job back.

I get up from my seat. Her gaze follows me as I walk toward her, shrinking the distance between us. The air around her smells unreal, mouthwatering like coconut and vanilla. "I understand," I say. "And I'm sorry that happened, but I have to admit, I'm glad to have you here. Especially at a time like this."

She cocks her head sideways. "A time like this? What do you mean?"

"I'm just going to be completely honest here." My breath escapes in a loud sigh. Better to get it over with now than later, even if it's still hard to talk about. "The children's mother—Jill—she's no longer around. We haven't been together for about a year now, and unfortunately, she doesn't want anything to do with the kids."

Addison's face is like a stone wall. "What do you mean? They're her kids too, aren't they?"

I nod, but that's all she's getting. I'm not going into the

nitty-gritty details with her about how Jill has always been a free spirit. About how she thought of me as the fun college guy who would make a great fling until I made the mistake of falling too far. About how she accepted my proposal because she liked the idea of a wedding but not a marriage. How getting pregnant with the girls during the wedding planning stage postponed everything. How she wanted to get back in shape after giving birth, only to get pregnant again with the boys. And then experiencing a postpartum depression after they were born that never left —a depression so bad that she wanted nothing to do with any of us anymore.

All she needs to know is why it's so important for her to be here. "The kids have had it rough the past year," I say. "But I'm hoping it's finally about to get better, because I'm getting married."

"Oh." She blinks a few times. "I didn't realize you were engaged. Congratulations."

"Thank you. I'm actually heading to Chicago two weeks from now to . . . visit my fiancée. But I'll do my best to help you get acquainted with the kids in the meantime. I know they can be a lot to handle."

"Don't worry," she says. "I have a feeling the five of us are about to become best buddies."

The kids are not, in fact, ready to become Addison's best buddies. This becomes abundantly clear over the next few days. First, Izzy convinces her siblings that making "paper snowflakes" out of Addison's packing cubes is a good idea.

Somehow, Addison remains calm, though I notice the way her mouth tightens when Izzy explains her intentions during the apology I force out of her.

The day after that, Moxie and Enzo get into Addison's makeup. It's been a while since something like this has happened because most of my nannies have been older; many of them did not have expansive makeup collections like Addison's.

When she brings me Moxie and Enzo, covered head to toe in lipstick and shimmering powder, I imagine what a field day Dad would have if he saw Enzo playing with beauty products. He used to yell at me for being interested in my mom's makeup, telling me I was a wuss and that I needed to find something more masculine to do.

The painful memory propels my next words. "Enzo, stay away from Addison's makeup. You understand?"

He crosses his arms and pouts.

"I mean it. It's one thing for Moxie to play with it, but you . . ." I trail off, unable to finish. It feels so wrong to tell him this. I don't have it in me. He's just a kid, and it doesn't matter to me if he wants to play makeup with his sister. So I say, "You need to ask Addison first if it's okay. Both of you."

Addison looks sheepish. "I didn't bring them in here to get them in trouble. I just wanted to know if it's okay for me to give them a bath, or if that's something you'd prefer to do."

I want to shake her, to ask her how she's fine with them messing with her stuff. None of the other nannies were. The fact that she's ready to roll up her sleeves and give them a bath? It's unexpected. It makes respect for her rise up inside me.

"I'm okay with it. But please, let me know if you need help." Our eyes connect, bringing forth a rushing in my veins, so I stare at the floor. *Inappropriate, Perry. You cannot be attracted to her. She's your nanny, for crying out loud.*

Over the rest of the week, Addison endures the same terrible treatment as all the previous nannies. The week mark is where most of them tend to quit, but somehow, Addison remains positive, even when Moxie gets into one of her dresses for the Miss Meadow pageant, and Abel puts twigs in her bed sheets because it's hilarious to him.

With disappointment, Izzy observes that Addison isn't getting frustrated like she's supposed to, which would be the last straw for me personally.

But Addison doesn't quit. On Friday, I walk into the girls' room to find Abel coloring while sitting on Izzy's bed. The other three kids are playing dolls with Addison. As ashamed as I am to admit it, I don't normally let Enzo play with dolls because I'm afraid it's just another avenue for my dad to torment me. With phrases like, 'You're too much of a soft boy, Perry. I didn't raise you this way,' constantly echoing in my head, I can't help but worry I've somehow passed my softness onto my son.

But Addison doesn't seem to find anything wrong with it, which only makes my attraction to her worse. There's something about her gentle confidence with the kids, her determination and drive to keep going that keeps pulling me in.

When she makes the kids' lunch every day, she always makes a plate for me, too. It's such a kind gesture, one I try to ignore and never completely acknowledge. Letting myself do so will only lead me closer to the slippery slope I'm avoiding —crossing the line between professional and inappropriate.

She's good. Too good. Almost a suspicious level of good. That is, until Friday afternoon. It's then that I hear panic in Addison's voice for the first time.

Chapter Seven

I CAN'T BELIEVE Abel would do this. The day with the water balloons, I fooled myself into thinking these kids liked me. But since then, they've pretty much made it clear they don't, no matter how hard I try to make their time with me as fun as possible.

"Abel." I knock softly on his bedroom door. "Please unlock the handle."

Silence.

"I'll do anything. Please."

We've been at this for twenty minutes.

At first, my knocks and pleas were met with entertained giggles from the other end. But it's been a while since that last happened, and now I'm starting to get worried. A montage of possible, deadly hypothetical scenarios plays through my mind. What if he found a small toy in his room and decided to put it in his mouth and now he's choking? What if he's coloring all over the walls? Or maybe he took off his diaper and had an accident on his bed.

The fact that I'm supposed to be looking after him and I have no idea what he's doing is terrible. If Perry finds out, he might fire me. Again. It's the only reason I haven't asked him for help yet, why I've tried numerous times to use a hairpin to unlock the door through the tiny circular hole in the handle where only a specific type of key would fit—the long, skinny kind— and it's nowhere in sight.

"Open the door!" My voice finally betraying my desperation, I smack my fist on the door. Still, Abel offers me nothing. Not a grunt, a laugh, or even audible footsteps so I know he's all right.

It might be officially time to ask for help. Because I've been up here so long, I haven't been keeping an eye on the other kids. They're all downstairs, getting into who knows what? It would be irresponsible of me not to fill Perry in by now.

I rush upstairs to Perry's wing and rap my knuckles on his office door. "Perry? There's a bit of a . . . situation. I really need your help."

No more than five seconds pass before Perry opens the door. His body is tense, and his eyebrows are pinched together. "What's wrong? What happened?"

"Abel got mad because his socks were bugging his toes, so he locked himself in his room. At first, he was laughing because he thought it was funny that I couldn't get in, but now he's silent and I still can't get the door open." I hang my head in shame.

"No. Not again." Perry's voice rises a bit, making my stomach drop. "He's done this before, but not since we lost the keys." He swears. "I knew I should have changed the doorknobs."

His steps quicken as I follow him downstairs to the second floor. Perry crosses his arms as he glares at the door. "Who else is in there with him?"

"No one. It's just Abel. The other kids are downstairs." *Do not cry, Addison.* I hold up my hairpin. "I've been trying to unlock it with this, but it's not working."

Perry takes it from me, trying for several minutes and swearing again when it doesn't work for him either. "Abel?" He shouts at the door. "Open up." His fist knocks harder than mine. There's no way Abel doesn't hear it, but there's no indication of what he's doing in there.

Perry exhales sharply. "Okay. Let me think."

"What happened to the keys?"

"Izzy threw them in the trash without telling me. By the time she admitted it, they were long gone."

A twinge of pity forms in my chest for Perry. Now I understand why he was so anxious on my first day. These kids really are a lot for one person, especially with Perry's restaurant business to manage on top of making sure stuff like this doesn't happen. I don't know how he finds time to take care of himself while he's trying to keep four tiny humans alive.

That's what he hired a nanny for, Addison.

"I'm so sorry," I mumble.

His gaze jumps to my face. "Over this? Trust me, this is nothing, and it's not your fault. I'm just trying to figure out the best way to proceed from here."

"We could remove the door?" I suggest.

But he shakes his head. "No. The hinges are on the

other side so we can't get to them, see?" He motions to it. "I'm going to have to kick it down." He turns around, putting his back against the door. Then he cranks his knee up, fully prepared to slam his heel into the door jam opposite of the hinges.

"Wait! That seems a bit excessive. Not to mention, you might scare him, or hurt him if he's on the other side. Isn't there . . ." I bite my lip. "What if we go through his bedroom window? Is there a way in?"

He glances at the stairs. "I have a balcony outside my bedroom, and Abel and Enzo's room is right underneath. There is a small ledge outside their window one of us could stand on. But it would be kinda dangerous."

I jump at his words, eager for a way to redeem myself. This was a massive slip-up on my part, and I want—no, *need*—to make it right. "I'll do it. Just help me down your balcony and I'll go through the window."

He stares at me for a long minute, debating. "I don't know, Addison."

"Come on. What's our other option? We could call the fire department, but this will be faster. He's been in there for twenty minutes now with no answer, Perry."

Some of the color drains from his face. "Okay. Let's go."

The next few seconds seem to pass in a blur. My heart races as I follow Perry into his room, barely registering what it looks like inside because I have tunnel vision for the task at hand. Perry opens the French double doors to the balcony, and we walk out onto it. I lean over the railing to look down, spotting the ledge he's talking about. It's a flat spot on the roof before it dips downward, wide enough for me to stand on, but if I trip or lose my footing, I'll end up falling to the ground from two stories high. "At least it's grassy down there," I say, laughing faintly.

"That's not funny. You don't have to do this."

"I'm doing it whether you help me or not." I step onto the bottom of the rail.

Without warning, he puts his hands on my waist and lifts me up so I'm sitting on the thin balcony railing. My brain fogs up at the contact for a moment before I snap out of it.

He's your boss, and this is an emergency. Focus.

"Don't worry," Perry murmurs. "I won't let you fall."

I nod, even though I'm shaking as I hoist one leg over the edge. Perry's grip moves from my waist to my hands, and I bring my other leg over the railing. He's the only thing keeping me from falling backwards now. I try not to focus on that fact as I slowly bring one foot down. The ledge outside Abel's window is too far down for my foot to meet, but Perry's grip on me is incredibly secure as he lowers me enough to let go. My feet hit solid roofing. The window is right in front of me now, and my worried reflection stares back.

"You okay?" Perry calls from the balcony.

"I'm fine." *Don't look behind you, Addison. And do not look down.*

I swallow my fear and start prying off the screen, almost crying in relief when I see the window is cracked open an inch. That will make things so much easier. My long, painted fingernails tear in the process to get the screen off, but I don't care. I toss it to the ground once it's off and slide the window open.

"I got it open," I tell Perry. "Meet me on the other side of the door."

"Okay, I'm going."

Thankfully, I'm in decent physical shape, so it's not too difficult to pull myself up and into the bedroom. A thud sounds through the room as I fall onto the wood floor. When I stand up and scan the room, my heart falls right through my stomach.

Abel isn't in here. The room is completely empty.

The two matching beds in here are mattresses on the ground with wooden frames in the shape of a house, the covers messy and unmade. I lift the blankets up to make sure Abel isn't hiding under them. I open all the drawers of the large, navy blue dresser against the wall. He's not hiding in any of them.

"Addison?" Perry's muffled voice is on the other side of the door. "Open up."

Tears cloud my vision as I unlock the handle and open the door. This is all my fault. His child disappeared on my watch. "He's not in here. I can't find him."

Perry frowns. He quickly scans the bedroom, then moves toward the closet. As soon as he opens it, a low chuckle escapes him. "Here's the little monster."

Hope rises in my chest. He moves aside to reveal Abel curled up in a ball, fast asleep on the closet floor. It's such a relief to see that he's okay; I could kiss him. My breath escapes in a loud exhale. I sink to the ground. "Thank God."

Perry smiles. "See? Everything is fine."

We leave Abel in his room to finish napping. Before Perry shuts the door, he ties a sock on the handle in an intricate knot to keep it from closing all the way. "I'll have Kiera replace the doorknobs tomorrow," he tells me. "And thank you for climbing through the window. That was brave."

The way he looks at me makes my stomach flutter, but I ignore it. "Of course. I'm just glad he's okay."

A loud crashing sound from downstairs makes me jump. "And with that, I better get back to work." I salute him like an idiot.

"Don't worry. You get Saturdays and Sundays off." He salutes me right back, a smile tugging at his lips. "And I'm still here if you need me."

I don't lose any more of Perry's kids. The rest of the day—mercifully—passes with ease, and the weekend offers me a much needed break. I knew this job would have its challenges, but I admit it's a lot harder than I thought it would be. And Perry? Well, it would be a whole lot easier to keep my head free of distractions if it weren't for him. Like, is it completely necessary for his voice to be so deep and gravelly that I can feel it in my chest, or for his smile to make my knees wobbly? I think not.

Regardless, I manage to make it through the next few days without any more emergencies taking place. I still don't know if the kids like me, even though I'm trying as hard as I can.

"Maybe this was a mistake," I tell Romilly over the phone Tuesday night. "Maybe I should have just gotten a regular job."

"But you love kids. And every job is hard at first. Remember how much you hated working at Rosemary Banquet when you first started? It's going to get easier, Addy. Just hang in there. By the way, I need your new address."

I sigh. She's right. I know she is. "Fine," I tell her. "I'm going to bed, but I'll call you tomorrow."

After we hang up, I text Romilly Perry's address and wince at the time on my phone. It's past midnight. As much as I'd like to watch some pageant videos, I know I'll regret it in the morning because the kids never sleep in past six.

I close my eyes and start to drift off, but don't get very far because my bedroom door bangs open without warning.

My eyes fly open, heart nearly pounding out of my chest. Abel is standing in the doorway holding his blanket. His blue eyes are red-rimmed. He doesn't say a word as he climbs into my bed with me.

"Oh. Hi, Abel. Everything okay, little guy?"

He whimpers in response.

And then I remember something Kiera told me during my interview—something about night terrors. "Did you have a bad dream?"

He hesitates before nodding. And then he scoots his body right up against mine and lowers his head onto my shoulder.

Something inside my chest melts a little.

"Aww, it's okay. You can sleep in here with me, alright?"

A nod, and then he closes his eyes. The front strands of his blond hair are plastered to his forehead with sweat.

"Addy?" Izzy's voice comes from the doorway. I sit up, squinting through my dark room to see her, Moxie, and Enzo peering at me. "Abel woke us up with his screams and now we're scared, too."

I want to laugh. They all look so cute, huddled together, stuffed animals in hand and faces pinched together. "Get on over here, then, you little chicken butts."

Moxie cracks a smile and Izzy laughs. The three of them climb into the bed with me.

The combined sound of all our breathing fills up the room.

"I scared," Enzo whispers.

I brush his dark hair away from his face with my fingers. Hair that very much resembles Perry's. "Don't be. Just think of happy things, and it will be easy to fall back asleep."

"Like what kind of happy things, Addy?" Moxie asks in a squeaky voice.

"Like . . . candy. And Christmas. Fields of flowers. Dandelions." My throat catches on the last one, so I clear it. "Think about the best day of your life and tell yourself to dream about it when you close your eyes."

They're silent after that. I can practically feel them all trying to do what I suggested, and somehow, it works. Within minutes, all five of us are asleep.

In the morning, things are different between me and the kids. There are no pranks. No more yelling and screaming. They listen to me the entire morning with no complaints.

It's almost as if they like me now.

Chapter Eight

PERRY

AT LUNCH TIME, Addison makes an extra plate for me and carries it upstairs to my office while I'm working.

I'm in the middle of renewing one of the restaurant's licenses when she comes in, but I turn off the computer when I see the plate of grilled chicken and sweet potatoes in her hands. The scent of it hits my nose when she sets in on the desk, causing my stomach to growl.

As she turns to leave, the urge to stop her seizes me. Since she climbed through Abel's window to unlock the door, I feel like we've gone from boss and employee to . . . friends? Close acquaintances? Nothing like an emergency with my crazy kids to create a bonding moment between me and my nanny. I'm not sure she feels the same way, but I enjoy talking to her. She's dramatic and funny, and right now, I want her to stay a minute longer because work is frying my brain.

"Addison? Could I talk to you for a minute?" The words escape me before I can stop them.

She turns back around to face me. "Sure." She studies my face like she's unsure of what I could want to say.

That makes two of us. To buy myself some time to think of something, I run my hands down my face. And then I remember I'm leaving for my trip to Chicago tomorrow. "I just wanted to remind you I'm leaving town in the morning."

"I have it in my calendar." She retrieves her phone from the back pocket of her jeans just to pull it out and show me. I want to laugh.

"Good."

"I hope you have a good time with your fiancée." Do I imagine the way it seems forced as she says it?

I clear my throat to keep from laughing. It feels silly now that I didn't just tell her the truth the first time I brought it up. After everything she's been through with my kids, I owe her a little bit of honesty. She's going to be sticking around for a while, hopefully, so it's probably time I filled her in on some things.

Blood rushes to my face, because I already know how stupid my next sentence is going to sound. "Thank you, but I'm not actually engaged yet. I'm leaving to meet with an agency that will match me with a list of potential wives because . . ." I cringe. "I have to be married to inherit my house, thanks to the will and trust my mother set up." I try to make it sound casual, but it feels like a confession, a shared secret between us as soon as it leaves my lips. "Kiera will be Lillian's point of contact while I'm gone, so she'll be pretty busy. You probably won't see her around until I'm back."

"Woah, woah, woah. Back up. Wait a minute. Are you

serious? You're looking for a marriage of convenience? Perry!"

The way she squeaks my name, it's like she already knows me. Like she thinks we're friends, too. I like it, and I can't deny it. "Marriage of convenience? You act like it's a bad thing. Or like it's common or something."

"Well, I wouldn't say it's common, or bad, per say. But it's a famous trope in romance books and movies."

I chuckle. "Technically, whoever I get paired with is looking for a marriage of convenience, too. And what else am I supposed to do? This house . . . there are so many memories of my mom here before, uh—" I clear my throat, "before we lost her. This is my home in every sense of the word. I can't just lose it to my sister over something like this. It's a screwed up situation, but I really can't risk it."

"Okay, back up again. What exactly are the terms of this will and trust thingy?"

I sigh, trying to remember the specifics. "My mother wanted me to have my childhood home once my dad was ready to retire. I could inherit it as long as I was married. If I wasn't, Rebecca, my half-sister, would inherit it if she was married. Which, she is."

"So, marriage trumps the fact that you have kids?"

"Oh, for sure. My parents wanted me to do things in the traditional order," I say. "Marriage, then kids. They wouldn't reward me for having kids out of wedlock."

"And your dad is ready to retire?" Addison chews her lip.

"Yep. I've already taken over his restaurant, and he's moving to Florida in January. Which means if I don't get married by the end of the year, me and the kids will have to move out, and Rebecca will own this house."

"Interesting." She tilts her head. "So, you're just going to marry a random stranger? Ew."

"Ew?" A smile tugs at my lips. "Ew? Really?"

"Yes. Ew."

"Well, I don't see you offering up your hand." As soon as I say it, I want to take it back. That was way out of line for me to say to my employee.

Pink spots form on her cheeks, but she doesn't look away. "Sorry. I can't get married. Not if I want to be Miss Meadow. And I can't have kids or step-kids either, so you can just count me out as an option."

"Really? That's a pageant rule?"

"A very firm rule, practically written in stone."

I laugh. "Kinda like the rules for me to get this house. So, when I get back, we can discuss whether or not my wife selection is still disgusting to you."

"Fine."

"Great." I pick up the fork and stab a piece of chicken. "Thank you for lunch, by the way. It looks delicious."

"You're welcome." She clears her throat, backing away from me and walks to the door, but she turns around to look at me again before she closes it. The way she twirls her curly hair around her finger makes me want to weave my fingers through it to see if it's as silky as it looks.

Bad Perry. Get a grip.

"Text me if you need anything," I say.

With a tight nod, she shuts the door behind her.

The rest of the day passes uneventfully until my dad calls me just before I'm about to drift off at my desk. I don't know why I even answer the call. I should expect by now that when he contacts me, it's never to say things like, 'I'm proud of you, son' or 'Good job handling the new vegan options on the menu' or even, 'Let's grab coffee because it's been a while.'

When he starts interrogating me about my imaginary fiancée, I shouldn't be so surprised. "I mean it, Perry. You've been talking this woman up for a month now. I can't wait to see if she's as great as you say on Saturday."

"Perfect."

"I sure hope she's good enough for you, son. If you want the house, you have about six months to make sure."

"Don't worry," I mutter. "She is good enough. I'm getting married and you'll finally have a less disappointing son."

There's a brief pause. His voice softens the barest hint of a fraction. It's so subtle that I'm probably just imagining it. "I don't blame you for what happened with Jill. And your mother chose these terms because she cared about you, Perry. She knew that finding that perfect person would make you the man you're meant to be. Marriage isn't for the weak—it takes commitment and sacrifice." His voice lowers an octave. It's the tone he only uses when he's giving me advice I didn't ask for. "I've already put you in charge of my five-star business. Now, you're about to fulfill the terms of the will. That's a good thing, son. You'll be setting a good example for your kids by settling down."

"Got it, Dad. It's in the works, like I said."

"Good."

"I'll talk to you soon," I mumble. "Goodnight." Hanging up the phone, I set it back down on my desk. I wish I could somehow stop caring about sentimental things, because it's not like they're going to bring my mother back. But I haven't exactly cracked that code yet. If Mom was still alive, I bet I could reason with her. She'd hear me out, just like she always used to, and there would be no more terms for me to adhere to. She'd be proud of who I am today, and as a result, Dad would be proud of me, too. But it seems like after she died, Dad has only gotten more critical of me. And that was when I was ten.

It's been eighteen years without her, and every single memory I have of my mom is almost completely tied to my childhood home.

I hate how much I care about this house.

But at least this time, I'm not choosing to care about something that can hurt me if I accidentally love it too much.

Chapter Nine

ADDISON

THE REST OF THE DAY, I tell myself I'm not going to stick my nose where it doesn't belong. I see Perry packing for his trip once he finishes work and mind my business, refraining from talking him out of his decision to marry a random woman. But by the time the kids are getting out the rest of their energy in the girls' room after dinner, I'm practically bursting at the seams.

His plan is a terrible one.

There's no way his future marriage is going to last if he's seeking it out purely for his gain. My parents knew each other for seven years before they got married, and it was still strained my whole childhood. I remember the constant fighting and screaming like it happened last week. If I'm being honest, I think caring for my brother might be the only glue left holding them together.

Perry choosing to marry a stranger just to keep his house is asking for trouble.

My resolve weakens when he comes downstairs from

his office to eat a late dinner. I plop down at the table and continue studying him as he serves himself a plate of the chicken parmesan I made. His cream shirt makes the golden-brown tones in his eyes and skin pop, and I'm having a hard time not noticing.

He's handsome—not that I'm checking him out or anything. His good looks are a simple fact, like the ocean being wet, or pink being the best color in the rainbow. Perry is probably the most beautiful man I've ever seen. He also has money, and his children are adorable. If he just took the time to get to know someone, I know they'd see all his positive attributes. He shouldn't have to marry a stranger.

He lowers himself into the chair across from mine and sets his plate down. "This looks offensively delicious. I can't wait to try it."

Against my better judgement, a question escapes my lips. "So, about this new wife of yours . . ." His fork pauses halfway to his mouth, but I continue. "What if your children don't like her?"

The fork lowers as he contemplates his next words. "Hopefully that doesn't happen. But if it does . . . then I guess we don't have to stay together."

I slap my hand on the table, making him jump. "And now you're already planning a divorce! I can't believe you."

"I never said anything about a divorce. Just that we wouldn't have to be together. Like, me and the kids wouldn't have to be around her."

"That's as good as calling it quits." I cross my arms.

"Addison . . ." He laughs incredulously. "It's really not

that serious. I don't understand why you're getting so worked up about it."

Why am I getting so worked up about it? Maybe it's because I've seen what Perry's life is like these past two weeks. I've witnessed the stress he constantly has to deal with. But somehow, this man still finds it in him to do things like speak politely and show concern when his kids are in trouble. Yesterday, Moxie cut her finger on some cardboard, and Perry drove to the closest city outside Meadow Hills to find a store with her favorite princess band-aids in stock.

He's . . . *nice.*

Even if he did have me fired.

"Because your trip is tomorrow and you're acting like you're fine," I finally answer. "What if your children are too much for your new wife to handle? What if you decide one day that you can't stand the way she chews her food? This is serious."

There's a brief pause as I stare at my hands, knotted on the table. When I glance back up at him, he's regarding me with tender eyes that do funny things to my stomach. "I'm sorry. You're right."

"What?"

"You're right," he says simply. "It is a big deal. *Marriage* is a big deal. I'm just trying not to think of it that way. This is something I need to do for me, and for my kids. I don't want them to feel like ever since their mom left, their life is falling apart. I want them to have stability, and I want them to feel confident that I'll provide that for them. Otherwise, first it's their mom, and then the only home they've ever known? What if they think it's going to be me they lose next? I don't want them ever to think I'd abandon them, too." Perry's voice cracks on the word *abandon*. I can't help but wonder if that's how he felt when Jill left. Abandoned. Because she didn't only leave the children, or the kind of life she was living by having them.

She left Perry, too.

He finally takes a bite of food, chewing it slowly, probably so he won't have to talk to me again.

"I get it," I say. "But why not just date someone and marry for love?"

He almost chokes on his bite. "Love? Seriously?"

"Yeah. You could date a nice girl. Get married when the time is right."

"I only have six months, remember?" His shoulders sag as he takes a deep breath. "*Love.* Look where that got me last time. How is 'dating a nice girl' any different from what I did with Jill? I loved her, but we never made it down the aisle."

"Fair point."

He nods. "There aren't any guarantees with love, considering my time frame. But at least there's a guarantee with a—what did you call it? A marriage of convenience." He crosses his arms, exposing the muscles from under his rolled-up sleeves.

"I know how you feel. My boyfriend dumped me last month. Before we got together, I told myself I wasn't going to date because, well, there's no point. I need to focus on the pageant, and dating is really just a distraction. Why tease myself?"

Perry searches my face from across the table. "I don't see how anyone couldn't like you. You're like a sweet little bunny or something. All cute and fluffy, hopping around like you don't have a care in the world. It's pretty adorable."

My entire face blushes. A laugh escapes without my permission. "I can't believe you just said that."

"Sorry." His lips part into a wide grin. "You're right. That was probably an inappropriate thing to say to my nanny. It's true though." Without preamble, he gets out of his seat. "I need to finish packing for my trip."

"You mean your wife shopping?"

"Wife shopping. Marriage of convenience initiation. Call it what you want, bunny. But to me, I'm securing my future."

I try desperately to hold in a laugh. "Then, by all means, don't let me stop you."

I take a shower after I put the kids to bed.

The water feels amazing against my skin. I shut my eyes and put my face in the stream, trying not to think about Perry.

Call it what you want, bunny.

Ugh.

Maybe taking this particular job wasn't such a good idea after all. I said it myself. The last thing I need is a distraction to keep me from my goals, but that's kinda what's been happening since I started working for Perry. I need to remember why winning is so important to me.

As painful as it is, I think back to that moment, that day, I realized I was never going to see Gran again.

Holding her hand in the hospital room as she took her last breaths, smiling at me with such love and pride. I remember thinking, *how do you say goodbye to the woman who practically raised you?*

Mom sat in one of the chairs, a sobbing mess who couldn't be consoled. She couldn't look Gran in the eyes, and I couldn't blame her. She and my dad spent the majority of my childhood with my brother and getting him the care he needed. When they weren't taking care of Finn, they were working. I know Mom felt guilty for pawning me off onto Gran so much as a result.

But I'm grateful they did. Otherwise, I never would have had the privilege of getting to know Gran so well. And as the first ever Miss Meadow, she was a fascinating woman. She taught me how to eat with etiquette, how to walk like a lady, how to retain information when I studied. She gave me my first custom ballgown at eighteen, when I decided I wanted to follow her footsteps and enter the pageant for the first time. I still remember the way her eyes shined with honor, as if it were a privilege to give *me* the gown, instead of the other way around. I could tell it meant a lot to her that I was determined to become the next Miss Meadow in the family, especially since Mom showed no interest in our small-town pageant.

Gran became my mentor, my teacher, my best friend. Year after year, when I'd lose to another local girl, she'd tell me to keep trying. "If that girl can do it," she'd say, "and if I could do it, Addy, then so can you. Don't stop trying, sweet girl. You just keep wishing on dandelions, and never underestimate the power of prayer. Turn that wish into a prayer for the Lord every time you blow one of these lovely flowers out."

We'd blow out a dandelion together every year before the pageant began. It became a sort of tradition of ours. Get our hair and nails done, practice speaking about my chosen cause to support, hold hands in prayer, and wish on dandelions.

I brought one with me to the hospital that day. As she faded away, I held out the fluffy flower to her and promised her I'd win. I promised her I'd never give up. And then we blew the flower out together. Her wheezy breaths didn't do much, but it still meant the world to me that she participated. Till the end, she never left me hanging.

I can't leave her hanging, either. No matter what, I have to follow through on my promise to Gran and show her I believe in myself as much as she believed in me. No more drifting. No more distractions. Especially Perry's marriage situation—and maybe even Perry himself.

I turn the shower off, ignoring the burning in my throat. As I get dressed, I make a point to choose something extra modest. A baggy T-shirt long enough to reach my knees, even though it's June. Boyfriend jeans. Hair in a bun. Anything that will repulse Perry, because if I catch him staring at me one more time, I just might let myself stare back.

And that would be the exact opposite of avoiding any more distractions.

Chapter Ten

PERRY

SAYING goodbye to the kids was harder than I thought. Moxie and Enzo, holding onto my leg, begging me not to go. Abel transforming into a crying heap on the floor. Izzy, pretending not to care as she crossed her arms and hid her quivering bottom lip.

I'm not sure who it was harder on—me or them.

I slide down the desk chair in my hotel room and close my eyes. The room is nothing special, and I could definitely afford better, but I've never really been a hotel snob, and this was the closest place to stay near the agency. I feel drained even though my flight was nothing to complain about. I'm supposed to meet Donna Caldwell, the international marriage broker for United We Band first thing in the morning, so I should probably get some rest soon.

My phone starts ringing just as I'm about to move from the desk to the bed.

At first, I'm worried it's Addison calling about the kids, but I relax when I see that it's just my buddy, Logan.

"Hey man," I answer.

"Don't you *hey man* me," he snaps. "We were supposed to hit the gym this week. This is the third time you've bailed."

Oops. "I'm sorry. I've just had a lot on my mind lately."

A beat of silence. And then, "I'm listening."

I fill Logan in on everything that's happened, starting with having to fire Addison at the restaurant all the way up to my trip here at the marriage broker.

"You need therapy," he tells me. "And I don't mean that as an insult. Think of it as brotherly advice."

"I appreciate it."

"So, this Addison girl," he says. I picture him rubbing his chin. "The way you talk about her makes it sound like you're into her."

Alarm bells ring in my head. "No. Of course I'm not into her. She's just my nanny. My employee."

"Mhmm." There's a smile in his voice. "I'll tell you what. If you need me to step in and help the rizz start flowing, just give me a call and I'll drive you two somewhere nice."

Logan has been working as a limo driver in between trying to make it as a pro surfer. I've been one of his best customers ever since, and I can't deny that it's awesome having my favorite friend drive me around instead of having to rack up miles on my car. "Will do."

"I mean it. Don't wuss out on her like you did on me with the gym."

"I didn't wuss out." I sound like a younger sibling

trying to defend himself against his older brother, calling him a doo-doo head. "And you're on. Let's see if your 'rizz' is all it's cracked up to be."

"I'm going to ignore that. We both know it is, my dude."

I hate that he's right. Logan isn't just a guy. He's *the* guy. Six foot four, velvety dark skin, and a blinding white smile that I've witnessed the aftermath of firsthand.

"I'll talk to you later." I hang up with him and sigh. I should go to bed now, but my open laptop stares at me on the desk, so I comb through my email inbox one more time to make sure there's nothing important I'm neglecting. Addison's job application catches my eye. It makes me wonder what she's up to right now, if the kids are behaving for her. Maine is only an hour behind Chicago, and it's 9:30pm here, so they're probably asleep, unless Abel is still wailing for me, which is entirely possible.

After the locked-bedroom incident, I've learned first-hand that Addison would rather handle everything herself than reach out for help, so a small text checking in on her couldn't hurt.

ME

How's everything going?

Several minutes pass without a response.

Oh, no.

What if my kids won't go to bed because I'm gone and are currently terrorizing her? What if she's packing all her bags this second, getting ready to dip out because they're too much? And I'm all the way in another state.

My knees bounce as I stare at the phone. It's hard not

to let my mind get carried away when I've had so many nannies quit on me in the past. Though I'll probably never tell her and risk scaring her away, Addison is number twelve in my long line of past nannies.

Everything's fine. She's probably asleep already.

Sleeping is what I should be doing, too. I have important decisions to make tomorrow. I need to make sure my head is on straight when I look at potential candidates to marry.

Her text message comes through, along with a picture of her lounging on a chaise in the backyard. Her long legs are crossed and there's a glass of white wine in her left hand. The green dress she's wearing falls gracefully around her knees. *How many sundresses does this woman own?* I read the messages underneath.

ADDISON

> You have quite the wine collection.

> Kids are in bed, BTW! Don't worry! hehe

> Hope it's okay that I have some! You told me to help myself that night Abel bit my hand, so I took a raincheck.

Her babble of messages makes me chuckle aloud. With a smile on my face, I type back.

ME

> Drink away. You deserve it. Those kids are something else.

ADDISON

> Ha! K, thanks

Also, they're not even bad. After you left, Enzo drew me a picture, and Izzy braided my hair into a crown. Think I might love them. Hope that's okay.

Hope swells in my chest, but I shove it down. Sure, she's made it longer than most of my nannies, but there's still time for things to go wrong.

ME

More than okay.

Goodnight.

ADDISON

Night!

By the way, I don't drink very often, and when I do, I only have one glass.

ME

I'm really not worried.

ADDISON

Okay. Goodnight for real this time.

I toss my phone onto the bed behind me and shut my laptop. By the time I strip down to my underwear and settle into the firm mattress, my mind is clear of worries. But as soon as I shut my eyes, Addison's teasing, dimpled smile flashes like a projector against a black backdrop.

Go to sleep, Perry. You're looking for a wife in the morning.

Somehow, I manage to turn my brain off. I have no idea how much time has passed since I got in bed, but I'm about to drift off. Finally.

My phone vibrates with a new message from Addison.

ADDISON

I know I lied and told Asher I already
have a new boyfriend, but I kinda want to
text him

I hate sleeping alone :(

Talk me out of it, Romilly!!!

The way I shoot up in the bed, sleep forgotten, is probably comparable to a man being electrocuted. I reread the messages several times just to make sure I'm not hallucinating. And then more come through.

ADDISON

And Perry isn't helping

Remind me again why Asher doesn't
deserve me, please

Romilly???

I blink away the shock. *Perry isn't helping?* What could I have possibly done from all the way over here?
My thumbs start typing before I can stop them.

ME

I'm not sure who Romilly is, but I'll
remind you. If you have to ask, the guy
doesn't deserve you.

And what am I not helping?

I wait up for another hour, perched on the edge of the bed like a maniac, but Addison never responds.

It's rough to wake up in the morning. I barely slept at all. Against my better judgement, I couldn't stop wondering if Addison ended up texting that Asher dude and inviting him over. My mind kept spinning out of control, imagining her inviting him into her room, letting him cuddle with her. Running his fingers through all that long, dark hair. Him whispering things in her ear to make her giggle, that sweet, charming little sound I've heard her make.

Focus, Perry. It's none of your business.

Either way, I overslept this morning and now I'm late. I tap on the handle in the backseat of my Uber, but the driver doesn't say much as he navigates the busy streets of Chicago to get me to my destination. We pass through the skyscrapers on Michigan Ave until we reach the smaller— but still quite tall—office buildings on Superior St. Big cities like this are fascinating to me, but all the hustle and bustle makes me happy to call a smaller town like Meadow Hills home. I hand the driver a wad of cash when he drops me off outside my destination.

I speed walk to the elevator and hit the button for the second-floor, as directed by Donna over email. The agency's door is propped wide open, so I go on in. A middle-aged woman is typing on a computer at the check-in desk, so I have a seat in the cluster of leather chairs off to the right. A few potted trees are staged against the light green walls, and the air freshener smells like a pleasant mix of mint and sunscreen.

"Mr. Whitmore?" The woman at the computer desk gets to her feet, walking over to greet me.

"Hi." I stand up and shake her hand. "You can call me Perry." I straighten my suit. I debated on wearing it, but decided to go for it in case there's a match here for me to meet today.

"Nice to meet you. I'm Donna. If you want to come on back to my office, we can get started." She rubs her hands together like she's about to dig into a box of donuts, smiling wide enough that the corners of her eyes wrinkle.

We walk together to her office down the hall. I know I should focus, but all I can think about at the moment is my kids. Will they be happy about this when they find out? Probably. They get excited when new weeds sprout up in the front yard. But what about in a year or two? I can't help but remember Addison's warning. That my kids might not get along with whoever I marry. Problem is, I don't really have another option, because losing my childhood home to Rebecca would be much worse.

And as for falling in love—Addison's other suggestion?

Marriage meant a lot to me back when Jill and I first got together. I saved up every hard-earned penny to buy her the ring of her dreams. We talked about how intimate our relationship would become, dedicating ourselves to each other and being together forever.

Turns out, it was all talk for her. I gave that woman my whole heart and then watched her toss it in the trash on her way out of my life and the kids' lives.

Now, it's hard to imagine love is even real, or worth it.

I sit across from Donna at a small round table in the center of her office. She's holding a tablet, and she slides it over to me. "Here's a list of potential matches for you, Perry. Based on the extensive questionnaire you filled out last month, I think you have quite a few great options." She beams at me, exposing all her teeth, and the smudge of pink lipstick stuck to one of them.

I swipe through the profiles of the women. Most of them are pretty, but none of them stand out to me, so I read their bios. Courtney likes dogs and Italian food. Amara enjoys hiking and beaches. Kim swears by essential oils and meditation.

Cool. Great.

I nod at Donna, pursing my lips to hide my disappointment. I thought it would be easy to look at these faces and pick the person who felt the most right. But I can't deny that I'm feeling pretty much nothing in this moment.

"Take your time," she urges. "And if you'd like, I can simply set up meetings with all your matches. That way, you have the ability to explore all the potential relationships. It's important not to make any rash decisions."

If by *rash decisions*, she means calling this quits and not paying her agency fifteen thousand dollars, I can see why she's worried.

"Yeah, sure." My shoulders sag. "Are any of them here today for me to meet in person?" *And convince to come home with me for my dad to meet?*

"Oh." Donna frowns. "No, no. We only set up in-person meetings after interest has been shown by both parties. As I'm sure you understand, it takes time to arrange travel on both sides until then."

My stomach drops. What am I supposed to do when my dad shows up in two days, then, fully expecting to meet my new fiancée?

My next words to Donna come out through my teeth. "Fine." I point to a random girl on the screen. "Can you have this one come to my house as soon as she can? That way, I can see how she interacts with my children."

Donna nods so fast I'm worried she might get a migraine. "Of course. I can absolutely do that, Mr. Whitmore. According to the schedule she gave me, Lisa could arrive in about three weeks."

"Great." The screech my chair makes when I get up rings in my ears. I can't help but wonder why I needed to be here for this in person. I imagine we could have done all this over email. But then again, United We Band probably wants to protect their candidate information, not just send it out online. "Is there anything else you need from me?"

"Just some paperwork signed and your partial payment, I believe. Then I'll shoot you an email when everything's squared away for that first visit." She squints at the screen. "Are you interested in meeting any other candidates?"

I scrunch my nose. "Nope. Thanks."

"Wonderful. Then I hope you have a safe trip home."

❧

I can't help but text Addison when I'm in another Uber, on my way back to the hotel.

ME

Guess what I just did?

ADDISON

I'm assuming you just picked out a wife like a new set of curtains. Shame on you.

ME

No need to get feisty. I didn't officially choose anyone yet. But a possible match will be coming over next month. Think you can behave yourself?

ADDISON

I'll put on the charm worthy of a pageant.

ME

Now, why haven't I seen this charm you speak of?

I'm totally lying. She's the most charming person I've ever met. I chuckle to myself in the back seat, and the driver looks at me like I'm crazy.

ADDISON

Because I've only been hired to charm your children. You, on the other hand, are my boss.

I can't help but grin as I read the text. Her boss. It's funny that I was technically her boss at her last job, too, even though we'd never met. And though she might think of me as her boss, it's hard for me to keep thinking of her as my employee the more I get to know her.

Especially after those texts she accidentally sent me last night. She still hasn't responded to them, even though the messages are staring her right in the face as we're texting right now.

I scroll up to read one of the messages again.

ADDISON

I know I lied and told Asher I already have a new boyfriend, but I kinda want to text him

I snort. Look at the two of us, both lying about having significant others.

And then the thought expands.

What if there was a way for us to help each other?

At first it seems like a crazy idea, but the more it unravels, the more I think that maybe, just maybe, I might have a perfect solution.

Chapter Eleven

ADDISON

"WHEN IS DADDY COMING HOME?" Moxie glances up at me, her bottom lip poking out a bit more than usual.

I stroke her hair. "Soon. Tonight, I think." We're lounging on the couch in the living room, watching videos of cats using the toilet. Moxie was giggling a few seconds ago, but now her tone is somber.

"Are you very sure he didn't leave forever?"

I laugh. "Of course not, Mox. He'll be back soon, I promise."

She turns her gaze back to the TV, seeming satisfied. Under her breath, she whispers, "Mommy left forever."

My stomach drops. I have no idea what to say to her, so I ask, "Do you remember her?"

She nods. "She's very beautiful, like a princess."

"I'm sure she is. So are you." I tickle her armpit, earning a fit of genuine laughter.

Izzy comes into the living room from the kitchen,

where she and the boys have been coloring. "Here, Addy. Your phone keeps ringing." She hands it to me.

"Oh, thanks." I glance at the screen. There are three missed calls from Romilly. She answers right away when I call her back.

"Hey!" Her voice is bright and cheerful as always. "Do you mind if I swing by? I miss you and I happen to be in the area."

I'm instantly suspicious. Romilly is never 'in the area' because she's always busy with a slew of charity work, church events, and running her dog-grooming business with her sister. She probably has something to tell me. "Of course. Come on over."

"Thanks. My GPS says I'm three minutes away."

"How is that possible?"

Her delicate laugh tickles my ear. "I told you. I was in the area."

"Uh, huh. See you soon."

We hang up, and I shuffle Moxie off my lap and onto the couch. She doesn't complain, eyes still glued to the screen. My gaze sweeps across the house. It's mostly clean, with the exception of a few dirty dishes on the counter waiting to be washed.

I know it's silly, but I check my appearance in the bathroom mirror next. Romilly has been my best friend since I was eighteen and has definitely seen me at my worst. But she also keeps me on my game, because she's so naturally beautiful that I can't help but feel frumpy in her presence sometimes.

The doorbell rings a Beethoven song, dragging me away from my thoughts.

Moxie skips around the living room, a bright smile on her face. "Daddy!"

My heart breaks a little at her excitement. Now she's going to be disappointed when she realizes he's not home yet. I grin at her, trying to influence her to be excited. "Actually, it's my best friend in the whole wide world. Want to meet her?"

All four of them crowd around me like magnets reacting to a pull. They nod, curiosity lighting their gazes. Their tiny, bare footsteps are like raindrops on the hard floor as they follow me across the foyer to the front door.

I open it, and just as I expect, Romilly is standing there looking like she just walked off a modeling set. Bright green eyes searing holes right through me. Jet-black hair framing her dark, heart-shaped face. Her long, elegant body dressed in a flowy white sundress. She's even wearing heels, for heaven's sake.

Capturing me in a squeeze, she whispers, "I missed you, my love." Her flowery scent swirls around me.

"Ditto." I squeeze her right back.

She releases me, peering over my shoulder at the kids. "These are them?" She whispers it like she's not allowed to speak loudly or something.

"Yep," I gesture to each one as I introduce them. "This is Izzy, Moxie, Enzo, and Abel." I caught her up on everything over text last night while Perry was gone, doing my best to keep her up to speed on everything—how my job is going, details about the kids. Perry.

"I brought prezzies for each of you," she tells them. Belatedly, I realize there's a woven basket hanging from her arm instead of a purse. It makes her look straight out of a fairytale.

Abel cocks his head sideways. "Prezzies?"

"Presents," I interpret with a giggle.

They all light up as she hands each of them a new toy. She even unwrapped them ahead of time so the toys would be ready to play with. "Who wants a castle, and who wants a toy gun?"

Izzy and Abel reach for the guns with glee. Abel wastes no time and pulls the trigger, releasing a foam bullet into the air.

Moxie and Enzo take a flat, polyester circle from Romilly, and she shows them how each one unfolds into a pop-up tent that looks like a castle.

Yeah. She definitely needs to talk. Otherwise, she wouldn't have appeared into thin air like Mary Poppins with a basket of fun to keep them busy for hours. I lead the way to the backyard. "Let's take all this outside, everyone."

They all race to the back, practically trampling over one another to get to the grass. Enzo sets his tent next to Moxie's and Izzy and Abel start launching bullets at them. Laughter emanates from inside the tents.

I turn to Romilly. "Sit."

She wordlessly plops into one of the chaise lounges on the deck. The warm sun wraps around me as I take the other one, searching her face. We're in the same spot I sat last night, when I thought I was texting her, but was really texting *Perry*.

My face burns at the memory.

"I have so much to tell you," she says. "Three big things, to be exact."

"Spill."

"Number one," she holds up a finger, "My sister and I are moving back home. Our dog-grooming business isn't exactly flourishing."

I wince. "That sucks. I'm sorry, Rom." I pat her hand and laugh without humor. "I bet Zara is so excited."

"She's *thrilled*." Romilly says sarcastically, her green eyes bright and shining. "So thrilled, in fact, that she's decided to quit grooming altogether and go back to college. Which brings me to number two." She takes a deep breath. "I'm not competing for Miss Meadow this year."

My brain struggles to process her words. "Excuse me? Why not?"

"Because of number one. I'll be too busy with finding a new grooming job to really have my heart in it."

I blink a few times. "I guess that makes sense. As long as you're not doing it for me. You know, to better my chances of winning or anything."

"Stop it." She reaches over and squeezes my hand. "You don't need me to drop out to win. You already have what it takes. This is your year, Addy. I know it."

My chest floods with warmth. Romilly is one of those freakishly beautiful women who is also smart, kind, and ambitious. Oh, and she has the most beautiful singing voice of anyone in her church choir. I'd hate her out of pure envy if she weren't such a genuinely sweet person who wants the best for everyone. Oh, and if I didn't already love her so much.

"The homeless are going to starve without your charity winnings," I tease. "They're depending on you, since you practically win every year."

She misses the joke, cringing. "Hopefully, the extra time I'm putting in at the church soup kitchen will help."

I resist the urge to snort. "What's number three?"

"Number three . . ." another finger pops up. "Things with me and Cole are, uh . . . moving really fast."

I squint at her, fighting a protective instinct. "What do you mean? Is he pressuring you to do things you don't want to?" For as long as I've known her, Romilly has wanted her first time having sex to be on her wedding night.

She was understanding when I broke the pact we made to both wait, but I know how guys pressuring her for sex is her biggest deal breaker in a relationship. Not that she's had many. She always has her hands so full of extra activities, she never has much time for relationships.

Romilly takes a deep breath. "Everything with Cole is great. I'm just not sure my heart is in it, to be honest."

"You mean he's okay with the whole waiting-till-marriage thing?"

"Yeah, he is."

"That's awesome. That's really great for you." Something twists inside my chest when I think about Asher. How I broke the pact for him and instantly regretted it. What he called me after I confessed I wanted to stop sleeping together. I stare at the ground, Asher's hurtful words echoing in my ears. *Just another pretty face. Nothing special. Not worth waiting for.*

Of course, Romilly wouldn't have to deal with something like that. She's the definition of the word special.

"Oh, Adds." Romilly glances around us, abruptly taking in the rest of our environment. "This house is stunning, by the way. I can't even imagine living here." A ghost of a smile surfaces on her mouth. "And from what I'm gathering, the owner of the house is pretty stunning as well."

I really want to tell her she's wrong, but I can't think of a way to do it honestly. I shrug instead. "Whether he is or not is entirely subjective."

Her grin widens. "And what is *your* subjective opinion?"

"He's . . ." I duck my head. But then his face comes to mind. His soft, hazel eyes framed by those thick, dark brows, and the way his serious expressions melt away when his smile lights up his entire face. I struggle to answer Romilly, my brain fogging up when next I think about the toned muscle I see peeking out of his tailored clothes sometimes when he moves. "He's the owner of Rosemary Banquet. He's the one who had me fired."

"Wait, seriously?" Her eyes widen, revealing the whites surrounding them. "You forgot to mention that little detail last night."

"Yeah. Kind of hard to like his beautiful face when all I want to do is punch it." *At least, that's what I should want to do. But Romilly doesn't need to know it's not even remotely true.*

"Beautiful? Did you just say his face is beautiful?"

Blood rushes to my cheeks. "Look, it doesn't matter. He's . . ." Something stops me from telling her about Perry's mission to get married. It felt like a secret when he shared it with me, and despite him not knowing him long, it doesn't feel right to break his trust. "He's engaged." It's not too much of a lie, since he *is* going to be engaged soon. "And I shouldn't be focusing on him, anyway. I need to keep my head on straight if I want to win the pageant."

"You *will* win." Her smile fades. "But don't deny yourself a chance at happiness in the process."

"Winning will make me happy."

"I know. But I also remember those texts you sent me, gushing about how hot Perry is and almost lonely-calling Asher as a result."

The voice that responds comes from behind us. "Funny. I remember some similar messages."

My head whips around to find Perry standing on the deck, hands shoved into his suit pockets and a smirk on his lips. My heart thuds in my chest when our gazes connect. For a minute, I forget what he's saying because it shocks me how good it feels to see him.

Romilly clears her throat, standing up to shake his hand. "I'm Romilly, Addison's bestie. Lovely to meet you."

He regards her with renewed interest. "Ah. So, you're Romilly."

She smiles like she has a secret. "Yes." Then she tosses an arched brow in my direction and hangs her basket back on the crook of her arm. "I was just stopping by for a quick visit, but I have to get going now. Again, great to meet you."

"You too," he says, watching her leave before turning back to me. The kids still haven't noticed him, absorbed in their game with the new toys, and he doesn't call attention to them just yet. Instead, he searches my face. "Hey, bunny," he murmurs.

His voice travels from my ears to my toes. Butterflies flutter in my stomach. *No, no, no. This can't happen. You can't officially have a crush on him. There are too many reasons why it's wrong!* "Hey," I say weakly.

"How much trouble have they given you?" He cocks his head toward the grass.

I belatedly realize he's referring to his kids. "Oh, no. They've been fine. Totally fine." *You, on the other hand . . .*

"Daddy!" The kids swarm him in an instant, jumping up and down and tugging on his expensive-looking suit. But he doesn't seem bothered, squatting down and gathering all four of them in a tight hug. He kisses the tops of their heads.

Abel points to the toys Romilly brought and proceeds to demonstrate how one of the toy guns work by unloading foam bullets on a tent. Perry grins, taking the gun from Abel and shooting a few times until all the bullets are gone. Abel runs off, eager to retrieve them all, but he gets distracted by Izzy's gun in the process.

With a sigh, Perry sits on the lounger next to mine, where Romilly was moments ago. My heart stutters. *Girl. Relax.*

"How was your flight?" I tuck my hair behind my ears.

"Fine." His lips pull up. "It's good to be back, even if I was only gone for a couple of days."

We sit in silence. I try not to be awkward, but it feels like there's an elephant in the room after last night.

"I'm not going to lie, Addison," he says. "I'm curious about one of those texts you sent me."

Oh, no. It's like he can read my mind. I school my features into a poker face. "Hm?"

"You said you lied about having a new boyfriend."

"Oh." I blink. Definitely not the message I thought he was going to bring up. "Yeah. What about it?"

"Is there a reason you told your ex you have a new man?"

"Well, it's kind of complicated, but basically he accused me of still being hung up on him, and I really want him to know that I'm not." I stare at my hands, which have begun fidgeting in my lap. "But I'm kind of in a pickle. Since he's the host for Miss Meadow, he has to come interview me, and he's expecting to meet this new boyfriend of mine. But my new boyfriend doesn't exist."

Perry's eyes sparkle. "And what on earth are you going to do when he arrives?"

"I'll probably make something up. Say he got food poisoning or something."

"Or we could help each other."

"What do you mean?"

Perry leans closer to me. "Would you believe me if I told you I'm in a similar predicament? I told my dad I'm already engaged, and he wants to meet my fiancée tomorrow night. Obviously, I don't have a fiancée yet."

I cover my mouth with my hand to hide my smile. "You want to be my fake boyfriend, don't you?"

"Fake fiancé, actually. What do you say?" The corner of his mouth turns up.

"What happens when you get engaged for real? You're just going to switch from one fiancée to the other?"

"Yep. Believe it or not, the will doesn't specify who I need to marry. Just that I need to be married once my dad retires to get the house."

I hold up my hand. "Wait a minute. Why do you need me, exactly? Why not just wait until you're engaged and have him meet your real fiancée?"

"I . . ." He hangs his head. "I didn't expect my dad to be so proud of me when I lied. I'm so used to him criticizing me, and it felt really good to have his approval for once. I know he's going to find out the truth eventually, but I'm not ready to face that just yet." He swallows hard. "I know the idea seems ridiculous, and I won't hold it against you if you don't want to. After all, you'd be in such an uncomfortable position, pretending to be romantically involved with your boss."

He's right. It would be uncomfortable, not to mention unprofessional. Who knows what playing the part of his fiancée would entail? And how the heck would it affect our dynamic after we stopped? I'd still be his nanny, and he'd have a new woman around. She'd be uncomfortable with me working for them if she found out.

But if I tell Perry no, what am I going to do about Asher? I could just come clean, admit I haven't moved on with anybody yet. Endure the way he'd look at me, cocky, triumphant, or even worse—with pity. The words from his text message flash in my vision.

I know you're still all hung up on me, but I swear, if you're trying to trap me with a baby . . .

Ugh. How dare he think he's that important? Like I'm just desperate to hang onto him? Plotting on the sidelines for ways to get him to come back? My blood boils just thinking about it.

But if he saw me with someone like Perry . . .

I imagine what Asher would think, seeing the attractive restauranteur at my side. That moment of realization that would smack him like a brick wall when he'd see that I have moved on. Moved on, and, dare I say, *upgraded?*

"I'll do it," I blurt. Perry's head snaps up. "I'll be your fake fiancée."

His answering grin is blinding. I can't look away and might even be drooling a little bit.

"Ah! Addison, you're the best." He stands up and hugs me.

The moment his arms wrap around me, I'm enveloped in his expensive scent. His biceps feel so hard. *Goodness . . .*

"No problem!" I laugh uneasily, and he releases me. "After all, I'm getting something out of this, too. Asher won't know what hit him."

Perry nods. "That's right. We're going to knock his socks off."

He looks so eager, like a puppy. It makes my cheeks lift against my will. "So, I'm meeting your dad tomorrow?"

The smile falls from his face. "Shoot. We have so much to do before he gets here."

"Like what?"

He winces. "If you're supposed to be my fiancée, there's stuff you'd have to know about me, and me about you. We'll have to get to know each other better in case my dad quizzes us or something."

I nod. "Okay. Tonight, after the kids go to bed?"

His shoulders sag in relief. "Perfect. I have a lot of work to do until then, but . . . it's a date, I guess." With a boyish grin, he waves as he walks toward the house backwards.

"It's a date." But the words sound more like a hushed, breathy whimper than a sentence.

Chapter Twelve

THE WAY ADDISON'S knees are bouncing as she sits on the couch, you'd think she's waiting to be called into a surgery she might not wake up from.

I offer her a calming smile from across the room, where I'm pouring us both a glass of wine at the kitchen island. I ignore tonight's dinner mess—half a massive onion sitting atop a cutting board and a pot still crusted with dry spaghetti sauce. Addison says nothing, only fidgets with the end of one of her curls. Actually, her hair is more of a wavy texture today, down, almost reaching her waist, and the warm beige jumpsuit she has on brings out the golden tones in her warm skin. She's so stunning, it's hard to look away.

I make my way over to the couch and sit beside her, handing her a glass. "Here you go."

"Thanks." She takes a sip immediately, making me want to laugh. I try to hide my expression with my glass by also taking a drink. She dabs at her lips with her sleeve. "Um, how exactly does this work? Other than with Asher, who was already my friend by the time we got together, I've never dated before."

I chuckle and duck my head. "Somehow, that's hard for me to believe."

"Really?" She frowns. "Why?"

"I . . ." My sentence dies as I stare at her, willing her to understand, so I don't have to make her uncomfortable by saying it. "Look at you."

It takes her a minute to catch up, but when she does, she blushes so hard, even the tip of her nose turns red. "I, um—" She giggles. "Thanks. So, how does this work? What do we do?"

"We should probably start by setting some ground rules. If we're going to do this, we need to be able to trust each other not to cross any lines."

"I completely agree." She bites her bottom lip. "For example, no touching each other underneath clothes."

I nod fast. "Yeah. Good one."

"And no kissing."

"Okay, what?" I frown. "No, that's ridiculous. We're going to kiss, Addison."

"We don't technically *have* to, though."

"It's going to happen. You must know that."

She clenches her jaw. "Fine. No kissing with tongue, then."

Just the idea of kissing Addison with tongue makes my head spin. "I think I can agree to that."

"Of course, kissing with tongue would only sell the relationship more."

My mouth twitches. "Just tell me what you're comfortable with, and I'll make it happen. How about that?"

We stare at each other for a moment. "Fine," she states. "Tongue."

"Are you sure? Because you look like you want to change your mind again."

"I'm positive."

I chuckle. "What about holding hands?"

"That's acceptable. But bed-sharing of any kind? Out of the question. And the fake engagement only lasts until you find a real fiancée."

"Agreed."

We both nod, letting our newfound set of rules sink in. When the room grows too silent, Addison squints at me. "Now what?"

"We get to know each other," I say. "Ask me anything, and then I'll ask you something. We'll take turns."

She scrunches her nose. "I can't just ask you something. You're putting me on the spot. And besides, the surface level questions that would be acceptable to ask you don't count as getting to know you."

"You have a point." I make a face, considering. "Ask me something *deep*, then."

"I can't start with *deep*, Perry."

She's right. Starting with deep would be weird.

An idea sparks in me. I hold up a finger. "Wait here." I leave my wineglass on the coffee table and grab what I'm looking for off the kitchen island. She blinks several times when I sit back down and hold up the remaining half of the raw onion from dinner tonight.

"What the—"

"Let's play a game." I hold it up in the air. "Shrek style. For every layer of this onion, one of us asks the other a question. Every time we ask a question, we have to remove a layer, and each question has to get deeper than the last."

"Okay." She covers her mouth to hide a smile. "But is the onion itself necessary?"

"I think it is." I nod seriously, but inside I want to laugh at her expression, at the silliness of the situation. "You seem to need a visual." With finality, I set the onion on the coffee table between us. And then I suddenly remember something she told me before. "So now, I'd ask you a question. For example, are you really deathly allergic to pineapple?"

"Oh, yeah." She winces. "My throat closes up completely. If I eat it, even a little piece, I could potentially die within an hour."

"Do you carry an EpiPen?"

"I used to." She shrugs. "But not so much anymore. I've gotten good at detecting when foods have it in them. Plus, being in the pageant has me eating pretty much the same healthy foods on repeat."

I feel a little queasy. "I'm going to start carrying around an EpiPen." I shake my head slowly. "All right, your turn."

The corners of her mouth turn up. "Okay." She ponders for a moment and then reluctantly reaches for the first layer of the onion. It makes a crunchy, tearing sound as she removes it, and the inevitable, strong scent fills the air. She sets her piece of onion on the table. "Do you have any other siblings besides Rebecca?"

"No. It's just me and her. She's actually my half-sister

from my dad's previous marriage. His ex-wife ended up having an affair."

"That's really sad. I'm sorry."

I shrug. "It's okay. But Rebecca and I have never been too close. And the fact that she might get this house . . ." My chest heaves, anxiety threatening to present itself. "This was *my* mom's house. I mean, it was my dad's house too, but they lived in it together and Rebecca was hardly ever here, always at her mom's until the weekend."

She nods. "You don't have to explain. I get it. What was your mom's name?"

"Marina. And my dad's name is Frank."

She nods. There's a beat of hesitation, and then she reaches over and pats my hand—just the briefest touch; but it sends tingles all over me, even with the moisture on her fingertips from onion juice.

I clear my throat. "It's my turn to ask you something." I tap my chin, pretending to ponder and earning a shy smile from her. There are so many things I want to ask her. So many things I'm curious about, but I don't want to scare her off, so for now I'm going to keep it simple. "What's your favorite color?"

She sits up straighter, like this question excites her. "Pink. Of *course*."

"What kind of pink? Like, beige-pink?" I ask, immediately thinking of her resume.

A single, breathy laugh escapes her. "Probably more of a sunset pink. No, wait! Ice cream pink!"

"Ice cream pink," I repeat to myself, laughing at her enthusiasm. "Got it."

She jerks her head at the coffee table. "Well, onion boy? Rip off a layer."

I do as she says, and right after, she takes a rip, too.

"How about you?"

"Yellow's cool." I shrug. "It's bright and happy."

"Like you."

I bark out a laugh. "Me?" I think she must have her words confused. She's the one who's all blossoms and sunshine. "That's not how I would describe myself. And I bet that's not how others see me." She looks confused, so I elaborate. "My life is kind of a mess, and I have a feeling I don't hide it very well. I'm sure I often appear stressed out. Tense."

"Maybe. But I can tell you're yellow on the inside." Simple as that. Like it's the easiest statement in the world.

Something cracks a little in my chest. "Well, thanks."

"My turn." She leans forward, eager. "What's your favorite TV show?"

"Oh. Gilmore Girls. One-hundred percent."

She beams, placing a hand to her chest like she's appalled. "Perry. I so did not expect you to say that, but I love that for you."

We go back and forth for a while, discussing all kinds of stuff about ourselves and tearing off pieces of the onion as we go. We form a sort of unspoken agreement to not tear off more than a tiny piece after a while because talking like this is fun, and I don't think either of us wants to run out of onion.

I watch her speak, mesmerized by her enthusiasm as she talks about her favorite ice cream flavor, rocky road, and why it's so important that everyone tries it at least once. She explains why orangutans are her favorite animal, talks about her pageant diet and how pleased she is by my grocery options, about how she often has to tone herself down so people don't get put off by her. She talks about growing up attending church with her grandma and how Romilly is the best Christian she knows and is secretly her role model. She scrunches her nose, pointing a finger at me. "If you ever tell her that, I'll be so embarrassed. I mean it!"

"Don't worry. I'm a Christian, too. I get it." I tell her about how I was led to God after Jill left, how He brought me a peace nothing and no one else could, which makes her relax a bit. Her expression becomes unreadable, but after a slight pause, she picks back up about a pact she and Romilly had before she broke it.

I'm transfixed. I can't help but notice all the cute things about her as she speaks, like the way she wiggles her hands back and forth for emphasis, the way her dimples keep showing themselves with every micro-grin, how her hair keeps ending up wrapped around her index finger.

I have no idea if I'm just as interesting to her. I can't imagine I would be. Still, I answer her burning questions, sharing with her a peek into my childhood, how I was into science kits instead of sports, and it annoyed my dad. How I used to cling to my mom's arm during scary movies, but insisted on watching, nonetheless. I share with her how much I love being a dad, even though at times it's really hard. She smiles at that admission, her face glowing.

I avert my gaze, because it's hard to make eye contact with her sitting this close while it's just the two of us. But when I do look at her again, she's chewing her lip nervously as she stares past me.

"What's wrong?"

"Hm?" Her gaze jumps back to my face. "Oh, nothing."

I arch an eyebrow. "Come on. Tell me."

"It's just that—well, it's silly really."

She looks . . . *embarrassed. Oh, now I'm intrigued.* "I'm all ears."

It looks like she might be holding her breath as she debates whether to tell me. "I don't want our first kiss to be in front of your dad or Asher."

"Oh." I frown. "*Oh.*"

"I think we should practice. You know, so it doesn't seem like we've never kissed before."

My heart is currently pounding in my ears, but I play it cool. "And you want to start right now?" I think I forgot my name. In fact, I have no idea what year it is, or what planet I'm on, either.

"If it's okay with you." She bites her lip again. "Your dad's coming tomorrow. What better time than now?"

She's technically right, but I'm having trouble thinking clearly. The thought of kissing her makes me feel like I'm in middle school or something, too nervous to even utter a word to a girl. *Come on, Perry. Be a man. You can do this. You're not as soft as your dad thinks you are.*

"Come here, bunny." I reach across us and take her hand, pulling her closer to me. Her hands are shaking, and it makes me feel so much better. Like, maybe she's nervous, too.

I touch her face with my free hand, brushing some of her hair back. It's just as soft as I've been imagining. Softer, actually, and it's giving off the floral, girly scent that I sometimes catch a whiff of when she's walking past me.

There's a buzzing in my ears from how silent we both are as we lean closer. Addison swallows, shifting her gaze to my mouth, and it's all the permission I need to close the rest of the distance.

Her lips tingle beneath mine, sending a jolt through me. I almost back away in surprise, but I'm worried if I do, the kiss will stop. Addison shudders, so I stroke her hair reassuringly, and she melts against me. When she kisses me back, her soft lips become urgent, rough. Her fingers find my face. Heat spreads through my body, unyielding as we continue. There's a voice in my head that shouts, *this is a terrible idea. You should have agreed to her no-kissing suggestion, and you need to stop right away.* But then a sound escapes her, and I have no choice but to pull her against my chest, wind my hands into her hair, push the thoughts away.

When we break apart, we're both frozen, staring at each other. I've never been this close to her before. But now that I am, I notice the subtle honey shades in her eyes.

My brain fogs up, and I'm left speechless as Addison backs away, scooting to the very edge of the couch.

I swallow hard, worried that I somehow crossed a line, made her feel vulnerable or too uncomfortable. "Are you okay?" I whisper.

She nods. "I'm fine." And then, as if by force, she smiles.

"Addison—"

"I think that's enough practice for tonight. Don't you?"

"Of course." My brows pull together. "We can pick back up tomorrow if necessary."

"Exactly. I have some pageant stuff to do before bed, so if we're all done here, I'm going to head upstairs." She stands without waiting for an answer, leaving me staring after her in bafflement as she all but sprints up the stairs.

I drag my hands down my face.

Great job, Perry. You scared her away.

Chapter Thirteen

I PRESS my back against the door the instant I'm in my room. My knees wobble, so I lower myself into one of the chairs by the fireplace.

I just kissed my boss.

And not only did I just kiss my boss, but he kissed me back like I've never been kissed before. Not by Asher, or anyone else before that. It wasn't the way he stroked my hair, making my scalp tickle in pleasure, or the way he seemed to breathe me in like I did his musky, teakwood scent, or even the way our lips intertwined like the meeting of waves and shore, a natural collision of desire and longing, leaving us both breathless in the aftermath. It wasn't any of that, but it was somehow . . . all of it?

It's a good thing we were kissing sitting down, because Perry made my knees weak.

I don't know how to face him now. That kiss is all I'm going to be thinking about every time I see him. How on earth am I going to function in his presence, knowing how manly his stubble felt on my palms, scratching lightly as his lips moved slowly against mine?

I'm going to melt into a puddle of desire. *Death by puddle.* That's what they're going to have to put on my headstone when it happens.

It's a good thing this event occurred tonight, because if it had happened tomorrow night in front of his dad, they'd both probably think I've lost my marbles.

I sink down in my chair. Then, I do the next most reasonable thing a girl can do: I call my best friend.

Romilly answers on the fourth ring. "Hey!"

"I kissed him. Perry. We both just smashed our lips together and our tongues danced, and I'll never be the same!"

Silence. And then, "Wait a minute. Back up, Addison. You *kissed Perry?*"

"Or he kissed me. I'm not totally sure. All I know is I'm starting to crush on him hard and I think this might all be a bad idea."

"What might be a bad idea?"

I launch into the story, explaining to her how Perry and I are supposed to be in a fake relationship now, for Asher's sake and for Frank Whitmore. Romilly listens quietly the entire time, and when I'm finally done talking, I wait for her to convince me I'm doing the right thing, or at least reassure me I'll get used to kissing Perry and the crush that's forming will go away soon.

"Addy . . . I'm not sure this plan of yours is going to work." She takes a deep breath. "What happens if you and

Perry start to develop feelings for each other? I'm talking about more than a crush."

"That's not going to happen. It can't happen, for obvious reasons. He needs to get married, and I have a pageant to win. Even if hypothetical feelings were to develop, it's not like *I* can marry Perry. Miss Meadow has to be unmarried, remember? And no children allowed, either."

"I'm well aware," she says evenly. "And for the entire year of her reign."

"Right. For the entire year of her reign. So, there you have it."

"Just be careful, Addy. I don't want to see you get hurt."

I roll my eyes. "No one's going to get hurt, Rom."

We talk a while longer; the topic shifting to the demented Labradoodle she groomed today. It feels good to talk about her, instead of my issues. Still, after we hang up, I'm left even more confused than before.

The next morning, I'm woken up by all four of Perry's children piling onto me. "Wake up, Addy!" someone shouts. Enzo, maybe? "Wake up!"

There's a chorus of giggles as I peek through one eye at them, and then rouse. Before they can expect it, I launch at them, tickling the two closest to me. The other two screech and run out of the room.

"Good morning," I say to Moxie and Abel. They must

be afraid I'm going to tickle them, because they run right out of the room as well. I giggle to myself. It's Saturday, which means I'm not working today. It's nice that Perry likes to spend the weekends with his kids; no work whatsoever unless it's something Kiera can't handle for him.

Ugh. That's right. *Perry.* I have to face him today.

My phone buzzes next to my head with a text message.

ROMILLY

Do you have a dress to wear for your interview with Asher?

ME

Not yet. Wanna go get one with me? I'm off today.

ROMILLY

I'll pick you up in an hour.

I grin at the screen. Excitement blossoms in my stomach, not just because I get to go shopping with my bestie, but because now I have a way to avoid Perry before dinner with his dad tonight.

I put on a green sundress with a cute cutout design at the waist, apply some makeup, and straighten my hair. By the time I'm done, Romilly texts me that she's here.

As I skip down the stairs like I'm in a music video, I see Perry and the kids eating breakfast at the kitchen island. My gaze locks with his, and his spoonful of cereal pauses halfway to his mouth. His eyes travel down my face, my body, lingering at my waist before he blinks and clears his throat. When he speaks, his voice sounds amused. "Going somewhere?"

"Shopping with Romilly." I avert my gaze and continue toward the foyer.

Perry stands up and steps forward, intercepting my path of escape. He crosses his arms and leans against the wall. "Listen, about last night. Maybe we should talk." His voice is low enough for only me to hear. The kids continue eating and talking about some cupcake show they like.

"What about last night?" I give Perry an innocent expression, even though I know exactly what he's referring to. *The kiss that will forever haunt my dreams.*

"Are you . . ." He contemplates for a moment. "Are you sure you're okay with this? The whole fake-relationship thing?"

Alarm bells sound in my head. Maybe he's having second thoughts. Maybe he realized how much that kiss affected me, and now he's worried I'm going to get too attached. Or worse, maybe he felt nothing at all and realized he can't even fake it in front of his dad. "Why? Did you change your mind?"

"Of course not. I just don't want you to feel pressured to do this because, well, because I'm your boss and you don't want to disappoint me or something."

"I'm not only doing it for you," I step past him so I can get to the front door. "This arrangement is seriously helping me out as well. Believe me." If only he knew how eager I am to dispel Asher's accusation, and hopefully wipe away the smug look he'll probably have on his face.

His gaze shifts to my hand on the doorknob. I know I look like I'm ready to bolt, but what he doesn't realize is that it's because I'm worried if I keep standing here with him, I'll grab his face and bring it to mine.

"We forgot to get you a ring," he says.

My stomach sinks. "Crap. You're right."

Izzy's voice interrupts us. "Why are you whispering?"

"No reason," Perry tells her, and then turns back to me. "Don't worry. I'll think of something. Have fun shopping."

If by *think of something*, he means to get me an actual ring, that seems like overkill. Unless it's an inexpensive dupe or something. Either way, I hope his idea will be convincing enough.

Romilly's car is waiting in the driveway. I sprint to where she's idling, and squeeze into the tiny passenger seat. "Thank God."

She tilts her head at me. "You okay?"

"Just trying not to jump Perry's bones. No biggie."

Her mouth falls into a shocked smile, but she only laughs. "Well, then let's get you outta here so you don't ruin such a professional work relationship."

We drive across Meadow Hills to the adorable downtown strip. The bakery, bike shop, ice cream parlor, and a cozy indie bookstore line the street, each window adorned with a hanging basket of wildflowers. We make our way into Iris Lily, a cute boutique with one-of-a-kind garments made by Iris Lily herself, the forty-something owner and seamstress. Romilly and I are regulars here. This place is our go-to for custom pageant gowns and most of our everyday clothing as well.

Romilly is like the other end of a magnet as she gravitates toward a rack holding flare jeans and frilly blouses. I peek at a rack of dresses, searching like a hawk for one that will be good enough for my upcoming interview with Asher.

"Do you have all your other gowns ready for the pageant?" She asks, her bottom lip sucked in with concentration.

"Pretty much. Hey, this is cute." I hold up a short black dress with a sweetheart neckline.

Romilly's eyes light up. "Oh. *Get it.* It's perfect for the interview."

She doesn't have to convince me. I can already imagine how it will fit based on my previous purchases from this shop. Iris Lily's sizing is always so spot on, I don't even need a dressing room.

"Is Rosemary Banquet still going to sponsor you?"

"I mean, I haven't heard otherwise from Lillian." A seed of dread sprouts in my stomach. "But now that I'm no longer an employee there, I think I'd feel super awkward accepting their support."

Slowly, she turns to face me, her eyes like round green marbles. "You're not thinking of switching your sponsor this late in the game, are you? Do you have someone else lined up already?"

I shrug one shoulder, but my insides are still whirring. I've been grateful to not have to worry about sponsorship since I joined the pageant. When Gran was alive, her gourmet jelly business was my trusty sponsor year after year. And when she passed away, I had Rosemary Banquet to rely on. But now? I'm worried it might not be so easy.

"Are you forgetting that Perry is the new owner, Rom? I'd really like to not involve him in every aspect of my life, if possible. It will be fine. I'm sure I'll find someone super quick."

She looks dubious, and rightfully so. Meadow Hills

isn't a bustling city. Most of the local businesses in town have likely already jumped on the opportunity to sponsor a Miss Meadow contestant. And with the rise of women entering the competition since it became televised four years ago, it won't be long before every local business is tied up into a contract with a candidate.

"What about Iris Lily?" She nods toward the register where the boutique owner is typing on her laptop.

"She has Hayden covered, remember?"

Romilly scrunches her nose. "Shoot. That's right."

"It will be fine, Rom."

She nods a little too quickly. "I'm sure it will be."

I stay out with Romilly as long as possible.

It's an ironic dilemma happening inside me: I'm desperate to avoid Perry, but there's also a very small— practically microscopic—part of me that likes the way it feels when he and I make eye contact. It's like downing an espresso shot or injecting the caffeine straight to my heart.

It's still light out when Romilly pulls into the driveway. "Good luck tonight, Adds. You got this."

"Thanks. I'll let you know whether I die of embarrass- ment or simply go into hiding."

"Perfect." She waves. "Love you!"

Getting out of the car, I make my way to the door, unlocking it with my key. I take my shopping bags filled with new clothes, including an outfit for tonight, upstairs. There is no denying I miss hanging out with the kids after spending the day away from them, but I need to freshen up before dinner.

I change into a mustard yellow blouse with matching pants that are fitted until they flare out a bit at the ankles. I pin the front sections of my frizzing hair back and touch up my makeup. There's still some time to kill before dinner, so I spend it watching pageant videos. I compare the dresses I have hanging in my closet with the ones the winners wear. I wish Gran was here. She'd tell me to stop analyzing things like dresses and to focus on the purpose of the pageant. *The charity.* It's what the sponsor funds contribute toward. It's the heart of the final phase of the pageant, the phase I've never once passed.

Stop worrying about appearances, and start worrying about what counts, Addy, she'd say. *Why do you want to win in the first place? What cause has been laid on your heart? That's what matters.*

When I emerge from my room hours later, I sweep my gaze across the foyer and living room. The kids must be asleep, because it's quiet in here, and the dim lighting creates a pleasant ambience.

Perry is cooking in the kitchen when I round the corner and the scent floating through the air is mouth-watering.

As if sensing me, he glances over his shoulder. A grin tugs the left side of his mouth up. "Hey. I didn't know you were back. Did you have fun?"

It's just a smile, Addison. Tell those flutters to cool it. "So much fun."

"Nice. I'm just finishing up dinner." He sets a wooden spoon on the countertop.

"I didn't know you cook."

"I do own a restaurant." He chuckles and runs a hand through all that thick dark hair of his. "But this is just spaghetti. Nothing special, but it's Dad's favorite."

We stare at each other. I fiddle with my hands. "I—"

Someone knocks—no, *pounds*, actually—on the front door. It's such a loud, jarring sound that I won't be surprised if it wakes the kids.

Perry exhales, deflating a bit. "That would be my dad."

I raise my eyebrows. "Does he always knock like that?"

There's a hint of a smile. "When I tell you he does it every single time, Addison, I'm not even slightly exaggerating."

I laugh. Perry goes to answer the door, so I fall back, lingering awkwardly. Before he lets his dad in, he squints at me standing in the living room and motions me forward with his chin. "Come here."

"Why?"

"So I can greet him with my arm around you. Get over here." He says it so playfully that I can't fight my smile. Dang it. He's so cute, and it bothers me because I really shouldn't think of him that way.

When I reach him, Perry sweeps his gaze over my body like he did when I first came downstairs this morning. He lifts his free hand, hovering it near my waist, and then looks at me inquisitively as if to ask permission to touch me.

I nod, and he settles his hand against the small of my back. Because of the exposed sliver of skin where my blouse and pants don't completely meet, I can feel his bare skin against mine as he moves his thumb back and forth.

I think I'm going to faint.

"Let's see how good your acting is," he whispers in my ear, sending goosebumps across my skin.

Acting. That's right. We're supposed to be acting.

I'm still trying to repeat it to myself as Perry swings the front door open.

Chapter Fourteen

MY DAD IS ALREADY SCOWLING when I open the door. "What took so long? Don't you have a maid?" He waves around vaguely. "Ah, what's her name? Kirsten?"

"I think you're referring to Kiera," I mutter, guiding Addison with me aside so he can enter. "And I've told you many times that she's my administrative assistant. She's not a maid."

He flicks one eyebrow dismissively, pursing his lips together. I know he probably has a whole notebook full of criticism for me on that front, but he holds it in and hones in on Addison at my side.

By the way his expression shifts, eyes glittering in interest, I know he must be seeing the same thing as me when he looks at her. A bronze, oval-shaped face containing big brown eyes, framed by delicate brows. Dark hair sweeping gracefully down her shoulders. Pink lips to match her nervous cheeks. Her hourglass figure that makes me stutter when I look too closely.

And dimples. Those dimples that pop out when she smiles, like right now. She reaches out to shake my dad's hand. "Hi, I'm Addison."

"Frank Whitmore," he says pleasantly. Well, pleasantly for him. His voice has a natural gruffness that hardly ever disappears, but Addison doesn't seem to notice.

"It's nice to meet you," she says. "I'm Perry's fiancée."

She says it with such confidence, even I almost believe her. I don't know how she does it, because I'm currently a mess of nerves, terrified of my dad derailing our act, and even more afraid that selling the story too hard will scare Addison off.

"Dinner is on the table," I announce, hyperaware of my hand still touching Addison's lower back. It's an unnecessary touch on my part, but every time my fingers graze her skin instead of her clothes, small shock waves of pleasure course through me. It's probably why I'm having such a hard time taking my hand away.

"I hope you made spaghetti," my dad tells me, and then turns to Addison. "Perry makes the best spaghetti on the planet. I don't know how he does it."

Addison sits across from my dad, chatting away happily. I get a bottle of red wine from the cellar and pour them each a glass. Other than a sweet "Thank you," from Addison, tossed in my general vicinity, the two don't break from their conversation.

It's amazing. Bizarre.

I'm not sure what I was expecting, but it definitely wasn't this—for her to hit it off with my dad like they've been the best of friends for decades.

I sit back in my chair and try to relax. Addison does

most of the talking, and a little moan escapes her when she takes a bite of my spaghetti. I try not to let it go to my head, but I can't deny the surge of satisfaction I experience.

Eventually my dad reaches for her left hand. "Let's see the ring."

Addison's eyes widen, but I wind our fingers together. This is the first time I've held her hand, and my brain screams how good it feels at me. "It's being resized," I tell my dad. Pulling Addison closer by the hand, I plant a kiss right on her mouth. At first, she stares back at me with open eyes in shock, and then seems to remember she should probably play along. She leans in and nuzzles her face against my neck in a soft, tantalizing way that gives me the jitters.

I expect my dad to be smiling at the show of affection, but his eyes only narrow in suspicion. "There's something about you that's familiar, Addison. Have we met before?"

Her body stiffens, but it's the only thing that gives away her nerves. "I can't imagine we have," she lies easily.

But I know where my dad has seen her before. At Rosemary Banquet, when he was still the owner. Since there's a typical turnover rate among servers, he's told me he doesn't make it his business to get to know each one very well. I'm just hoping he doesn't put it together, because that would lead to him discovering she's the same waitress who slapped his customer.

"It's a small town, Dad. I'm sure you've bumped into her a time or two."

His mouth twists into a grimace, but before he can go on one of his usual rampages about how he may be old, but his memory is plenty reliable, I collect the empty plates of spaghetti. "You finished?"

He nods. "I should probably get going. It was nice to meet you, hun."

Hun? Who is this man, and what has he done with my father?

Addison brightens. "It was so nice to meet you, too." She's full of enthusiasm as she uses her hands to talk, even as she picks up her wineglass. "Now I know where Perry gets his stunning good looks."

Before I can analyze that one and let it sink in, she stands to walk my dad out and trips on the leg of her chair. I reach for her, but she catches herself before she can fall. Her wineglass, on the other hand, flies across the room. The sound of glass shattering fills the air, and the crimson red wine from her glass splatters across the floor, the walls, and the curtains, like a murder scene.

Addison gapes in horror, but my dad starts laughing, a deep guttural bellow of laughter so hard he has to hold his stomach. He's bent over. "Perry, she's perfect. Where the heck did you find her?"

Addison sprints for a dish towel and immediately starts wiping up the mess. "I'm so sorry!"

"Sweetheart," my dad gets out between laughs. "I've been telling Perry this place needs redecorating for years. It's been missing a womanly touch. Good work."

Addison stares at him in disbelief before he sees himself out. She kneels to the ground near the far window in the living room.

"Addison." I make my way over to her. She's scrubbing the bottom of a curtain frantically, and it takes a lot of self-control for me not to cover her hand with mine and stop her. I can tell she's horrified at the mess she's made, but there's a part of me that—like my dad—finds the whole situation pretty funny. "Please. I don't care about the stains."

"You care about your house!"

"I care about the *memories*." I display a wide grin. "And I'm not gonna lie. This was a really good one."

At that, she lifts the rag from the curtain and swats me with it. "This is so not funny, Perry Whitmore!"

"It's actually *quite* funny."

"IT IS NOT."

"It really, really is."

She huffs, returning to the mess when she realizes I'm not budging. I chuckle under my breath and go to the kitchen cabinets, retrieving a stain remover that's saved my butt on more than one occasion after the kids got a little too rowdy with acrylic paints.

Kneeling beside her, I spray the wine stains on the curtains and squeeze it with my towel. Just as I expect, the marks are practically gone when I take the towel away.

Addison gasps. "Give me some of that. Like, right now."

I laugh as she seizes the spray bottle from me and gets to work on the rest of the house. I fold my arms across my chest and lean against the wall, watching her and fully embracing the amusement bubbling in my gut. She cleans all the stains pretty quickly, and when she's done, she sets the bottle on the table. "There. Now it never happened."

"Oh, it happened." I smirk. "Consider me an eyewitness."

She tries to glare at me, but a smile creeps onto her face. "Whatever."

I can tell she's about to go upstairs, so I think of the first thing that crosses my mind to get her to stay. "It's a good thing we practiced kissing, because my dad totally bought that."

Do I imagine the way a brief flush creeps across her cheeks, the way she immediately glances at the floor instead of my face?

"True. We were pretty convincing."

"You know what else I'm going to need you for tomorrow, bunny?"

She swallows. "Hm?"

"We need to go on a public outing. A date. People around town need to see us if we want to make this whole thing more believable. Especially when you get interviewed for the Miss Meadow pageant." I try to sound aloof, practical. But the truth is that I really just want to take her out so I can listen to her laugh some more, watch the way her gaze refuses to land on me for more than a minute without her blushing. I want to watch her fiddle in her lap and randomly talk really loud when she's passionate or excited. I want to feel the buzz I get every time she finally makes eye contact with me.

"Who is going to watch your children while we go on this date? Do you have a backup nanny hiding in the basement?"

"I can hire someone for the day. They'll most likely only last a few hours, but that's fine." I lower my voice, take a step toward her. "A few hours is all we need."

"Fine." She drags out the word dramatically, a little smile on her lips.

I watch her go upstairs, wondering when this shift happened inside me, where I suddenly don't want to stop spending time with her. *This is all just an act,* I remind myself. *One that's supposed to buy you time until you can find the girl you're actually marrying.*

At least my car is clean. It really shouldn't matter, because Addison is well acquainted with my kids and how messy they are, but still. I want to impress her. And I hate that, because I don't want to care, and I don't want to like her. Liking someone just leaves a person more vulnerable to get hurt when they eventually leave.

Yet, I can't deny how pleased I am when she gets in the passenger seat of my black SUV the next day, and hums when she sniffs the air inside. "It smells so good in here."

Thank you, sage and eucalyptus car spray.

"Really? Thanks." I try to keep my eyes on the road as I start driving, but the frilly, light blue dress she's wearing snags my gaze. Especially the way it lands just above her knees, pooling in against the shape of her thighs.

"I hope that lady you hired will be nice to the kids," she murmurs, bringing me back to attention.

"Me too. Her profile says she's a mom of six fully grown adults, so hopefully she'll be well equipped to handle mine for the day." It doesn't seem like a farfetched concept, but apparently, I've been wrong about every single nanny I've ever hired.

Except the one sitting next to me.

Addison squints at me. "What's in your pocket?"

Ha. I knew this moment was coming. With my eyes still on the road, I remove the cylinder tube from my pocket and hold it up for her to see.

She gasps. "Is that . . . you seriously got an *EpiPen?*"

"That's right, bunny. Kiera picked it up for me this morning." I beam proudly.

"You're unbelievable!"

"I can't very well have my fiancée dying on my watch."

"Fake fiancée." She crosses her arms.

"You can now feel safe eating whatever your little heart desires as long as Perry Whitmore is around."

She remains speechless the rest of the drive, but when I glance over at her every few minutes, I swear she's fighting a smile.

It takes ten minutes to arrive at the breakfast lounge I'm taking her to. This place reminds me of her; bright and cheerful, with cozy leather seats and yellow accents every-where. And of course, they have amazing coffee, which is very important.

When I park, Addison squeals and claps her hands. "Softly Poached? I love this place!" She bounces in her seat until I turn off the ignition. Being near her is like getting a second-hand dose of happiness every few minutes. I'm learning that this is part of what makes her so addicting to be around.

She reaches for the car door handle, but I gently grab her elbow to stop her. "Let me get the door for you, silly," I say. "We're on a date."

She blinks. "Oh. Right."

I get out and come around to her side, opening the door. Her seatbelt clicks as she unbuckles, and I reach for her hand to help her down. I keep hold of it even after she's out of the car. She avoids my gaze the entire time, so I make it my mission to get her to make eye contact with me for at least a full minute during this date.

As we walk together, I notice the lingering glances of those we pass on the sidewalk. I spot Mr. Sanders, owner of a local landscaping business. He raises his eyebrows as he looks at us, like he's trying to process why Addison and I might be together, at this spot, in our pretty outfits, holding hands. I recognize a few other familiar faces, no one I'm close enough with to greet, but people who have lived in Meadow Hills long enough for me to know by name. I nod at a few, feeling a little bit like a small-town celebrity with Addison at my side. She's probably well-known around here as a Miss Meadow contestant. I can't help but wonder what everyone thinks, seeing the two of us together.

As we enter the restaurant, Addison leans in to whisper in my ear. "People are staring at us." Her sweet breath tickles my ear.

"Get used to it, bunny. I have a feeling this is only the beginning."

When we check in, the hostess glares at Addison like she personally offended her. Addison's grip on my hand gets tighter. I rub small circles against hers with my thumb, but she doesn't release her iron grip until we're seated at a small booth near the entrance. She slides into the seat across from me and picks up a menu, careful not to look at me.

And the challenge starts . . . now.

"You have to try the coffee here. It's to die for."

She grins into her menu. "Oh, I'm aware. It's haunted my dreams a time or two."

My laugh echoes in my ears as it booms, attracting the attention of the couple at the table next to us. The woman sitting there stares at us a few seconds longer than necessary before turning back around.

I watch Addison search the menu. I have suspicions that she's only doing it to busy herself, because if she already knows how good the coffee is, she probably already knows what's on the menu.

"Do you know what you're getting yet?" I ask.

"Probably eggs and oats."

Come on. Look at me.

"I think we should sit next to each other," I blurt.

That gets her attention. Her eyes land right on mine, sending a flutter through my stomach. "Now?"

"Right now." I nod. "While everyone's looking."

Her lips part. That adorable flush covers her face as she nods right back. "Okay. You're right. We should." She swallows. Licks her lips, and stays right where she is.

I stand up and slide in next to her on the booth seat. Up close like this, I can smell her vanilla perfume, and even see my reflection in her eyes. My pulse is sprinting in my neck, but I can't show her nervous I am, how addicted I'm getting to all her reactions, because she'll end this arrangement before one of us gets too attached. I should definitely stop letting myself have fun with this. This should be a strictly practical arrangement. I know this—I really do.

Reaching up to touch her cheek, I'm vaguely aware of

all the curious eyes on us. I stroke her cheekbone, and her eyes drop.

"Look at me," I whisper. "Right up here."

Our gazes connect again. I could stay right here, just like this, and it would be more warming than drinking the coffee we're about to order.

I lean in close, enjoying the way her eyes don't shift elsewhere, remaining transfixed on mine. I know this is probably overkill, but I tell myself it's necessary, just so people get the picture.

She presses her cheek against mine. "This is uncomfortable," she whispers, so only I can hear. "Having everyone watch us like this."

"Then block them out. Pretend they're not here. Pretend it's just me and you, and I gaze at you adoringly like this all the time. Pretend you live for it. You love that I only have eyes for you."

To anyone who's watching, we look like two people who can't wait to be alone. Her mouth is right up against my ear, so I hear the little sound she makes in the back of her throat.

"Can I get you two something to drink?"

At the sound of the waitress's voice, Addison scoots all the way to the other side of the booth seat, as far away from me as she can get.

In a daze, I look up at the waitress, but I can still feel her cheek against mine, burning through all my thoughts and senses.

I have no idea how long our server has been standing here, but I clear my throat and order our coffees. Addison adds a chocolate milk to the order—of course she does—and then we're left alone again.

I feel her finally glance up at me. "Do you think we're being convincing enough?" Her voice is almost a whisper.

"Of course."

"Then why do people keep looking at us?"

Because you're beautiful and they're probably wondering how someone like me landed, someone like you, I want to say. Instead, I offer her a reassuring grin. "We have plenty of time to work out the kinks. All that matters is that Asher and my dad buy this relationship, and they will."

"Promise?"

She looks so hopeful; I don't have it in me to tell her I'm just as nervous about the truth being discovered as she is. "Promise."

Chapter Fifteen

ADDISON

THE DAY ASHER is scheduled to interview me comes much too quickly for my liking. But now that it's officially July, I only have two months left until pageant time, so the interview was bound to happen sooner or later.

Seeing his name come up on my phone brings back the familiar heaviness in my stomach.

ASHER

What's your address again?

I type back, giving him Perry's address.

ASHER

You moved?

ME

I sure did!

He doesn't respond, but honestly? I'm totally cool with that.

Romilly comes over in the morning to help me get

ready for the cameras. This interview won't count toward pageant scoring, but it will be televised as an introduction for Meadow Hills viewers to get to know the contestants, if they don't already. Since Romilly's not competing this year, I can't help but wonder if this scratches some sort of itch for her.

She gets to work immediately, wetting my hair and adding in product to accentuate the curls, then diffusing it dry. She gives me an elegant, no-makeup makeup look and takes a proud photo of me after I put on the black dress I picked out while shopping with her. Somehow, we squeeze all the getting ready into nap time, but by the time she's out the door, the kids are all waking up.

"Ooh, you look really pretty, Addy." Moxie's eyes get large and round as she takes me in. "Like a princess."

I ignore my nerves and smile at her. "Thanks, Mox."

Izzy points to my shoes. "Those look like stilts from the circus we saw one time."

I snort. "Good observation. They definitely feel like stilts."

The girls follow me to the boys' bedroom, where Abel is crying. I pick him up, careful to avoid anything from his trickling nose ending up on my dress. Normally, I wouldn't dress like this while taking care of them, but Perry is finishing up work, and Asher is supposed to be here any minute.

Ugh.

I have to see Asher again.

An onslaught of memories plays in my head. Him taking my hand backstage before it was my turn to model the evening gown. The hushed breaths we shared in my room at The Orchard Inn, where the pageant is held, late at night when everyone was asleep. The way he'd roll his eyes whenever I started talking too loud or told me I'm just a pretty face. Not special enough to wait for.

I think of his text message, the last time we talked.

I know you're still all hung up on me, but I swear, if you're trying to trap me with a baby . . .

The memory makes me burn with rage. I still can't believe he would think that. My desire to prove to him he never meant as much to me as he thinks is the perfect reminder of why I'm playing this part with Perry.

My determination makes me pat Abel's back a little too hard, and he screeches right in my ear. "Oh," I whisper. "I'm sorry, little guy. Addy's sorry."

Enzo watches me from his bed, completely content, swaying back and forth as he holds his feet with a smile on his face.

"Addison, are you ready?" Perry's voice floats up the stairs. "That interview is supposed to be starting in a few —" His voice cuts off as he enters the room. "...Minutes."

His eyes devour me, starting from my feet and slowly traveling up to my face. And then he blinks, clearing his throat and suddenly finding the floor fascinating. It makes me blush.

He looks gorgeous himself. He's dressed in dark jeans and a white button-up with a fitted blazer over the top. His usually messy hair is tame for once, except for a few thick tendrils falling into his face.

I shift my weight between feet. "Asher will be here any minute."

"Okay." He runs a hand through his perfect hair,

messing it up already. "Wait! Give me Abel so he doesn't ruin up your dress."

I nod, crossing the room to where he's standing and pass the clinging toddler to him. Abel doesn't complain. He's just happy to be held.

Moxie tugs on the corner of Perry's blazer. "Daddy, do we get to be in the interview?"

"It's up to Addy."

She turns to me, a desperate plea already visible in her blue eyes, but it's unnecessary. I smile at her. "Of course you can be in it. You, Izzy, and your brothers are the coolest. It would be silly to hide you all away."

Perry looks surprised by my answer, but he mouths *Thank you* to me. It feels warm, like an invisible hug.

The doorbell rings, and all the nervous jitters inside me seem to multiply. After today, all of Meadow Hills will absolutely know about my "relationship" with Perry—if they didn't already. I can't help but wonder what people will think, considering all the letters I received when my relationship with Asher went live last season. I can only hope the production crew doesn't decide to paint me in a negative light, in a way that could possibly affect the judges' opinions of me. According to the Miss Meadow rulebook, judges don't take anything from the television aspect of the pageant into consideration when making decisions. Personally, I don't buy it.

I can only hope the rulebook is right.

The doorbell rings again, and Perry grins at me, boyish and sexy. "Let's do this, bunny."

I help him bring the kids downstairs, and we set them up at their coloring table.

"I'll let you know when it's time for you guys to join the interview," I whisper to Izzy and Moxie while Perry goes to the door. "And if you two keep your brothers in line and behave, I'll bring you candy later."

Their eyes widen simultaneously. They both nod seriously and then pick up some crayons, turning to the coloring books with intense focus.

Perry opens the front door, revealing Asher's short but strong frame standing on the other side. He has the Miss Meadow filming crew with him, and a flood of old memories resurface when I see them all. I lift my hand into a little wave, and a couple of them return it. The others are struggling under heavy camera equipment, so I usher them in and point to where they can set it up.

I feel Asher's presence beside me before I see him. "You sure are comfortable here, Ad."

I finally meet his eyes, and he cocks his chin to the place where I had Maya, one of the filming crew, set her camera.

"I live here, Asher," I say cooly. "Of course I'm comfortable."

He nods, flashing his crowd-pleasing smile that doesn't reach his eyes despite the ever-present crow's feet. "Well, come here, you." He pulls me into a tight hug.

I keep my arms hanging at my sides. The last time I saw him was the day he dumped me. I'm still too mad to hug him back, and I don't care if he knows it. Today is about making a good impression on camera and proving him wrong. Showing him he's not the precious gem he thinks I regard him as.

"So, tell me, Ad." The way the nickname rolls off his

tongue irritates me beyond belief. He's always called me that, even though he knows how much it bugs me, even occasionally lengthening "Ad" into "Advertisement" to be funny. Asher lifts one eager brow. "Where's this mystery boyfriend of yours?"

"Perry Whitmore," Perry says from behind us. I've never heard him use such a firm tone before. Asher spins around to find Perry's hand outstretched toward him. "Nice to meet you."

"Likewise." Asher returns the handshake with ease. Always showing a pleasant face, no matter the circumstances. "Lovely place you got here. Did you say Whitmore?"

"Sure did."

"Doesn't your father own Rosemary Banquet?"

Perry smiles tightly. "I'm the new owner, actually."

I see it then; the moment I've been waiting for. Not only does Asher look impressed, but his expression changes, as if seeing Perry in a new light. Like he's realizing I not only have a new boyfriend, but a handsome, wealthy boyfriend from a family he's heard of.

He stands up straighter as he mingles with Perry. But Perry's expression remains hard and unyielding while he's talking to Asher. I'm probably the only one who notices, but still, it's there.

After a few minutes, Asher claps his hands. "Let's get this interview started!" His booming voice makes the kids gasp at their coloring table. He eyes them curiously before returning his attention to Perry. I motion for them to keep coloring, and Izzy nods. She puts a sheet of blank paper in front of the boys, and they immediately resume their scribbles.

Good old Izzy. All it took was candy bribing all along.

I plop down onto the sofa. *Here goes nothing.* If this fails, I've decided my chosen path is to go into hiding due to humiliation.

Perry sits next to me. The soft fabric of his blazer grazes my bare leg as he reaches for my hand. When I take it, I don't miss Asher's gaze following the action. I know it's just for show, but his warm, steady touch lessens my nerves a bit.

It takes a few minutes for the crew to set up and for us to start rolling. When Steve gives us the signal that we're on, Asher readies his first question on his tablet. There will be no introduction from him in this interview, because the intro and backstory for each contestant is always voiced over by him separately. His first question comes out smoothly, as if he's practiced it over and over. "Addison, can you tell us what you've been up to this summer?"

I know what I'm supposed to say. Something relating to my chosen cause of families with special needs children, along with hobbies that make me look interesting and admirable to viewers. But all I can think about is what I've been actually doing.

I try not to look at Perry as I formulate an acceptable answer.

"This summer has provided me with so many unique opportunities." I grin at the camera, even though on the inside I feel like I'm collapsing. "A passion of mine has always been working with children, and this summer I've had the pleasure of getting to know four wonderful kids who have really helped me grow as an individual."

I can feel Perry's gaze on my face, but I refuse to look at him yet. I don't want to know what he thinks of my answer.

"And who are these wonderful children, exactly?" Asher asks.

The camera pans outward to include Perry in the shot. I lift our joined hands with a wink. "They're my boyfriend's kids, actually. Perry and I have been dating for . . . a few months."

"Perry," Asher hums. "Are you the same Perry Whitmore who owns Rosemary Banquet, the much-revered restaurant local to Meadow Hills?"

Perry nods. "Yeah, that's me."

For some reason, a giggle escapes me at the way he answers. Perry doesn't have a camera voice, and it shows. He sounds just like he would if this were a regular conversation, and it's somehow so cute.

Asher's gaze jumps to me. "Anything to add, Addison?"

"Umm . . ." My heart races as I struggle to think of something. The crew will most likely cut out any long pauses on my behalf, but I'm still always worried that one day they'll edit the footage to make me look silly, or worse, dull. "Perry is a fantastic business owner. He's full of integrity, drive, and honesty."

Asher nods slowly. A faint smile spreads across his mouth. "Right. I'm sure you would know, considering you used to be a server at that restaurant before being let go. Or am I mistaken?"

Anxiety floods me like I'm drowning. I know Asher hates me, but still. This is a low blow, even for him. A Miss Meadow contestant has never, ever been exposed for getting fired. I would know. I've seen every preliminary interview ever filmed.

My face burns with shame.

Perry cuts in smoothly. "Actually, her leaving Rosemary Banquet was a mutual decision on both of our behalves. We didn't think it was appropriate to continue having a work relationship while forming such a strong romantic attachment."

Okay, what was that I said about Perry not having a camera voice? My jaw drops for a second, but then I quickly recover, nodding in agreement with his statement.

"Interesting." Asher frowns, like he's confused. "So, you ended the work relationship because of the romantic relationship, but proceeded to hire on Addison as your children's nanny. Can you elaborate on that contradiction a bit, Perry?"

Silence. I think I've lost the ability to speak. How does he even know that? This feels more like a murder trial than a Miss Meadow interview. I try to remember any mention of me nannying in our messages, but I know I never told him. The only other person who knows is Romilly and—

Bronwyn. He must have stopped by my old place to interview Bronwyn. I remember her unimpressed, stoic expression the day I moved all my things out, stating that I got a live-in nanny job.

Ugh.

Perry leans forward. "Addison is not my nanny. She's my girlfriend."

I think he almost says fiancée, but realizes that might not bode well with the pageant, since being married is against the rules.

Asher tilts his head sideways. "That doesn't align with the info given to me by my sources."

"Your sources are wrong." Perry's voice turns menacing. Dark. Even I feel intimidated. "Maybe you should invest in quality control."

Asher's face turns red. "Or . . ." He nods toward the children. "Maybe we should get their opinions."

Perry shakes his head. "I don't give you permission to film them. And these questions hardly seem relevant. What kind of crooked pageant is this, anyway?"

My eyes widen. "Please, cut that," I mouth to Steve. He winks at me and smiles kindly, nodding. I try to sound upbeat. "Okay, let's get back on track. Asher, what other questions do you have for me that are related to the pageant?"

He continues his glaring contest with Perry for a few more seconds before returning to me. "What cause will you be highlighting this season, Addison?"

My thoughts immediately travel to Finn. All the years my parents sacrificed to help him.

Even though my chosen cause is one I could cry over, one that I think about constantly, it's hard to sound open and vulnerable because Asher is the one listening, so I give him my rehearsed, diplomatic answer. "My philanthropic support lies with the same cause I've chosen for the past eight years. I wish to raise funds for families who have special needs children. I'm hopeful and optimistic that this is the year I'll finally get to offer mine and the pageant's support to something so close to my heart."

The interview continues, now sticking with the usual questions. Perry isn't mentioned again until the end.

"What plans do you two lovebirds have before the preliminaries begin?"

Perry throws his arm around my shoulder, pulling me close against him. I can feel all his muscles flexing as he moves, and it makes my head buzz. "I'm taking her and the kids to our summer cottage tonight, actually. It's a beautiful, romantic vibe over at Goose Rocks Beach. I've taken the kids a couple times, but this will be Addy's first time with us."

Asher narrows his eyes. "Goose Rocks Beach? Funny. I have a place over at Old Orchard Beach, about twenty-five minutes away. Maybe I'll pop in for a bit and the grownups can grab some drinks."

"Absolutely." Perry doesn't falter. "We'll be there all week."

They continue staring at each other. Is Perry baring his teeth, or am I imagining it?

"I think that concludes today's interview." Asher stands. All traces of the kindly, open host are gone. Now he's the Asher I know, the one he only shows people when the cameras are off. He gestures to the filming crew to start packing up before turning back to me. "Enjoy your romantic getaway, Ad." The way he says it makes me think he doesn't believe us. Like he knows Perry and I are putting on a show for his benefit.

As if he's in sync with my thoughts, Perry nuzzles into my neck. "She's going to love it." He presses his lips to a sensitive spot beneath my earlobe. I feel a tickle all the way down to my toes. I turn my face toward his, and he doesn't wait for permission, just moves his lips from my neck to my mouth, holding onto my waist while he kisses me like he knows I might faint.

When we break apart, Asher practically sneers. "See you both there. Later." Perry gets up to walk everyone out. Asher speed-walks to the door, not bothering to hold it open for the crew, but Perry grabs hold of it so everyone can exit without dropping any equipment.

And then they're all gone.

Finally.

I turn to the kids. "You all did so good. Thank you for sitting so nicely and coloring all that time."

"You picked really good pictures." Moxie holds up a coloring book. "And thanks for the stickers."

"Don't forget our candy," says Izzy.

A laugh escapes me as I take in the boys, faces covered in animal stickers like chicken pox.

Perry shoves his hands in his pockets. "We better get packing. We have a beach trip to get to."

"Yay," Enzo yells. "Beach, beach, beach!"

I gasp. "Wait, we're really going?"

"Of course. I said we were, didn't I?" He offers me a lopsided grin.

"Well, yeah. But I thought that was all for show."

"We can't let him get there and find out it was a lie, right?" There's a mischievous twinkle in his eye that gives me shivers.

"I guess I better get packing, then."

His answering smile is blinding.

A few hours later, there are four designer mini suitcases by the door, ready to go. Even the kids have quality luggage. Perry sets his bag on top of one.

"Addy helped us pack those," Izzy tells him.

Perry glances at me and turns back to her. "Awesome. Did you thank her?"

She taps a finger to her chin. "I think so. I can't really remember."

I laugh. "You did thank me, Izzy." I walk over and smooth back her blond hair. I try to avoid looking at Perry as I say, "I can't believe we're leaving tonight."

"Why? Do you need more time? Because we can leave tomorrow if you want."

I stare at my shoes. "No, tonight's fine. I'm just surprised you can drop everything for an impromptu getaway."

"That, bunny, is the beauty of being a business owner. I get to make the rules." He rubs the back of his neck. "It also helps having a wonderful assistant like Kiera to help me when I need a break."

"Does she know we're leaving?"

"Already e-mailed her."

"Huh." I twirl a lock of hair around my fingers. "Where exactly does Kiera live? When I first met her, I thought she lived here."

"Here?" Perry laughs. "No. She's only around here sometimes. Most of her work is running errands and doing all the little but important things that make the business world go 'round. She lives across town, kinda near Old Joe's Diner and The Orchard Inn."

I beam. "The Orchard Inn? That's where the pageant is held, you know."

He nods appreciatively. "I could totally see that. The place is . . . ornate."

I snort. "Alrighty, then. I'll go get my bags. They're still in my room."

"No, please allow me."

Before I can react, Perry is heading upstairs. The moment he's away from me, I release a long exhale. Nervous jitters are coursing through my body. Not because we're going on a getaway. But because it's supposed to be a romantic one. I can't help but wonder how much pretending this trip will actually entail.

All I can hope is that I'll somehow be able to tell the difference between pretend and real. Because thanks to my very annoying and inconvenient crush on Perry, the lines seem to only be getting blurrier for me.

Chapter Sixteen

PERRY

I DECIDE to take my friend, Logan, up on his offer from forever ago and let him drive us to the beach. It's been too long since I last saw him anyway, and—much as I hate to admit it—he really does bring the "rizz" along wherever he goes.

We do our secret handshake when he pulls up to my house. Over my shoulder, he catches sight of Addison coming outside with the kids. His brows shoot up to his hairline. "That's your nanny?"

"That would be her."

Logan whistles. "My man . . ."

"I know."

"She's—"

"I *know.*"

He chuckles. "Just lemme know when, not if, you need my help." Shaking his head with a goofy grin on his face, he gets into the driver's seat before Addison notices him.

The last thing I need is him making some sort of innuendo toward her.

Thankfully, riding with the kids in the limo for two hours isn't bad at all. A bottle of champagne does its job to keep me and Addison company. She also brought the kids all kinds of activities to keep busy, like coloring books, puzzles, and other cute stuff. I doubt I could have gotten them here without yelling if it weren't for her.

I have a chance to check in with Kiera during the drive. She's doing a restaurant visit and inspection, and I've been eager to read what she has to say about Rosemary Banquet in her emails.

Mr. Whitmore,

I checked in with Lillian, the restaurant manager. Apparently, Rosemary Banquet has seen a significant decline in customers over the past month, beginning nearly a week after Miss Ellsworth was let go. Lillian insists the lack of traffic is directly linked to Addison leaving, stating that the regulars found out about her dismissal. Lillian has witnessed some of the servers telling customers about the incident with Lyle, and they all feel she's been unjustly let go.

The man she assaulted was apparently just passing through town from further inland to get to the beach, so he had never met her before.

I'm not sure if you'd like to consider reinstating her here, sir, but Lillian let me know

SHE'D WELCOME HER WITH OPEN ARMS. THERE HAVE BEEN NO SIGNIFICANT CHANGES WITH THE ESTABLISHMENT, OTHER THAN THIS.

SINCERELY,

KIERA FANG

I peek over at Addison. She's currently helping Moxie build a snowman out of playdough. They're both smiling so big, it's infectious. Seeing my kids happy again, at last, feels like releasing a breath I've been holding for too long. The fear that they've been scarred, doomed with abandonment issues like me, has kept me up at night. But with Addison here, those fears seem ridiculous.

For a minute, I allow myself to flirt with the idea of what life would look like if we were a real couple. Just for that minute, I see her bright smile in my kitchen, smell her vanilla perfume all over the furniture, and feel her lips against mine like a live wire. I see my kids happy—actually happy.

It's foolish, because Addison is only human, like Jill. Sure, she makes my children light up like a Christmas tree every single day. She allows a part of me I long ago buried to feel alive again, and she makes this challenging life I'm stuck in seem possible to endure, but she's just as capable of abandoning us as Jill was. Even more so since these aren't even her children.

I could always let her go *first*. I could be the one to end things so she won't have the opportunity to hurt us. I could call up Lillian and reinstate her previous employment. But the thought of her going back to her waitressing job makes me want to lock her in this vehicle and never let her leave.

Despite my fears, I need her here. Though I'd like to think my reasons come down to nothing more than the kids, or keeping me from losing my home to Rebecca, I'd be lying to myself if I tried to believe that. Deep down, I know I want her here for selfish reasons, too.

I like her. I want to be around her.

And it terrifies me.

I nod off as we drive along the sandy coastal stretch. I know we're almost there when I spot a towering lighthouse. About thirty minutes later, the summer cottage I purchased last year comes into view. It's two stories, with a pointed roof and gray paneling. The best part about it—sand is the only thing separating it from the ocean.

I squint around the dim limo. The kids are all asleep. Addison's eyes widen a fraction when we pull up, taking it all in.

Logan stops in the driveway and lets us out. Seeing him here reminds me of when I first visited these beaches just a couple hours outside of Meadow Hills, where I met him at a bar, and we ended up having a drunken heart-to-heart. That first meeting was when he told me he's trying to make it big in surfing but drives limos on the side.

When I hand Logan a generous tip, he rolls his eyes but bumps my knuckles. "Have a nice night, and remember, I'm only a phone call away if you need help removing your foot from your mouth." He waggles his eyebrows for emphasis, which I choose to ignore.

The sun is setting, so it makes sense to keep the kids asleep and put them straight in bed. Addison waits in the car while I carry each one inside, one at a time. They stay asleep, even through the sound of seagulls calling to each other as they glide above us, effortlessly through the salty air.

The cottage only has two bedrooms, something I forgot about when I announced we were going on this trip. I bought it before Jill left, so the amount of space was perfect at the time. Two bunk beds for the kids in one room, and one queen bed in the other for me and Jill.

I wonder how Addison will react. I'll definitely enjoy seeing her expression get all wide and alarmed *before* I tell her I'll be sleeping on the couch tonight.

Once all the kids are in their beds, I head downstairs. The sight of this place instantly makes me happy. For one, there's the epic view of the sea stretching to the horizon through windows framed by billowing white drapes. The rhythmic crash of waves against the shore is audible, even from within this cottage. There are sea salt and coconut-scented candles filling the space with a subtle tropical ambiance. Addison must have lit them while I was moving the kids.

She's walking around the cozy, honey-oak kitchen, biting her lip. Her steps are light and slow, like she's worried she might fall through the floorboards if she walks too hard or fast. It makes me chuckle.

Her head whips around to face me. "What?"

"You worried about breaking something, bunny?" Waving a hand at her feet, I add, "You can walk around less carefully, you know."

"I don't want to wake the kids." Her eyes flicker to mine briefly before falling away. It irritates me, so I say something to make her look at me again. "What ever happened with Asher that night I was in Chicago? Did he make it over?" *Please say no.*

Two bright pink spots appear on her cheeks. "Um, no. He didn't."

Something inside me loosens. "I bet he's regretting that after seeing you today."

Her mouth twists. "I never ended up asking him over. I don't miss him *that* much. I just hate sleeping . . ." she trails off, biting her lip like she's afraid to say what she's thinking.

She doesn't have to. I remember what the messages said. "Sleeping alone?" It's a loaded question, because she could mean plain old sleeping, or she could mean, ahem, *sleeping.*

The alcohol in my veins propels my next honest words. "Believe me. I hate sleeping alone, too."

"Yeah, I bet it's been a while." Then she covers her mouth with both hands like she didn't mean to say that. "Not that you—I didn't mean it like that, obviously, because *look* at you. It's just that . . ."

"Relax, you're fine." If Logan were here, he'd be dying of laughter right now.

"Good. I was worried I offended you, and you were about to fire me again." Her words slur a little. She's probably feeling tipsy, too, otherwise I doubt she would have said that.

"Still mad about that, huh?"

"Not really. It's your loss since you fired your hardest worker. Me." She points to herself as if I don't know who she's referring to. And for someone who's worried about waking the kids, she sure hollered that last part.

Yeah. The wine is definitely affecting her.

"Addison." A rough laugh escapes my mouth. "I can see that you're a hard worker, and I admit, I probably shouldn't have fired you. But I promise that mistake has nothing to do with you and everything to do with my dad pressuring me to make tough choices."

She fights a smile. "Can I have my old job back then?"

I immediately think of Kiera's email and my chest reacts, tightening painfully. "No way. You're the best nanny I've ever had, and I'm enjoying you being around way more than I have any right to."

Our gazes linger together for a moment before we both glance away.

"I, um . . ." She suddenly finds the wood grain on the floor fascinating. "I should probably go to bed."

"Same here." I blink a few times. "I'll sleep down here on the couch. You take the bed."

"There's only one?" She exhales a humorless laugh. "Of course there is."

"It's okay. That couch is pretty comfortable." I cock my head backward in the general vicinity of the living room.

She glances at the weathered wicker sofa with soft, plush cushions piled high. "Um, no. That doesn't look big enough for you to sleep on."

I arch an eyebrow. "If you think I'm letting you sleep out here, you're crazy."

"I'm not letting you sleep on the couch in your own house."

I shrug one shoulder. "Then I guess the only solution is for us to both sleep in the bed."

"No. Bed sharing is strictly prohibited for us, remember?"

"True."

"But then again, you're way too big for that couch."

I smirk. "We'll just have to make an exception, then. Won't we?"

"Fine." She walks backwards, inching her way toward the stairs.

"I'll see you up there."

The sound of massive waves crashing against the shore fills the otherwise silent kitchen after Addison goes upstairs. I stare out the window above the sink, thoughts in a blur.

This is supposed to be fake. Convenient. Stop flirting with her, Perry.

Because I'm so attracted to her, the wisest thing to do at this point would be to call everything off, but we still need each other. I need her until I can find a real fiancée, because I'm not ready for my dad to find out the truth yet. And she needs me to get under Asher's skin—which is, admittedly, *so* much fun.

But I'm worried if we keep doing this I'm going to fall for her so hard, I won't be able to pick myself back up. Falling for her—or for *anyone*—would be a terrible idea. After all, there's a reason I'm choosing to marry someone I feel nothing for—so that someone can never shatter my heart the way Jill did.

I lean against the kitchen island. I stare at my shoes like they're going to solve my problems. And then I go up the stairs.

The worst part is, the closer I get to the bedroom, the more intense the excitement, the feelings in my stomach get. I try to make them go away, reminding myself of all the reasons I don't want to open up again after what Jill did to me. But listening to those reasons feels like reading a language I don't know.

I stop at the bathroom to change into sweats and take off my shirt. When I go into the room, I catch a glimpse of Addison's face through the mirror hanging on the wall. She's lying on her side with her back to me, and her eyes squeeze shut as soon as I crack open the door. Her delicious aroma is all over the room, probably clinging to the walls and sheets.

Perry, you got this. Just get in the bed with her. It's no big deal.

My pulse sounds like an R&B drum beat in my ears as I peel the blanket away and get in. Thanks to the high quality of the mattress, there's no creaking noise from my weight. But the cushy, foam material dips as I settle myself in.

And then I notice all the pillows crammed between me and Addison. I laugh, breaking the silence in here. "Seriously?" I pick one of the fluffy pillows up and toss it across the room.

"Don't ruin the pillow wall!" Addison shoots up in the bed.

"Aha!" I smirk at her. "You *were* pretending to be asleep."

"I was not pretending. You woke me up when you threw the pillow."

"Pillows are known to be virtually silent, bunny. Nice try." I squint at her through the dim light, barely making out the way her mouth is twisted in fury.

"The couch is sounding really great right about now," she huffs.

I hold back my amusement for her sake. "Okay, I'm sorry. Look, I won't touch you if that's what you're worried about. Not a single finger or toe of mine will touch a single finger or toe of yours, Addison. I promise."

She pouts as she tries to determine whether I mean it. "Good. Thank you."

We lie back down.

Knowing she's just on the other side of those pillows is torturous. I can practically feel the warmth radiating off her. The sound of her even breathing relaxes me, and that thing she told me resurfaces in my mind, that she hates sleeping alone. Part of me wonders if this counts to her as not sleeping alone, and if she likes it. I know better than to ask her though, because she'll probably get embarrassed and go downstairs.

I shift onto my side so I'm facing her. I think I hear a little whimper come from her, but I'm probably imagining it. Something tickles my forehead, and when I look up, I realize it's a thick piece of her hair. I leave it right where it is and whisper, "Goodnight, Addison."

She doesn't respond, but later, when I'm almost asleep, I think I hear her whisper it back.

Chapter Seventeen

ADDISON

PERRY SLEEPS without his shirt on. I know this firsthand, because when I open my eyes in the morning, my cheek is pressed right up against his bare chest. He must still be asleep, because if he wasn't, surely, he'd politely scoot me back to my side of the bed to spare us both this embarrassment.

I blink a few times, and as I do, my eyelashes get caught in his fine chest hairs. At first, I don't know where I am, but then I see the sunlight filtering through sheer curtains, casting a warm glow across weathered wooden floors. Whitewashed walls are adorned with nautical-themed decor—seashell wind chimes, framed beach landscapes, and tiny prints of vintage surfboards. A small wardrobe is in the corner of the room.

Perry hums and the arm that's draped across my shoulders moves downward, landing on my lower back.

Oh. My. Gosh.

I'm painfully aware of his touch, and every hard

muscle on his body pressed against me. Tucked into the crook of his shoulder, it's no wonder I slept like an angel all night.

Except right now, this close to Perry, the thoughts I'm having are anything but angelic.

I need to move. Now.

Slowly, I scoot away from him. It takes a genuine effort because he's stronger than me and his arm is heavy. But after what feels like forever, I'm finally back on my side of the bed, facing *away* from him.

That little hum happens again, and the next thing I know, Perry's spooning me. Yep. That's right. His chest is against my back, and his arm slides around my waist. I know I should wake him up, but it feels really . . . good to have him wrapped around me like this. And that's so wrong of me.

Even though I'd secretly like to stay wrapped up in him all day, I pinch his hand to wake him up. Hard.

He gasps, shooting up like I electrocuted him, and I pretend to stay asleep. I feel it then, the moment he realizes we've been cuddling in our sleep, because he removes his skin from mine like I burned him and swears under his breath.

The moment he gets out of the bed, it's both a relief and complete, utter torture.

I spend the next two days trying to occupy myself with helping Perry's children build sandcastles and collect seashells. I stay out of the water whenever Perry goes in it, and I pretend not to check him out when he takes his kids into the ocean for a swim, wearing nothing more than a tight pair of swim trunks that leaves me with nowhere else to look other than places I really don't want to be looking. Like his torso and arms, covered in a light layer of soft, dark hair that does nothing to hide the toned muscles beneath.

My phone chimes with a text from Romilly.

ROMILLY

How's the trip so far?

ME

There's only one bed, so we've both been sleeping in it together and it's starting to feel impossible not to jump his bones.

ROMILLY

Um, wow

Okay

Don't panic. We can work with this

ME

Are you sure? Because I keep catching him staring at me all dark, broody and sexy, but I'm his NANNY. He's getting ENGAGED and then MARRIED soon, and here I am thinking about him constantly.

ROMILLY

He's not officially engaged yet, right?

ME

No. But he's going to be soon. Still, not in a position to eat my face in the kitchen like I want him to.

ROMILLY

I mean, kitchens are technically for eating.

I release my phone and run my hands down my face.

I'm so doomed. Even just watching Perry play with his kids in the water right now is making me feel like I need a cold plunge.

I close my eyes and try to enjoy the beach. With my lids shut, it's easier to focus on the briny scent of seawater in the ocean breeze, mingling with the earthy aroma of driftwood and sun-warmed sand.

"Well, if it isn't Advertisement."

My gaze darts to my left by instinct, but I don't even need to look to know who it is. I'd know that voice, and that nickname, anywhere. "Asher." I run my hands over the towel I'm sitting on and squint up at him through the intense sunlight he's trying to block with his body. He's wearing blue swim trunks and a tank top with a palm tree at sunset on the front. It's probably the most casual I've ever seen him. "Wow. You really weren't kidding about showing up here."

He barks out a single, loud laugh. "Of course I wasn't. By the way, we still need to film your interview footage, and after I left, I realized I left out some questions that I meant to ask. Too bad the camera crew isn't here. This beach would make a great filming location."

His head turns to follow my line of sight from a few seconds ago, landing directly on Perry and the kids splashing around. He makes no comment on them, but I register the way his posture grows rigid.

I shake my head. "I can't believe you're here." In the six months we spent dating, we never went on trips like this together. I can't help but find it a bit ironic that our first time on a beach together is nothing more than a product of his jealousy. *So much for not being special.*

"Well, I didn't come just for you." He scrunches his nose. "I brought the parents. We come to another beach close by every summer so Mom can day drink without being judged."

"Ah. Good for her." And then I remember something important. "By the way, can you add me to the unsponsored section of the pageant website? I'm hoping a business will reach out and send me an offer."

"You mean . . ." He narrows his eyes. "You don't have a sponsor yet?"

"Well, I did. It was Rosemary Banquet. But that was before—"

"You started dating the boss," he says it like it's funny to him.

I clear my throat. "Anyway, I'd really appreciate it if you could add me on there."

"Of course. It's no problem."

We smile thinly at each other as silence stretches between us. Suddenly uncomfortable, I stand up to dust the sand off my butt.

Asher watches, his gaze lingering on my bathing suit, which rides up uncomfortably when I bend down to brush some sand off the towel.

"You look great, Addison." The words sound regretful coming from his mouth. "I miss you."

His words mean nothing to me now, but they're exactly what I wanted to hear a few months ago, the day he dumped me. "I don't put out anymore, and I'm still intense, you know. Those are the parts you didn't like, remember?"

He shakes his head at my teasing tone and shoves his hands in the pockets of his shorts. "Maybe I was an idiot."

"Perry and I have been talking about engagement." I know it's a low blow, but I don't care. Asher still seems to think he can weasel his way back to me, which means I must really need to drive my point home. And it's not too far of a stretch, since Perry's dad already thinks we're engaged.

"Don't be so dramatic." He sighs. Putting one hand on each of my shoulders, he spins us so I'm no longer facing the shore. As if I can't concentrate on his words while Perry is still in view or something. "Look, I know it's not my business, but think about what you're doing for a second."

"Meaning?"

"I know you. You get way too excited about everything and tend to overlook potential problems. You're trying to be Miss Meadow this year. Isn't this your last chance before you're too old?"

I wince at *too old,* but nod. "Obviously."

"Well, part of the reason you didn't want to hook up with me in the beginning was because you were worried about having feelings and getting distracted." He winces, like he's about to hit me with terrible news about myself I don't even know yet.

"Okay? And it turns out I was fine. I'm not distracted by Perry, either. How is this relevant at all?"

He presses his lips together like it's obvious. "How you were just looking at him? I've never seen you look at me like that, not even while we were dating."

I want to deny it. I want to so badly, but I can't.

He squeezes my shoulders with his hands, hard. "Despite what you may think, I still care about you, Advertisement. You should listen to me and pull back. He isn't worth losing your chance over."

I cringe at how tightly his nails are digging into my shoulders and try to shake him off in a friendly way, but his grip is too tight. "Let go."

He shakes his head. "If you just listen to me—"

"Take your hands off her." Perry's voice comes from beside me.

Asher releases my shoulders, but the way he smiles at him reminds me of an unfriendly dog baring its teeth.

Perry's gaze connects with mine. "Are you okay?"

"I'm fine—"

"Relax, dude," Asher cuts in. A cocky smirk appears on his lips. "I used to date this girl, remember? Whether you like it or not, I've touched her before."

They stare each other down wordlessly. It's like a ridiculous macho stand-off from a cheesy movie.

I roll my eyes. "It was nice to see you, Asher." It's the perfect dismissal—polite, but clear. *Time to go, buddy.*

He seems unbothered as he murmurs in my direction. "Just remember what I said. Think about it." With a meaningful glance at me and one last scowl in Perry's direction, he heads down the sand toward the parking lot.

"So . . ." I turn to Perry. "Asher's here. Great, right?" I laugh to lighten the mood, but he doesn't smile or answer.

Beside him, all four children are wrapped in towels and watching us curiously. He seems to notice at the same time I do and swears, staring up at the sky. "Kids, let's go back inside. I think we've all had enough excitement for now."

Izzy taps Perry's arm. "Hey, Daddy. You sound jealous of that guy who was talking to Addy."

"What's 'jealous' mean?" Enzo tugs on Izzy's towel.

"It's when you feel bad because you want something that's not yours." A giggle escapes her.

"Observant, as always, Izzy," Perry says.

The rest of them chorus a laugh with her, leaving me blushing with nowhere left to look. I don't know how much of that exchange they witnessed, but apparently it was enough to be funny to them.

"Daddy, we don't want to leave yet. We want to sign up for the junior lifeguards." Moxie stands, making her lower lip pout. She gestures down the sand a bit, where an umbrella stand is set up.

I start walking in the direction of the stand. "I'll go sign them up so you can rinse them off inside." Before Perry can respond, I'm already on my way over to the stand.

A middle-aged couple with smile lines greets me when I approach, handing me fliers and a clipboard to sign the kids up. My eyes widen when I see how much it's going to cost for all four of them to spend two hours a day this week "learning to be lifeguards," which by the look of the activity list is really just them playing with other kids, using binoculars, eating snacks, and building more sand-castles in a group setting. I can see why they want to join so badly. And it's not like Perry can't afford it.

When I'm finished signing them up, I walk back to the cottage. Slowly.

Despite what I told Asher about Perry not being a distraction, I can't help but admit to myself, very begrudg-ingly, that he's right. Perry has been nothing but a distraction since I met him, and it's only getting worse the more time we spend together. I should be more focused on the pageant than ever before, but it's starting to feel like it's falling to the wayside.

His words ring in my ears. *You should listen to me and pull back. He isn't worth losing your chance over.*

Chapter Eighteen

THE TERM *FAMILY trip* leaves a bad taste in my mouth. When I think back to what things were like when Jill was still in the picture, what I recall most was me doing as much as possible so she wouldn't have to lift a finger. Managing the screaming kids alone. Preparing all our meals. Singlehandedly packing and lugging all the bags around. Hanging back in our room with the kids so she could explore our destination without us ruining her fun. Anything to keep her happy.

As it turns out, none of it was good enough.

Addison is the complete opposite. I try not to compare her to Jill because it's probably not healthy, but I often catch myself pleasantly surprised when she scoops two kids up into her arms at once, something Jill refused to do because apparently, even one kid was too heavy for her.

I remind myself Addison's only doing it because it's her job.

The next day, she suggests we take the kids to a nearby

field to pick flowers. Begrudgingly, I dial Logan. He arrives at the cabin within twenty minutes to take us to the field Addison shows him on her phone map. *He better keep the jokes to himself.*

"Addison, this is my friend, Logan."

A sly twinkle enters his eyes. "You're the nanny, right? Perry's told me . . . a *lot* about you."

I'm going to kill him.

She giggles and ducks her head. "Actually, I'm Perry's girlfriend."

With his polite smile in place, Logan simply shifts his gaze in my direction.

I. Will. Never. Hear. The. End. Of. This.

"Right. I knew that. It's nice to meet you, Addison," he says.

"Nice to meet you, too. Do you live in the area?"

"Nah, I'm from Meadow Hills, like you. But any chance I get, I stay over here to surf. It's part of why I agreed to drive this lazy bum around." He squeezes my shoulder, earning a glare from me.

Addison laughs. "How nice for us."

She helps me place each napping kid in the back of the limo with a blanket, and when she gets in with the rest of us, she's blushing.

I arch an eyebrow. "Something on your mind?"

"Nothing." She clears her throat. "It's just that your friend is very cute. And nice."

I can't stop the jealousy from reappearing, just like it did on the beach when I saw her talking to Asher. When I saw him *touching* her. It's not fair of me to get mad about her thinking Logan is a good-looking guy, because it's not even an opinion. It's a straight up fact.

She watches my face, biting her lip to keep from smiling. It's almost as if she *likes* this, watching me react to her statement. I'm just glad all the kids are still sleeping so they don't get to watch too.

"You like making me jealous, don't you?" I practically growl.

"I mean, it's not boring, that's for sure."

"Keep it up, bunny, and I'll get rid of every pillow in the house, so there's nothing between us tonight, and we'll see who has the touching problem."

Her mouth falls open.

Satisfied, I rest both arms behind my head and settle back to get more comfortable. Neither of us speaks again until we arrive at the field, but I notice the way she fidgets with the ends of her hair the entire ride. I wonder if she has any idea just how cuddly she gets as soon as she falls asleep. I'm not complaining, but I find it funny that I'm the one she keeps warning to keep my hands to myself.

Logan lets us out of the limo. I want to smack something when Addison smiles at him and murmurs, "Thanks."

As soon as she's out of earshot, he grabs me by the arm, a Cheshire grin on his face. "Girlfriend, huh?"

I sigh. "Remember the marriage terms in my mom's will I told you about?"

"Oh, it just gets better and better. Y'all are engaged, aren't you?" He raises his eyebrows. "And I get to hear about it from her? Why haven't you been bragging about it to anyone who will listen?"

Because you're my friend and I'd feel bad lying to you.

"I'll explain later. It's a long story."

"Good, because I'm invested now." He shoves his hands in his pockets and leans against the limo. His smile still hasn't gone anywhere.

"Thanks for the ride."

Logan watches Addison and I shake the kids softly awake. When they realize we're here to pick a bunch of flowers, it doesn't take much else to get them out of the vehicle. Addison hands each of them one of the woven baskets she brought from the cottage pantry, and they take off running.

She lingers behind to help me grab the blankets and cooler we brought for lunch. When she bends over to reach for them in the trunk, I come up behind her, placing my hand on the small of her back. Her pink sundress feels soft under my touch. I don't even ask if it's okay, because we're fake dating and Logan is here. I'm pretty sure he counts as someone watching, even if I plan on telling him the truth eventually. "I got all this."

"I got it, too." She stands, holding the giant cooler in one hand and the blankets under her other arms.

"Give me the cooler before you hurt yourself."

"It rolls, Perry. See?" She sets it down and pulls the handle until it extends up to the right height.

"I don't care." I take it from her and start rolling it toward the field. "If I don't have something to keep my hands busy, I'm worried about where they'll end up." Wait a minute . . . did I actually just say that?

She giggles, and the sound goes straight to my gut. I'm painfully aware of her trailing behind me as we make our way to where the kids are plucking away at all kinds of different flowers. Their baskets are huge, so it looks like they're going to be at it for a while. Moxie is even attempting to tie the stems of her flowers together to make a crown, or a necklace, maybe.

Addison lays the four blankets out on the grass, giving us a huge area to spread out. I try not to stare when she sweeps all her hair to one side, revealing the thin straps holding her dress up.

She sits down, and I lie next to her on my side, facing her, with my head propped up on my elbow.

She lowers herself so she's flat on her back, staring up at the sky. I watch her take it in, fascinated by her fascination. Her brown eyes look lighter under the sun, and there's a healthy glow surrounding her bronze skin. The gentle wind makes her thick curls float around her like there's no gravity.

"What's your favorite flower?" she asks, breathing the words into the silence.

I frown, actually giving it some thought. "Sunflowers, I guess. They're so happy and positive." *Like you,* I want to say, but I keep it to myself. "What's yours?"

"Dandelions. I love them and I hate them."

"Why?" I frown at the emotion in her voice.

At first, I don't think she's going to continue, but after a moment, she takes a deep breath. "They were Gran's thing with me. We'd always wish on dandelions before a pageant. It became a sort of tradition of ours, wishing that I'd win, right before the preliminaries. But I never did win." A glossy shine appears on her unblinking eyes. "I brought one with me to the hospital when she passed away, and we blew it out together. I wished for her to get better, and she wished for me to win. But obviously, neither one happened. I'm pretty sure it's the last time I ever wished on one of those stupid flowers." Her voice catches at the end.

Something breaks inside my chest. "Hey." I reach over to her hands, because she's twisting her fingers together and it looks painful. I lace my fingers through hers. I probably shouldn't do something like this in front of the kids, but they're distracted with the flowers. *And it's just for a moment,* I tell myself.

"Sorry. That was probably way too heavy." She tries to laugh, but it comes out more like a sad breath.

"No. I like hearing about your life. Tell me more."

"Before Gran died, I used to also wish on dandelions for my brother, Finn, to get better, even though I knew it wouldn't happen. But it was kind of a selfish wish, anyway. It's never bothered me that he has special needs, but I used to get really upset when my parents spent more time with him because he required a lot of special services. He still does. I don't blame them now, but it sucked not seeing them that much when I was younger."

"Where did you go while they did all that?"

"With Gran. She practically raised me." She smiles faintly. "Did you know she was the very first winner of Miss Meadow? She joined the pageant the year it began."

"I get why it's so important to you. Winning, I mean." I release her hand and roll flat onto my back. "You want heavy? Get this." She shifts onto her side so she can face me. There's a curious glint in her eyes that I can't deny I really like. "My house is the only place I can remember my mom. No matter how hard I try to recall memories of her that aren't attached to those walls, I can't. And as sad as that makes me, I also feel like I get to keep part of her with me while I'm there. Like, she's still with me or something."

"She is with you. Of course she is."

"I don't understand why my sister even wants the house. Like I've told you, she and I have different moms, and even though she technically spent time there too, it doesn't have much sentimental value to her."

"I might pretend otherwise, but I get why you're so willing to marry a stranger."

"You mean you're no longer repulsed by my life choices?"

"Let's not get ahead of ourselves." Addison smiles coyly. "But to be honest, I love the idea of marriage. I've always thought that God has marriage in His plans for me, but I'm not even entertaining that idea until I win. Even if I want . . ." She swallows, her gaze cutting away from me.

My gut tightens. "Addison . . ."

But she shakes her head before I can finish. "This *thing* between us? We can't entertain it."

Thing? Is she . . . is she admitting she feels something for me, too? It takes me a minute to clear the fog in my brain because hearing what she might be implying makes me feel like I'm not crazy after all. I'm not imagining any of it.

But she's right. We can't keep entertaining it, teasing ourselves with it, no matter what we might be feeling. It's unhealthy, considering our futures, and it's only going to set us back.

"Fine," I growl. "But at least admit—"

"Stop." She places a finger against my lips, which does

strange, sinister things to my body. "Let's not go there. It will only make things worse."

After a long moment, I nod. Releasing a heavy sigh, I change the subject entirely. "Tell me more about your brother. How old is he?"

She seems surprised by the question, but answers regardless. "He's thirty. He still needs full-time care, so my parents moved to Vermont with him because there are better services for him there."

"Why didn't you go with them?"

"Because I haven't won yet, and in order to compete in the pageant, I have to live in Meadow Hills."

"Got it. So, growing up, what was it like having a brother with special needs?"

She shrugs. "I mean, I don't have anything different to compare it to. I loved him. I still do. And I used to hate when people would make fun of him. It was the only time I'd ever, ever lose my temper and snap."

As soon as she says it, the puzzle becomes complete. It all makes sense. The real reason she slapped that customer at Rosemary Banquet. I remember her telling me she did it because the customer was making fun of a regular with . . . what was it? Sensory issues? It reminded her of her brother. I swear under my breath. "I feel like a complete jerk. I get why you slapped that customer now."

She smiles sadly. Shrugs. "I guess I haven't grown up all that much."

"Look what we found, Addy!" Izzy practically trips over herself trying to get to us. Her basket is filled to the brim with colorful flowers, mostly yellow. But in her hand, there's a giant white dandelion, much bigger than all the others around us.

All the kids are crowding around it like it's made of gold. Izzy hands it to Addison. "We've been fighting over who gets to make a wish, so we thought you should decide."

I know the way she swallows hard as she takes the flower from Izzy is only obvious to me. "Well, there's only one correct answer. You all should wish at the same time, of course. I'll hold it for you and count to three, and then you all have to blow it out together."

Their excitement as she counts down is obvious. But there's a sad part of me that recognizes how hard it must be for Addison to act excited as the children blow it out, whether it's because she misses her grandma, or because she's only prolonging the sad truth from these innocent kids: that wishing on flowers won't really make their dreams come true.

Chapter Nineteen

ADDISON

I TRY to stay in good spirits the rest of our time in the flower field. I giggle as the kids watch Perry feed me strawberries and grapes to get them to eat theirs. I help Izzy and Moxie finish their flower crowns and put one on my head too so we all match. I cuddle the twin boys when they randomly get frustrated about the fact that Christmas is in the winter, not summer. I reapply sunscreen on the kids at least twice, careful not to put it too close to their eyes.

Perry and I talk some more, and he plays with my hair as we lie there. I don't know if he even realizes he does it. But it tickles my scalp in a way and makes my tummy feel warm, especially when we lock eyes occasionally as we tell each other our birthdays, who our childhood best friends were, where we'd travel if life couldn't get in the way.

I can't deny he's really good at distracting me, but still, my spirits are down. And it's all that silly dandelion's fault. It brings back all the memories I've tried so hard to ignore, especially my parents constantly pawning me off onto

Gran so they could focus on Finn. Even when they moved away, their offer for me to come along didn't feel sincere enough. And that was fine. I didn't want to leave Meadow Hills and abandon all the wonderful memories I shared with Gran, anyway.

Deep down, I knew I wasn't good enough for my parents to choose me too, not just my brother. Maybe part of why I want to win so badly is to prove to myself I'm good enough; that I have what it takes. It's something Gran always knew. I just need to see it, too.

Perry's teasing voice breaks me out of my trance. "You still with me, bunny?"

"Yeah." I shrug. "No."

His expression shifts, the amusement melting away into something else. A knowing, sort of comforting look. Like he wants to share my sadness with me. Wordlessly, he reaches his hand out to me. I know I shouldn't, but I take it, letting him thread our fingers together. Some warmth makes its way back into my chest.

Okay, I was wrong. I'm not sad only because of the flowers, reminding me painfully of Gran and all I have to lose, but because of these children. This trip. Perry.

It's too easy to pretend, imagining myself as their stepmom instead of their nanny, and that this is one of our family vacations. Lying here next to Perry, talking so openly with him, feels good. Too good. This is a dangerous game I'm playing—allowing myself to confuse this fantasy with reality. And the reality is that I'm these children's nanny, nothing more. I'm not Perry's real fiancée, no matter how many times I've allowed my brain to tiptoe into that small, nuclear fantasy.

Under different circumstances, this wouldn't be a life I'd reject. I love kids, and I have nothing against marriage, even for younger couples. When it's love, it's love. There's something about the forever commitment, the vows. The idea no one is supposed to give up and walk out on the other person. Besides my terrible decision to date Asher, I've always tried to push my hopelessly romantic thoughts away because of the Miss Meadow pageant, locking them in my brain, within a filing cabinet neatly labeled: Do not open or think about this till you're twenty-seven.

The more time I spend with Perry and his kids, the more jealous I'm becoming of whoever gets them all in the end. But even if I plucked one of these dandelions from the ground and wished for things to be different, I know they couldn't be. If I become Miss Meadow, I won't be free to get married for a year. By then, Perry's deadline will have already passed.

When we get back to the cottage, the kids put all their flowers in their shared room for safekeeping. I promise to guard them while they're at junior lifeguards' class, and Izzy nods, thanking me profusely.

Logan arrives to drive them to their class, and I cross my arms when the limo disappears from view. "What am I supposed to do while the kids are gone?"

Perry opens the fridge, producing a bottle of fancy white wine. Before I can protest, he's pouring me a glass. "Now remember," he murmurs. "As good as this would look all over the furniture, I'd prefer if it stayed in the glass this time."

"Hilarious." I take the glass from him carefully and lift it to my lips, smacking them together after I swallow. "This is really good."

There's a mischievous glint in his eye as he smiles. "You know where it would taste even better? The jacuzzi."

His wide grin reminds me of a child. It's so excited and endearing that it makes me laugh. "You're really enjoying this, aren't you?"

He takes another sip. "The fact that my kids are elsewhere for a minute? Yes, I really am. And you should be, too. You finally get a break from them, bun." He gives me a pointed glance. "You. Me. Jacuzzi. Let's go." He's already in swim trunks, so all it will take for him to get ready is removing his shirt—revealing his body, which I most definitely won't be drooling over when I'm stuck in a hot, steamy tub with him.

It's just a jacuzzi. A friendly body of warm water where two friends—coworkers—fake fiancés—whatever, can wind down! Nothing dangerous about it at all. It's what I tell myself when a flurry of nerves swarms my body.

I lift my glass to Perry, wincing when the liquid nearly sloshes over the edge. He stares back at me with amusement.

"I'll go change and meet you out there," I say.

A moment later, I'm in the primary bedroom where my open suitcase is waiting on the floor. The bed is still messy and unmade from last night. I feel kinda bad, putting all those pillows between us. He's so much bigger than me, and he probably loses a lot of space on his side. But I know myself, and if there's nothing separating us at night, I don't think the concept of personal space will exist anymore on my end.

I change into my strappy red one-piece. It's the bathing suit that placed me in the top six three years ago for Miss Meadow, and I know it flatters my skin tone and body shape.

Grabbing the wineglass, I sling a towel over my shoulders before heading back downstairs. I linger by the sliding back door in the dining room, my nerves catching up with me.

When I open the door and peek outside, Perry is already in the jacuzzi with his eyes closed and head tilted back. His hair is soaking wet and pushed away from his face. While he's not looking, I take a moment to commit the planes of his face to memory, letting my eyes linger on his muscled arms resting on top of the rim of the tub.

It's warm outside. The sound of laughter and chatter carries over from neighboring cottages, mingling with the distant melody of an acoustic guitar. This place has a comfortable, casual vibe that makes me feel like I'm at home.

I set my towel next to a rattan basket overflowing with colorful beach towels and drain my glass before leaving it on the patio table next to me. The sound of it clinking makes Perry's eyes fly open, and his gaze zeroes in on me. He flexes his jaw and then stares at the sky.

"Wow, Addison."

"What?" I frown at him as I inch myself in. The hot, bubbly water feels amazing against my skin as I sink down, leaving only my neck and head exposed. We're on opposite sides, finally looking directly at each other, and it's making the adrenaline in my veins rush through me at an alarming speed.

"You, uh . . ." He clears his throat. "You look gorgeous. That's all."

There should be alarm bells ringing in my brain, but I can't deny how good it makes me feel to know he thinks that. "That's an inappropriate thing to say to your nanny, if you ask me."

"True." He comes closer, the water between us lapping up his chest. "But it's not such a far-fetched thing to say to my fiancée."

"Fake fiancée."

I try to steady myself, reaching forward, but he drapes my arms around his shoulders. I wrap my legs around his waist, because I can't help it. There's not really anywhere else for them to go. His hard abs graze my inner thighs. I barely move an inch, frozen in shock and desire.

Wordlessly, we take each other in. It's like our conversation from earlier didn't happen, because here we are, both torturing ourselves.

"I think I need a refill," I say, disentangling myself from him. I snatch my towel from the basket and wrap it around my torso. The air feels cold on my skin as I walk back inside. Good. Maybe it will wake me up. But when I get into the kitchen, my brain is still completely foggy.

What did I come in here for again?

Perry's voice cuts into my thoughts. "You forgot your wineglass." There's a towel around him too, and as he comes closer to hand me the glass, I see the water drip from his hair into his eyelashes. He holds the glass out to me, but I don't take it, so he sets it on the counter. "What's wrong?"

"What? Nothing is wrong."

"Tell me."

"It's nothing."

"Addison."

Okay, so he's not going to drop it. I sigh. "You're just so . . . overwhelming."

A frown. "What did I do?"

I think about the buzzing beneath my skin whenever we make eye contact. The annoying things his voice does to my body that I can't seem to ignore. How warm and inviting it felt to wake up pressed against his chest. His close proximity to me, here in the kitchen. "You didn't do anything. It's just part of your personality, I guess. You probably have women tell you all the time that you're over-whelming."

Perry laughs incredulously. "Look. I can't believe I'm admitting this, but I was painfully shy until I'd almost finished college. I've never been called overwhelming, and I was afraid to talk to women the majority of my life."

I ponder that, thoughtfully, and say, "Just so you know, I would never guess by the way you kiss."

The corner of his mouth pulls up. "So, what you're saying is there may be some truth to those texts about me you sent Romilly? You like me more than you want to admit?"

"I was drunk. I didn't mean any of that."

"Oh, really, miss 'I-only-have-one-drink-at-a-time'?" I'm silent, breathing harder, so he continues, his voice hinting at amusement. "You're not enjoying being in a fake relationship with me? Not even a little?"

And then he tucks a strand of my wet hair behind my ear. A strangled sound escapes me.

Part of me knows I definitely shouldn't let him engage with me like this. But the other part of me is way too buzzed from the wine to care.

"You're getting married soon. It wouldn't be responsible to let this go any farther than pretending, like we've been doing."

"Believe me. I know." His gaze travels from my eyes to my mouth. "But if you think those kisses were good, imagine what it would be like if I kissed you while I'm not pretending."

An extremely long pause stretches out between us. My heart thunders in my chest. "Fine," I say. "Show me, then." The words come out hushed, like I'm afraid to speak them.

"Are you sure? Because that didn't sound very confident, bunny." He leans forward and trails his nose along my neck.

I let my head fall back, whimpering when he presses his lips against the sensitive skin above my collarbone. "Show me, Perry," I mutter. "Please."

It's all the permission he needs from me. He wraps his hands around my waist and lifts me onto the island.

Then he positions himself between my legs. My towel pools down around my waist, still damp.

"Last chance to change your mind," he says, and I can tell he means it. If I don't want him to kiss me for real, he won't.

I shouldn't want him to do this. But I do. I really, really do.

"Why?" I whisper. "Worried you won't be able to back your words up?"

He laughs without humor. As Perry leans in closer, I try to remain calm. His fingers slowly trail up my arms, leaving a path of tingles along my skin. He puts one hand on the base of my neck. With me sitting on the island like this, our faces are level. It's the first time I haven't had to look up at him.

He doesn't kiss my mouth right away. He takes my hand in his free one and lifts it to his lips, gently keeping his eyes on me as he kisses it, as if to observe his effect on me. It's so intense, I almost can't hold his gaze. But I know if I don't commit the way he looks right now to memory, I'll kick myself for it later. So, I take note of every detail, the way he's staring at me, kissing my hand with his head slightly bowed, hazel eyes searing holes right through me. My blood heats up like molten lava beneath my skin.

He kisses his way up my arm, taking his time, and I smother a nervous giggle. But the laugh quickly transforms to a low, throaty sound as he kisses up my collarbone, as if he hadn't had enough of me from the first round and wants another taste. Every time his lips come down in a new spot, my senses feel like they're going to explode.

Perry doesn't pause, continuing his tongue's devastating dance up my neck until I have no choice but to grab fistfuls of his dark hair to keep from falling off the counter.

"Don't worry, I've got you," he murmurs, tightening his grip on my waist.

He buries his face in my hair as he tips me backward

and scoots me to the edge so I'm lying flat, beneath him on the island. I cling to him desperately as he teases me with his mouth, kissing all the areas around my neck, my collarbone, leaving me desperate for more. I think I might die of desperation, in fact.

He kisses his way up my neck until he reaches my face, and doesn't hesitate, parting my lips with his and taking my tongue into his mouth. There's only a brief moment where the kiss is soft, caressing, and then we're crashing our mouths together, kissing as if we're coming up for air. Our tongues slide together, and his grip on my waist is slippery from the water. I practically burst into flames as he kisses down my neck, muttering a stream of gibberish.

The taste of wine is everywhere, shared between us, but underneath it is the sweet taste of Perry.

He whispers against my mouth, "Bunny, you're making it hard for me to stop." And then he's kissing me again. I tell my tongue to behave itself, but it disobeys, tangling with Perry's in a delicious rhythm that makes my heart scream at me. Whatever crush I've had on him triples into something else the longer we stay connected like this. It's dangerous, the little game we're playing, especially since it's not a game at all right now. Still, I can't find it in me to break away. I reach up to hold his face with both hands. His stubble is rough against my palms as I breathe him in, enjoying the way his weight presses down on my body.

"How do you always smell so good?" he mutters between kisses. He doesn't wait for a response. It's not a question. He says it and keeps kissing my lips, over and over, like doing so is bringing him back to life.

I don't know how much time passes, but I do know that I don't want it to end. He was right. He was so right. The way he kissed me under the guise of our fake relationship was nothing compared to this. And now that I know, I don't know how I'm going to go back to the way it was before.

When he releases me, my limbs feel loose and wobbly.

And then he's scooping me up and carrying me upstairs. My brain doesn't process anything but how strong Perry must be to carry me like this as he gently nudges the door open with his foot and sets me on the soft mattress. He tosses the pillows onto the floor, like he's been annoyed with them and has wanted to do so since we got here, and then the mattress dips under his weight as he joins me, pulling me closer to him so our damp bodies are flush together.

He kisses me again, this time deeply, slow and heady. The faint tang of sunscreen lingers on his sun-kissed skin. He gives me a moment to breathe, his mouth traveling down my body. The combination of his warm, soft lips and prickly facial hair turns me on even more as he kisses the side of my stomach, teasing me by kissing everywhere I'm exposed in the bathing suit. His mouth explores me frantically, and I'm practically out of my mind, digging into my own palms and overcome with desire.

Oh, God. Give me strength to resist. I want more. This is torture.

As impossible as it feels to do, I come to my senses and remember.

No more distractions.

This is exactly what I was trying to avoid.

"Perry," I whisper. "We have to stop. Right now."

He sits up and our eyes lock. "What's wrong?" He must see the turmoil in my eyes because he's instantly next to me again. His hand grazes my cheek, his thumb gently moving back and forth. "What's wrong, Addison?"

I shake my head hard enough that his hand falls away. "We can't do this. Ever again." I stand before I lose my train of thought. With him so close, it feels practically impossible to stick to my point right now. I want nothing more than to climb back in the bed with him and let him have his way with me.

Nothing more, except the Miss Meadow crown.

"No more kissing. Especially like that. Not unless it's because someone's watching. And—and even if someone's watching, you don't need to kiss me like that again."

His concern melts away. Now he looks like a wolf who just ate a piglet and is very happy about it. "Got it. No more kissing. But just so we're clear, what else exactly is off the table?"

"Everything. No more touching, no more flirting, no more anything." I pace back and forth.

"Don't be silly, bunny. Those things are going to happen whether you like it or not." He doesn't look at all worried about it, which proves I'm the only one whose heart is turning to mush the more we cross lines that have been drawn for a reason.

He's right, though. We need to keep this ruse going. If Asher finds out my involvement was all for his benefit, I will quite literally pass away from shame.

That means flirting. And touching. And . . . kissing.

A knot forms in my throat.

"This is too much," I say. "You're too much. I should be focusing on the pageant while I have time away from the kids. Perry, I haven't been doing anything I should be. There are interview questions I should be going over, exercise routines I've been skipping. Philanthropic education I've been avoiding." I pinch the bridge of my nose. "And you're always around, taunting me. Every time you kiss me, or touch me, or look at me, even, I want to do other things with you."

His mouth twitches. "Other things? Just say it. Say what you mean."

I glare at him. "You know what I mean. Don't make me say it."

"Sex," he says. "You want sex."

"Yes. But when I broke my pact, I had a pregnancy scare, so I got off birth control to deter myself, to make sure nothing like that would happen again. I can't risk getting pregnant, because then I'll be eliminated from the pageant." Tears spring to my eyes. "My focus hasn't been in the right place all this time. It's been on you and the fake relationship, and—"

He gets up from the bed and gathers me in his arms. "Shh, it's okay, Addison. I get it." He strokes my hair in a slow, soothing motion that makes my throat burn when I swallow. "I—I won't touch you again. I won't flirt with you anymore. Not unless you want me to. I promise."

"That's the problem. I do want you to." I pull out of his embrace.

He stares at me, looking torn. Neither of us speaks. Eventually, he rubs the back of his neck, walking back and forth across the room. "Like I said, I won't distract you anymore. I mean it."

"Thank you."

"I know we're leaving in a few days, but I'll sleep on the couch from now on."

"I can sleep on the—"

"Absolutely not," he says firmly. "You're sleeping in here." Perry gathers up a few of the oversized pillows and retrieves a comforter from the wardrobe in the corner of the room.

And then he goes downstairs.

As he leaves, I try not to replay what just happened over and over, but I can't help it. In fact, I think I'm ruined from having other thoughts ever again.

What were we thinking? What did we just do?

This man is trying to find a wife. He's about to get engaged, for real. And here I am, his child-friendly nanny, letting him kiss me like a starving man at his first buffet. But even worse, the thought of him getting married fills me with a sense of dread so heavy, it's alarming. I can't help but wonder if Gran—if God—would approve of my behavior.

I doubt it.

Please, heart. Go back to the way you were before.

But if my heart is anything like me, it probably won't listen.

Chapter Twenty

PERRY

IT TAKES every ounce of my control to keep my promise during the remainder of our vacation. I barely talk to Addison, barely look at her. Every time I want to, I think about the panic on her face when she thought she might not win the pageant because she's distracted.

By *me*.

I wouldn't be able to forgive myself if I were the reason she didn't win. So, I keep my promise, as hard as it is.

I leave her alone while she exercises in the mornings. While the kids are gone, she practices some kind of speech in the bedroom. I'm tempted to knock on the door and ask if I can help her, but I'm worried that's exactly what she doesn't want. So, during her pageant prep time, I go jogging on the beach with Logan. It's nice, having him to talk to. And the gentle rustle of palm leaves swaying in the coastal breeze is definitely not unwelcome during our jog.

"So, what are you going to do when your dad finds out you lied?" he asks after I've finally caught him all up.

"I have no idea." I stop running for a minute to catch my breath.

"You could always stage a breakup so he thinks it was real."

"True."

He winces. "But then you'd still have to deal with him being disappointed, wouldn't you?"

"What else is new?"

Logan offers me a pitying glance. "Let me know if you need my help. For real."

"Thanks, man."

"And when you're nice and married and Addison's free to date again, go ahead and pass her number my way."

I resist the urge to punch him.

Despite everything, our trip ends too quickly for my liking. It doesn't feel like a week has passed, but sure enough, the emails come through about the girls' kindergarten registration and the boys' preschool enrollment, just as scheduled.

I text Addison the addresses while we're in the limo on the way home. When she sees it, she pouts at me. "If they're going to be in school all morning, why do you even need me?" She says it jokingly, dramatically, but I answer her anyway.

"Because I need someone to take them there and pick them up, then manage them after that until I'm finished working."

"Daddy's really busy," Moxie adds.

Izzy nods in agreement. "Yep. But we like you, Addy, so it's okay."

She smiles down at Izzy. "I like you, too. And don't

forget, Perry, since it's Saturday, I'm going to finish my solo interview with Asher tonight when we get back. He's already home, and he just sent me a reminder text."

I look Addison over. She's dressed in skin-tight jeans and a white, frilly blouse. Her cleavage peeks out just under the neckline, and her long, dark hair is in defined curls that cascade down her back.

Before I shift my gaze away, she notices me noticing her, and clears her throat before looking out the window. After a few minutes, a bunch of text messages blow up her phone. She winces and starts texting back.

"Who is that?" I ask.

"Asher."

Something catches fire inside my chest. What could he have possibly said that made her wince like that? I try not to let my voice reveal how I feel, because it will probably scare the kids. "What does he want?"

Her gaze darts to my face and narrows, which makes me realize I'm not hiding anything from her. "He wants to get drinks before the interview," she says evenly. "But I'm not sure I'm comfortable with it."

I cross my arms. "Tell him no."

"It's not really something I can get out of. It's just another pageant thing I'm very much required to do."

"The interview, yes. But not the drinks. Not if you don't want to."

"Why don't you like Addy's friend, Daddy?" Izzy asks.

Addison's expression tightens as she waits along with Izzy for me to answer the question.

"Well," I ground out, "he stopped being friends with her once over a very silly reason, sweetie. I just don't think that's the kind of person who deserves her . . . *friendship* anymore."

Moxie frowns. "Like the time I stopped being friends with Kayla because she picked the same crayon as me when she came over? You told me that was silly, but we're still friends." Her bottom lip wobbles. "Am I like Addy's friend?"

Addison covers her mouth to hide a smile.

"No, no, of course not, sweetie." I pat the top of her head. "You're wonderful, and so is Addy's friend. I just don't want him to be mean to her again. That's all."

Izzy and Moxie nod, seemingly satisfied with this answer. The ride is quiet again, the boys deeply invested in the singing puppet video playing on their tablet, and the girls start playing with the dolls they brought.

Addison returns to her phone; and I want to yell in frustration. But then my phone buzzes with a text from her.

ADDISON

Would it be too much to ask you to drive me there?

If we're really getting drinks, I don't want to drive or carpool with him, like he wants.

ME

Yeah. There's no way you're carpooling with him.

ADDISON

Right?

Thank you.

ME

> I still don't understand why you won't just tell him no?

ADDISON

> What if it makes him mad and then he has Steve the camera man edit our interview to make me look bad? Asher is the host. I may despise him but when it comes to this, I don't want to step on his feet.

ME

> I do. I'd really love to step on his feet, in fact.

ADDISON

> Besides, it's not like you driving me would be weird or anything. We're fake engaged until you get real engaged.

I don't respond, because the text makes my chest feel tight. *Until you get real engaged.*

❧

It feels good to be home. As always, the comforting sights, sounds, and smells from my childhood home lift my spirits significantly. When I look at the kitchen, I still see my mom making my favorite chocolate cake with strawberry frosting for my birthday every year. I see my parents cuddling in front of the fireplace and hear Mom's laughter whenever Dad would accidentally come down the stairs in an outfit that matched hers. Believe it or not, it happened pretty often, which makes me think they must have been soulmates. It's probably why my dad never remarried after Mom passed away.

Kiera looks up from her laptop and waves at us from the kitchen when we come in. I had her order dinner for everyone from my favorite Italian restaurant downtown, and it's steaming at the table.

"I'll be right back," Addison murmurs to Kiera before going upstairs.

Kiera makes a face at me. I texted her in the limo, asking if she could help with the kids tonight so I could go with Addison, and thankfully, she agreed. Once Addison is out of earshot, she says, "You owe me big time, Mr. Whitmore."

"I'll pay you time and a half."

She blinks a few times and nods her approval.

I serve myself and the kids, setting a plate aside for Addison, too. Even after I take a few bites of rigatoni Bolognese, my stomach is tied in unsettled knots, so I push my plate away and stand up. Closing my eyes, I press my forehead against the stair railing.

As if on cue, Addison comes down the stairs in a completely different outfit than before. She looks absolutely devastating in a short, black dress that hugs every curve of her body. Her curls are no longer tamed, but wild and free around her face and shoulders. She's wearing more makeup now, too, with dark eyeshadow around her brown eyes that make them all-consuming and haunting. And her lips . . . they're soft and swollen in a way that reminds me of how they look after being kissed.

As good as it feels to be home, in this moment, all I

want is to take her back to that tiny bedroom in the summer cottage, before I promised to leave her alone.

She meets me at the bottom of the stairs, smiling a little. I'm at a complete loss for words, so I motion toward the dining table. "Dinner is ready. Do you want to eat before we go?"

"No. I'm not hungry." She bites her lip.

"You should eat something."

"Can't. Too nervous."

"Okay. I'll get my keys." I retrieve them from a tiny ceramic bowl on the kitchen counter and scoop her dinner into a plastic storage container to take with us, in case she gets hungry on the way.

The doorbell rings. Addison walks stiffly to the front door and swings it open.

Asher's tanned, smug face is in the doorway. His stupid mouth parts when he sees Addison in that dress, his gaze sweeping up and down her body like he owns her. It takes everything in me not to shut the door in his face and beg Addison to stay. I know she has to do this interview, and I hate it. Especially since I can tell she's uncomfortable with the whole thing.

If the kids weren't seated at the table, watching all this like one of their tablet videos, I'd probably give up trying to rein in my expression.

"Hey," he says, his voice husky. "Look at you." He pulls her into a hug. "Come on. Let's get out of here. Steve and the rest of the crew will meet us at the inn when we're done with drinks."

He barely finishes his sentence before I'm standing next to her. "I'm going to drive her." The words come out a little too rough, and Addison must notice, because squeezes my arm tightly. *So much for being too soft. If only Dad could see me now.*

Asher's eyes are wild with amusement as they take us in. "Is there a reason you don't want to ride with me, Ad?"

"Do I need one?" she asks.

"It's not another couple interview. This really doesn't concern your boyfriend, so he doesn't need to be here."

I cross my arms. "If it concerns her, it concerns me."

Asher's gaze jumps back and forth between the two of us. "Look, I'm the host of the Miss Meadow pageant. I shouldn't have to remind either of you that I'm in charge here."

I narrow my eyes at him. "Are you trying to say that if I drive Addison to get drinks with you before her interview, it's somehow going to undermine your authority?"

He doesn't answer, but his cheeks turn slightly pink. He looks to Addison for help, but I put myself in between them to shield her gaze from his. This woman is bringing out a feral instinct in me that I can't suppress. That I don't want to suppress.

Addison places both fists on her hips. "Sorry, Asher. But this isn't up for negotiation."

I can tell Asher is trying to keep his cool in front of her. He makes no other comments about me coming along, but there's obvious tension in his shoulders, especially when my hand finds its favorite place on the small of Addison's back as we all go outside. I notice Asher's eyes linger on my hand, touching her there, and his face seems to get redder than before. I know it's probably immature of me, but I make a show of rubbing my thumb back and forth.

He gets inside his silver convertible and slams the door a little too loudly.

"Ready, bunny?" I smirk down at Addison.

She sticks her lower lip out at me, but there's a sparkle in her eye. "Do you think we hurt the poor baby's feelings?"

"I really hope so."

"Who knew you could be so protective?"

"When it comes to you? Always."

Her breath hitches at that. I lead her toward the garage off to the side of my house. We cross the little stone steps leading the way, and with a button in my pocket on my keychain, I open the garage door where my black SUV is parked.

The car beeps as I hit the unlock button. I open the passenger door for her. "After you."

After we're both buckled in, I start the car and back out of the driveway. I have no idea where we're going, but I follow behind Asher as he annoyingly leads the way.

"Kiera is never going to forgive you for leaving her with the kids."

"She'll be fine. She's watched them before."

She arches an eyebrow at me. "How many times?"

"Once or twice."

"Seriously?" She rounds her eyes.

I laugh. "She knows what to do. She just doesn't like doing it. Kiera very much prefers the administrative tasks I hired her to do over babysitting. She's not a huge fan of kids, but she'll never admit it."

Addison ponders this in silence. I try to keep my eyes

on the road instead of staring at her, especially since it's so dark out.

"Do you think I'm overreacting, having you come along? Maybe Asher doesn't have any bad intentions, wanting to get drinks."

"Oh, please. I think he forgot to wipe the drool off his chin when he saw you."

She giggles. "You're so cute when you're jealous."

I snort, remembering what Izzy said on the beach. "Jealousy is when you want something that's not yours. As far as he or anyone else is concerned, you're already mine, bunny."

I might be imagining it, but I swear she sucks in a sharp breath.

Asher parks on the street next to a pub that transforms into a small club at night. Flashing lights and music emanate from inside.

Addison frowns. "I thought we were going to Old Joe's Diner for beers." She takes out her phone to look at past messages. Another one comes through. "Great. Asher just told me this is the place he wants to go to now."

I park us in a quaint lot down the street from the pub. We're isolated, with no other cars parked near us. Only in Meadow Hills would there be plenty of parking available at a club on a Saturday night.

I reach over to brush her hair out of her face. "Do you want me to take you home?"

"No."

"You're okay with going into that club with Asher—alone?"

She hesitates, then nods.

As if on cue, her phone buzzes on the passenger seat. The preview of the text comes into view.

ASHER

I'm here. Where are you?

I open the door for her. "I'll be waiting here."

"You don't have to do that. Asher can drive me back."

"I'm well aware. But I'll be waiting here, regardless."

She doesn't argue. Just nods at me and reaches into the passenger seat for her phone and the tiny purse I didn't even notice she had.

Chapter Twenty-One

ADDISON

"WHAT TOOK YOU SO LONG?" Asher's gaze sweeps over me like a mother hen checking its chicks for injury. "Where'd your boyfriend go?"

"He's waiting in the parking lot for me." I try not to roll my eyes at his tone. "So, let's get this going."

Asher orders us drinks at the bar. For the few cars I saw outside, it's still loud in here. So loud, I don't know how the bartender even hears him. There are people crammed together on the dance floor, people who probably didn't drive here on their own.

Once our drinks are in hand, we make our way to a booth in the back corner of the club, away from the booming speakers. Asher squeezes in right next to me, so close I can feel the heat from his body.

"I'm going to be honest, Ad. I don't like the way Perry looks at you. It's like no one else is allowed to talk to you."

"He's my boyfriend. What do you expect? And he's also a dad, so it's practically part of his personality."

He snorts. "Right. I almost forgot. What is he, like fifty? And where's his baby mama?"

Asher's tone makes my cheeks hot. The instant urge to defend Perry shouts at my brain. "He's twenty-eight. Same age as you. And the children's mom isn't . . . in the picture."

His eyes probe me as he waits, probably hoping his silence will keep me talking. I take a sip of my drink—a margarita—and glance out the window next to our table.

"Ad, I need to tell you something."

"What?"

"I was an idiot to end things between us."

My gut ties itself into a knot. I shake my head. "Don't."

"I mean it. I wasn't thinking, and I didn't realize how good I had it with you. I didn't appreciate you like I should have."

"Thanks, Asher." I wait for his words to mend the part of me that's been angry at him, but it's like there's nothing left to be mended in the first place.

He takes my hand. "You look gorgeous, by the way."

I take my hand away, biting my lip. "I don't—"

"We were good together, Addison. I understood your goals. I never pressured you for marriage or babies because I knew you couldn't have those things yet. And," his voice creeps down an octave, "I was the best you ever had."

His words make me want to put distance between us. I know his cocktail—empty now—is probably hitting him, otherwise there's no way he'd be so brazen.

I clear my throat. "Let's do our interview."

"First, let's dance."

Before I can respond, he's pulling me out of the booth by the hand, towing me behind him to the dance floor. As

we walk, I check my phone. There are two texts from
Perry.

PERRY

How's it going?

Everything okay?

ME

Everything's fine.

Asher's buzzed already, and he just
professed his love to me. So
uncomfortable haha

PERRY

Yikes.

Do I need to come in there? My
superhero cape is in the trunk, and I've
been itching for a reason to try it on.

His response makes me snicker. I'm about to type
Sorry, but you'll have to stay Clark Kent for now, but
someone bumps into me, and I accidentally send a blank
text instead.

Asher's hands appear on my waist. He pulls my back
against his front, forcing us to sway to the music together.
His grip on my hips is iron tight, even as I try to squirm
away from him little by little.

"Asher," I yell over my shoulder. "Stop."

"You look so hot." He speaks directly into my ear, loud,
moist words that make my eardrums buzz.

"We still need to do the interview." I yank out of his
grip, practically flinging myself against a girl dancing next
to me by accident. I cross my arms as I face him. "Let's get
out of here. I want to leave."

He wraps his hands around both my wrists. "No. Don't leave."

I grimace. "That hurts." The feeling of him holding me in place by my wrists leaves me panicked, the thought of not being in control making my heart race. "Let go!" I throw our hands in the air together, but his remain locked, too tight.

"Ignore her again. I dare you." Perry says from behind me, and my unease and fear instantly melt away. Relief settles in my stomach, the feeling of safety overwhelmingly present.

"Screw you, dude." Asher rolls his eyes. "You're overreacting."

"Maybe. But if she's telling you to let go, and you're not listening, then I don't really care." Perry looks pointedly at Asher's hands still locked around my wrists.

"Don't forget, she was mine first. But here. Take her." He throws my hands in Perry's direction. "You can just forget about your interview, Addison." He stumbles away in the opposite direction.

I know he's bluffing, otherwise I'd be freaking out. He may be the host of the pageant, but part of his job depends on him collecting all the interviews in time for preliminaries.

Perry cups my face in his hands. "You all right, bunny?" His gaze searches my face.

All I can do is nod. There's an overwhelming feeling unfurling in my chest at having him advocate for me. Maybe because he just got accused of the same thing Asher used to always say to me.

You're overreacting.

Over time, I became so afraid of hearing it, I'd try to tone myself down for him, not react. Not feel. But Perry standing up for me over something this small feels so . . . validating. Like I still deserve to express my feelings, whether they seem dramatic or not.

"Let's get out of here."

The entryway is dark when we get back to Perry's house, and Kiera and the kids are nowhere to be seen. We make our way upstairs as quietly as possible. Once we reach the third floor, I open the door to my room and plop onto one of the chairs by the fireplace, patting the chair next to me. "Care to join me?"

But he just shakes his head and leans against the doorframe, an amused smile on his face. "You know, I think you've ruined this room for me. Every time I come in here, I think about the day you came out of that shower, wrapped in nothing but a towel."

I laugh, looking around as if doing so will make me see that moment from his perspective, but that day felt like a different lifetime. Now, this room just feels like home to me. And that kinda alarms me.

Don't get used to it, Addison. This won't be home forever.

Perry finally takes the seat next to mine and looks at me in a thoughtful, absentminded way. Butterflies swarm my stomach.

He picks up something from the end table between the

chairs, and as soon as I realize what it is, my cheeks heat in embarrassment.

Perry flips through the pages, furrowing his brows. "Is this a Bible?"

"It's a book of church hymns and Bible verses. It was my grandma's. I like to read it sometimes."

He stops on a page, clears his throat, and reads aloud, "Song of Songs, chapter one, verse two. 'Let him kiss me with the kisses of his mouth: For thy love is better than wine.'" He arches an eyebrow at me, waggling it a little. "Better than wine? I might have to get me one of these books."

I laugh, reaching for it. "Oh my gosh, Perry. Stoppppp."

He chuckles, keeping the book out of my reach as we wrestle, and by the time I finally snatch it, we're both leaning toward each other, much too close.

"I should probably go to bed now," he says.

"Thank you for coming along tonight. And for overreacting for me in the club."

"I'd overreact for you anytime."

My heart tangles in my chest as he murmurs the quiet words.

Too soon, he gets up and crosses the room until he's standing in the doorway again.

"Goodnight, Perry," I whisper.

"Goodnight." And then he smiles at me, soft and gentle, making the butterflies return all over again.

They'll go away soon, I tell myself. *You're just romanticizing all this. There's no way you're in love with him already, because that would be ridiculous and you can't be.*

He turns the light off and shuts my door as he leaves. I can't help but wonder if he would have stayed longer if I asked, even though I made him promise to leave me alone. I tighten my arms around myself, wishing, even if just for tonight, that he'd forget everything I said.

Gran's voice suddenly pops into my head. *Never underestimate the power of prayer and keep wishing on dandelions. Turn that wish into a prayer for the Lord every time you blow it out.*

As much as I wish I had a dandelion right now, I know deep down I don't need one. Not at all.

I close my eyes as tight as I can and pray, *Please Lord. Either help me stop feeling this way—or find a way for him to become mine.*

I wake up to seventy-three new emails in the morning. The endless pinging from my phone became part of my dreams while I slept. But now that I'm awake, I know exactly how real this is, especially when I see that all seventy-three subject-lines share a common word: Sponsorship.

I shoot straight up in the bed.

The emails are endlessly kind. Personalized. Almost all of them mention Perry and my relationship with him at some point, stating they'd love the opportunity to sponsor me, and that they're huge supporters of his restaurant, Rosemary Banquet.

Oh, and they love us together. They really, *really* love us.

All of this can only mean our interview has been

posted to the Miss Meadow site and sent out to the email subscribers.

I swing my legs off the side of the bed. The hardwood floor is cool against the bottoms of my feet. It feels nice, because it's warm outside; so warm, I can feel the heat coming through the windows in my bedroom.

I put on a yellow sundress, ignoring the fact that it's Perry's favorite color. My hair is a mess from last night, so I wet it down to reform the curls, do my makeup, and brush my teeth.

I speed-walk down the stairs, still reading some of the emails on my phone, when I crash right into a solid body and smack my head on the hardness. "Ow!"

Perry steadies me before I can go toppling down the steps. "Careful, bunny. Are you all right?"

"Yeah. Just clumsy." I laugh faintly, holding up my phone. "Don't text and walk, they say."

His mouth curls. "Exactly. You're a danger to everyone on the road right now."

"I was actually coming down to show you this." I rotate the screen so it's facing him. "I just got a bunch of emails offering me sponsorship, and apparently it's all thanks to you."

He frowns. "Me? How?"

"Everyone loves us together. They saw our interview."

"Ah." He smirks. "Well, of course they love us together. Who wouldn't?" He takes my hand, pulling me down the stairs with him.

"Hm. I don't know. Asher, and maybe whoever you end up proposing to for real, but hey, that's just a guess."

He chuckles. We walk into the kitchen together where

the kids are eating pancakes. I don't know why it still surprises me when Perry cooks something delicious. I mean, he's been cooking long before I arrived.

"OOH, YUMMY!" I sing, taking a seat at the table.

Izzy laughs, but Moxie shushes me. "Don't talk so loud, Addy."

"How can I talk quietly when there are PANCAKES?"

That one gets her to crack a smile.

Perry sits with us. As I shovel the food into my mouth, I help Enzo and Abel take bites since they still have trouble using their forks.

"You don't need to do that," says Perry as he watches me. "It's your day off."

"It's no biggie." What I don't tell him is that I stopped thinking about taking care of the kids as work a long time ago. To me, this feels as natural as drinking water.

Chapter Twenty-Two

PERRY

WHEN THE KIDS FINISH EATING, they start a wrestling match in the living room.

Addison sighs across the table. "So, who do you think I should choose for a sponsor?"

I glance at the kids, playfully trying to pin Abel down. For all I know about pageants, she'd do just as well getting their opinions. "Hmm. That's a tough one. Pick who feels right to you?"

She gives me a look that says, *come on.* "No. Help me! Pretty please?"

I laugh. "Okay, let me see the emails." She hands me her phone and I look through them. I recognize the names of almost everyone in her inbox because they're all business owners here in Meadow Hills. I've grabbed drinks with some of them. I've let them put their flyers on the bulletin board hanging in the waiting area of Rosemary Banquet. Others have reached out to me a time or two, asking for business advice and start-up tips.

It's too hard to just pick someone. But two emails in particular jump out at me. "There's Mrs. So's old ballet studio. It says here she's desperately trying to increase enrollment, and I know her. She's a really sweet lady. Either that, or the local children's hospital because, well, how can you say no to that?"

Addison's face falls. "Ugh. How am I supposed to say no to either of those?"

"Don't worry. I doubt it will be the end of the world for either of them if you say no. But here, let me show you Mrs. So's studio. Maybe it will help." I take out my phone and open the website for the studio, So Ballet Academy.

I hand Addison the phone. "Check it out. Tell me what you think."

She takes it from me and examines the pictures of the studio, but her expression freezes after a minute. There's something in her eyes that wasn't there before. I doubt anyone else would notice, but I've learned how to read her like a book. "What's wrong?" I ask.

She shrugs lightly, despite the face she's making. "Oh, nothing. It looks like you have an email. I swear I didn't mean to read it. My thumb tapped it on accident when I tried to swipe it away."

I take my phone back. And then I see it.

Mr. Whitmore,

This email is a reminder that your match from United We Band is ready to meet you. As discussed at our last meeting, she will be arriving at your home in two days to meet you

AND YOUR CHILDREN. IF YOU NEED TO RESCHEDULE, WE HAVE APPOINTMENTS FOR EARLY NEXT YEAR.

REGARDS,

DONNA CALDWELL

UNITED WE BAND COORDINATOR

I clear my throat. "Kids, want to play outside in the sprinklers?"

All four of them gasp in excitement from the living room. Abel releases Enzo from being pinned on the ground. "Yeah!"

Izzy squeals. "Ooh, can I set it up, Daddy? I know how. Please?"

I nod. "Go ahead. And help poor Enzo up."

She claps. "Okay, come on, Enzo. Let's go!" She takes his hand, and the four of them sprint outside, voices mixing together in enchanted unison.

My gaze cuts to Addison. "I'll call it off."

"What?"

It's hard to keep my breathing steady, but I lean forward. I mean every word I'm saying. "Just say the words, and I'll call the whole meeting with this match off."

A little V appears between her eyebrows. "Perry, what are you talking about?"

I sigh. "Addison . . ." *Come on, Perry. Just tell her. Tell her how you feel.* "You and I both know we're not faking it anymore. We haven't been for a long time. I . . ." Deep breath. "I don't *want* to fake it with you. I want the real thing. So just say the words. I'll email Donna back right now and tell her I'm out."

She's stunned into silence. Her bottom lip wobbles slightly. "You'd do that for me?"

"Of course."

She stares into my eyes for a long moment and then shakes her head as if to clear it. "We can't." She blinks like there's something irritating her eye. "I mean, I knew this was coming. It's no big deal. Really."

The way her words cut into me like a knife is unexpected. I clear my throat. "Addison. It's okay for things to not always go according to plan. I know you want to be Miss Meadow, but—"

"No buts." She holds up her finger. "There are no buts, Perry. This is my last shot and unless you want to go house shopping for a new place to live, you need to get married. End of story."

A spark of anger appears in my gut. She's making it seem so transactional, like there were never any blurred lines or mistakes made by either of us. "So, you're telling me you feel nothing?" I motion the air between the two of us. "You feel literally nothing?"

Her gaze darts to the table before returning to my face. "That's right."

"I don't believe that for a minute," I growl. "Tell me to call the wedding plans off and I will, bunny. I will do it, but only if you tell me the truth."

"I don't want you to call off your plans!" She all but hollers it as she gets up from the table. "Now stop it! We can't do this." She's breathing heavily, eyes wild and crazed.

I clench my jaw. "Why not? Talk to me." When she can't meet my eyes again, I finally realize what's happening. "You're scared. You're falling for me the same way I'm falling for you, and it terrifies you. You don't know what you want more; me or that pageant crown."

A glassiness appears on her eyes. She doesn't cry, but it looks like she might until she blinks a few times.

"Perry." Her voice is hoarse as she paces back and forth. "If we let this go too far, guess what's going to happen? One of us will have to give up our dream. I'm not ready to let mine go without accomplishing it. And I wouldn't want you to do that, either. You need to stop, or I'll have no choice but to quit to keep that from happening. So please." The last word comes out in a broken whisper. It breaks my heart; almost as much as what she just said.

She would leave us? Just like that, like it's nothing? The stab of betrayal, of anger I feel, is too intense. It feels like Jill all over again.

She must know her words are a step too far because she shakes her head. "I'm sorry."

I press my lips together. Run my hands over my face. "I get it," I say. "Don't worry. I'm, uh . . . I'm going to play with the kids outside. Enjoy your day off."

She nods. Doesn't try to stop me. She lets me leave, even though the way she's looking at me makes me think that perhaps she doesn't mean anything she just said. Maybe she's lying through her teeth about quitting and not wanting to be with me.

Even if she's lying, there's a truth to her words I can't deny. One of us would have to be willing to give up our dream to make it happen.

I just can't remember when exactly my dream stopped being holding on to this house and started being *her*.

Two days passes quicker than I expect, and before I know it, my first match is on her way. Donna sends me an email in the morning alerting me. I tap the link included in the emails and her profile comes up along with basic details about her. Lisa Parker, 31, likes hiking and chardonnay. She has a daughter and finds joy in decluttering. Her round, friendly face is pleasant enough in the photo. Bright blue eyes. A wispy, blond haircut that frames her jaw. She's cute. Pretty, even. I should be excited someone out there is crazy enough to want to marry me despite all my baggage.

I sigh and shove my phone in my pocket, getting up from my desk chair. I try to hype myself up as I walk down the hall, because it's time to finally tell the girls what's going on. I'm not concerned about Enzo or Abel because they're too young to understand, and it will probably be better to just ease them into things rather than complicating the situation for them with an explanation. Plus, they're still napping.

I open the girls' bedroom door and peek inside. The room is clean, but the scent of concentrated sugar dusts the air. Izzy's toy kitchen stands in the corner, the smell of forgotten, fresh-baked cookies coming from the plastic oven. Moxie is wearing one of her princess dresses, sitting beside Izzy on the ground in front of the dollhouse. Addison lies on her stomach next to them, feet crossed in the air as her animated face provides the doll in her hand with dialogue.

I know I came in here for a reason, but I'm struggling

to remember what it is, watching the three of them play. Like always, it does strange things to my heart. It's like whatever feelings I have for Addison double whenever I see her with my kids. Those feelings are impossible to ignore right now, and they make my heart thud when I finally pinpoint *what* they are.

Love. I love her.

How did this happen? I try to replay all the moments leading up to now since I met her, struggling to narrow down when exactly this happened. All I know is it's very real, and the knot in my throat won't go away no matter how many times I swallow.

She finally feels me staring at her and glances up from her game with the girls, eyes questioning. "Everything okay?"

Izzy and Moxie turn to look at me over their shoulders. "Oh, hi, Daddy," Moxie says. "Didn't know you were there."

Izzy digs around in one of her toy bins. "I think there's a prince in here somewhere if you want to play." Her tongue pokes out of her lips as she frowns in concentration.

I hold out my hand. "No, that's okay."

The three of them wait. Addison struggles to make eye contact with me, saying nothing. I want to scoop her up into my arms and take her to my room. I want to lock the door so she can't leave and no one else can get in, and I want to bury my nose in her hair, breathe her in and never let her go.

But she wouldn't want that. She's made it clear that she wants me to go forward with the original plan, no matter how much it makes me want to rip my hair out. "I need to talk to the girls. Would you mind giving us a few minutes?"

"Yeah, sure." She hops up and closes the door softly behind her as she exits the room.

And then I'm left alone with my daughters. I release a long breath. I can't remember the last time I had to tell them something this serious. In fact, I don't think I ever have. When Jill left, they were younger, and I never really sat them down and explained everything to them. Their repeated "Where's mommy?" inquisitions died out eventually after they finally realized they weren't going to get a response. I swallow the knot in my throat, but it still refuses to go down.

Moxie tilts her head at me. "Are you sad? You look sad."

"Yeah," nods Izzy. "What's wrong? Are you okay?"

"Nothing's wrong, girls. I have something exciting to tell you, actually." They don't look convinced. Under different circumstances, their pinched eyebrows and incredulous eyes would be comical. "I'm getting married, you're going to have a new mommy figure, and we'll get to live in this house forever!"

Simultaneously, the suspicion melts away. Their eyes round as they smile at each other. Izzy squeals and bounces up and down. "Is it Addy? I hope it's Addy!"

Moxie gasps. "Are you marrying her, Daddy? Because she'd be the best mommy ever! Even better than our real mommy."

Ouch. I didn't realize my heart was capable of breaking any more than it already had, but here it is. It's like my heart is made of glass and it just got dropped on the floor.

"No." My voice comes out too quietly. "I'm not marrying Addy. It's someone else. We're going to meet her today."

The smiles slowly fade off their faces. Izzy shrugs "Oh. Okay, I guess."

Moxie sighs dramatically. "Is she nice?"

"Of course. I'd never marry someone who's mean to you. I promise, girls." I pat each of their heads, trying to imagine what the future will look like married to some random woman. Waking up next to her every morning, going on family trips, and sharing stories. Her tucking the kids in at night.

I can see it all so clearly, and it even makes me excited for a moment. But as soon as I realize why, the hard knot in my throat returns. This woman I'm supposed to share my life with, my children's lives with, is only easy to imagine because it's Addison's face she's wearing.

Chapter Twenty-Three

ADDISON

LISA IS THE WHOLE PACKAGE. She's pretty, nice, and mature. She uses her inside voice, and doesn't spill the wine Perry gives her, not even once. Her clothes look ironed. I bet she makes really good pies.

I watch politely from the kitchen island sink, doing dishes and glancing up occasionally to see Lisa smiling or laughing at something Perry says. I catch him stealing a glance now and then at me too, but ignore it, my gaze immediately darting back to the dishes. My cheeks burn when Perry looks at me for the fourteenth time and Lisa follows his gaze, her smile frozen on her mouth.

He tells her to wait a minute, and she sits perched on the edge of the sofa. Perry crosses the room to me. My senses are hyper aware of him, skin practically tingling as he makes his way closer.

"Can you please bring the kids down?"

I nod too fast. "Mhm."

"Addison."

I finally look up at him. He's closer than I realized, his entire frame blocking my view of Lisa. I ignore the flutters from our eyes meeting. "What?"

"Just say it, and she goes away. That's all it will take." His voice is a deep murmur that penetrates my senses.

"I'll be right back with the kids." I dry my hands on the dishtowel next to the sink and spin on my heel toward the stairs.

As I go up, I hear Lisa ask Perry, "What do you do for work?"

His response is delayed. "I own a five-star restaurant here in town."

She makes an impressed clucking sound. "That's right. I recall seeing that on your profile." I don't wait to hear the rest. My thighs burn as I take the steps two at a time to the second-floor. I open the girls' room and poke my head in. "Your dad wants you both downstairs." I do a double take when I see them both pouting on Moxie's bed together, arms crossed. I open the door wider. "Everything okay in here?"

Moxie shakes her head, and Izzy informs me, "Daddy's getting married, but we want you to be our new mommy. Not somebody else." It comes out shy and raspy, nothing like Izzy's usual bold, clear tone.

Something inside me melts. "Oh, honey." I walk over to where they're sitting and smooth down their hair. Moxie hugs my arm. "I'm sure whoever she is will be wonderful." I try to smile at them, but there's no point. They aren't looking at me. They both have downcast faces. "I'm going to go get your brothers and then I'll meet you guys down there."

I leave them in there and pick up the now-awake boys from their floor beds. When I bring them, whining and squirming, downstairs, Lisa's face lights up.

"They're so cute, Perry." I have to stop my mouth from twisting when she says his name. I don't know why, but I hate it. It sounds so intimate, and it makes me want to tell him the truth about my feelings, just to make her go away. Just so I never have to hear her say his name again. But I smile back at her and hold out one of the twins for her to hold.

Her smile wobbles a bit as she takes Abel from my right arm. Perry looks nervous as he processes this exchange. It almost seems symbolic, like I'm passing the torch, handing over the kids I've spent time bonding with to a complete stranger. A complete stranger that Perry fully intends to marry.

Abel squints at Lisa and grimaces. Then he shrieks and tries to throw himself out of her arms.

Lisa's grip tightens, which only aggravates him more. "I'm Lisa," she says in a formal tone. "Nice to meet you."

Abel grunts and tugs on her shiny pearl necklace, breaking it off and sending all the small, white pieces scattering across the wood floor. Some of them roll under the couch.

Lisa gasps and puts Abel on the floor, where he continues to twist and cry. I pick him up with my free arm, shushing him and gently bouncing in place until he quiets down. His little fists grips my T-shirt so tight, the skin around his fingers turns red.

Perry and I watch Lisa scramble on the ground to collect all the pieces of her necklace. It's like witnessing a car accident happen; impossible to look away. If I wasn't still holding both kids, I would get down on the ground and help her look for the rest.

Perry, however, has no excuse. I don't exactly want to assist him with her, but this is painful to watch. I shoot him a menacing glance and mouth: *help her*.

"Let me, uh, give you a hand there," Perry says, kneeling down. He sounds so confused, I almost laugh.

The girls never come downstairs on their own. Perry ends up dragging them down screaming and kicking. I'm guessing the outcome might have been different if I'd been the one to retrieve them, but the boys wouldn't let me go.

Izzy and Moxie continue to pout as they wave hello to Lisa. Thankfully, they don't mention anything about wanting me to be their mom instead of her. It's already too awkward to stomach another minute down here. Unfortunately, though, it's my job to manage the kids, even in situations like these. After hours of being the middle person between them and Lisa, sitting through an extremely awkward dinner, and then finally, *finally* putting all the kids to bed, I come back down the stairs to get a glass of water.

I expect to see Lisa in the living room, still stiff on her seat on the sofa. What I don't expect is to see her pressed up against Perry in the wine cellar, his back to the stone wall and her directly in front of him. She looks up at him from behind her eyelashes and runs her fingertips along his shoulders.

An icky, angry feeling boils under my skin, making my blood feel hotter. I can barely see straight, and I'm grateful, because if I have to watch her touching Perry for one more second, I'm going to explode.

I run back up the stairs to my room and shut the door behind me. I'm breathing heavily, my chest heaving up and down like I just ran a marathon. What if he takes her to his bedroom tonight? The thought of them sleeping together makes me want to sob into my pillow.

Oh Lord. There's really no denying it anymore.

I love him. I love him so much it actually hurts.

I take Gran's hymn book out from my mattress, crack my door open, and tiptoe down the hall to Perry's room. I haven't been in here since Perry helped me over his balcony to rescue Abel, but I'm craving the feeling of him being near. I...miss him. Hesitantly, I sit on his bed. His comforter is cushy and soft, gray linen with a down-feather material underneath. There are charcoal curtains drawn over the windows, and dark wood accents from the hanging photo frames, and the dresser against the wall. It smells like him everywhere in here, like teakwood and warmth—and Perry.

I flip open the pages of Gran's book until I find the verse about love that I'm looking for.

> Love is patient and kind; love does not envy or boast; it is not arrogant or rude. It does not insist on its own way; it is not irritable or resentful; it does not rejoice at wrongdoing, but rejoices with the truth. Love bears all things, believes all things, hopes all things, endures all things.
> —1 Corinthians 13:4-7

I read it over and over, wondering how I can possibly

endure this. I know it says that love doesn't insist on its own way, which points me to the answer I'm dreading. I need to let Perry continue dating Lisa. I won't be free until next year if I win, which is six months past his deadline. He'd lose his house over me trying to stop him. That would be the opposite of selfless.

Tears prick in my eyes. I need to get out of his room.

Before I get up, I look around the room, taking in the rich, dark wood furniture. The heavy, ornate curtains covering the windows. The framed canvas of four child-sized handprints, each one in a different paint color. The lingering scent of Perry's cologne in the air. I run my hands along the silky, high-thread-count sheets peeking out under his unmade comforter.

Okay. Time to go.

The doorknob turns, and Perry enters his room alone. He flips on the light switch and his stare hones in on me sitting in the center of his bed. "Well, well. What do we have here, bunny?" A smirk lifts the corner of his mouth.

I clear my throat. "I was just, uh . . ." but I trail off, coming up empty. I definitely didn't expect him to catch me in his room, and now that he has, I don't know what to say.

He sits next to me on the bed. "What are you doing in here?"

Finally, I come up with something. "I was curious to see if your mattress is as comfy as mine." I shrug. "It's close, but mine's better. Goodnight." I start to get up, but he takes my hand, sending goosebumps across my skin.

"You're not jealous, are you?" The deep rumble of his

voice travels straight through me. "Because that would be ridiculous."

"No, it wouldn't be." My voice is quiet. Wounded. It's embarrassing, so I look down to hide behind my hair. "She's perfect. You guys will make a great couple."

"Don't you realize what I've been trying to tell you?" Hesitantly, he lifts my chin back up. Tucks my heavy hair behind my ear.

"We can't be together, so there's no point in telling me."

With a frustrated grumble, he tilts my face up, forcing our gazes together. "You're impossible, you know that?" The way his gaze meets mine sends chills down my spine.

"Where's Lisa?" I whisper.

"She's sleeping in the office."

"She's right next door? I should go. She wouldn't be happy if she knew her *fiancé* was in her alone with his fake fiancée."

"We're not engaged. We haven't even talked about it. This trip is about us meeting and getting to know each other to see if we're compatible."

"So . . . you're not together yet?"

He shakes his head. Pulls me closer to him.

I'm still worried that me being in here with him alone is wrong, so I pull away. "No one's watching us." It's a silly thing to say, because our fake relationship technically ended the moment Lisa arrived.

But he doesn't laugh. He just kisses me. "Perfect."

Another kiss. And another. My throat burns with emotion. This feels different from the other times. This kiss carries a weight so heavy it feels like it might crush me.

I bring my hands up to Perry's face, pulling him closer and deepening the kiss. We both must know it's the last time we'll ever do this. It has to be. I'm painfully aware that after this, I'll have to let him go.

When our faces break apart, I swallow back my tears. I wish more than anything we could be back at the beach house, sharing that bed with all those pillows stacked between us.

Perry hesitantly tucks my hair behind my ear. "Stay with me tonight?" My eyes widen, but he chuckles. "No *other stuff*," he says, mirroring my phrase from before. "I just want to hold you. Just for one night."

I know this is a bad idea. There's a good chance that if I say yes, it's only going to make saying goodbye to him that much harder. But at the same time, denying myself this one thing when I already have to let him go feels unbearable.

I nod.

Perry's limbs loosen a bit, like he's letting out a relieved breath. We lie down on the bed, facing each other. We don't kiss again, but Perry captures me in his arms and closes his eyes.

I rest my head against his chest. Our combined breathing is the only sound in the room.

It feels like a sick joke that I have to untangle myself from him and go back to my life tomorrow. I know I have to do it, but for the moment, all I want to do is lie here with him and pretend this moment can last forever.

Chapter Twenty-Four

PERRY

ADDISON ISN'T in the bed when I wake up. The emptiness I feel now that she's away is like a missing organ, vital for my survival. I hate it. I'd *give* a vital organ just to have her back in here with me for a little longer. Actually, that wouldn't be long enough.

I hear the bright tinkle of her laughter coming from downstairs, so I sit up. The sheets fall down, pooling around my waist. What time is it and how long has she been up?

I get dressed in to jeans and a button-down and slip on a pair of socks. When I get downstairs, I find her at the stove with a spatula in hand, serving pancakes to Lisa and the kids with a smile on her face. She's wearing baggy grey sweatpants and a white tank top, her hair in a messy top knot, but to me, she's never looked more sexy. Her dimpled grin lights up her entire face as she interacts with the kids.

When she sees me standing at the base of the stairs, her smile falters only briefly before it's right back in place. I'm guessing all those pageants she's done have given her that uncanny ability to hide her distress and smile, even when she doesn't feel like it.

Lisa follows her stare and brightens when she notices me. She gets up from the bar stool at the island and saunters over. Why does my entire body have to stiffen whenever she gets too close? It feels like being a kid and having to hug a distant relative during the holidays—awkward and uncomfortable. Like we both know, any chemistry between us is forced, since we both want to get married as quickly as possible for our own personal reasons. I have no idea what her reasons are, and to be honest, I'm struggling to remember mine.

Lisa places her hands on my shoulders and squeezes. It takes every ounce of self-control I have not to remove them, to take a step back and put some distance between us. Something sits painfully undigested in my stomach.

I don't think I can do this.

If I can't even stomach her touching me, how am I going to spend an eternity married to the woman?

"Hey Lisa," says Izzy, coming up to us. Her face isn't as pouty as it was last night, which gives me a tiny inkling of hope. If she can find a way to warm up to Lisa, maybe the rest of the kids can, too. Me, though? I can't warm up to anyone but the woman I'm already burning for.

I glance past Lisa to Addison, who's watching Izzy with curiosity.

Izzy shoves a piece of her pancakes into Lisa's hand. "You can have my pancake. It's so yummy."

Lisa grimaces, shaking the food off her hand and letting it fall onto the floor. "No, thank you." I think she's trying to keep smiling, but it looks like she's baring her teeth. I can't believe how much the expression turns her pretty face into something completely unattractive.

"Izzy, don't put food into people's hands without asking first." I sigh, running a hand down my face. "Sorry," I tell Lisa.

Her genuine smile is back. "Don't be. She'll learn." She finally backs away to go wash her hands at the sink. Grabbing a paper towel and wetting it, she dabs at the dressy black trousers I didn't notice she was wearing.

It's at precisely that moment that Abel—completely covered in syrup and jam—chooses to hug her clean leg.

"Oh, no, sweetie." Lisa shakes her leg a little to get him off her, but Abel just laughs, thinking it's a game. "Get off, please." Her voice comes out a little lower, firmer. "These pants are new."

Addison moves to get him, but Abel makes a show of wiping his dirty hands up and down the side of her pants.

Lisa scoffs. "Okay, get off me!" She shakes her leg hard enough to send Abel onto the floor. His mouth curves downward, and he starts wailing.

Addison picks up Abel and glares at Lisa. "You don't have to be so mean. He just likes the texture." She starts swinging him gently, immediately making his tears stop. "You okay?"

Lisa completely ignores Addison and shoots me an icy smile. "I think my pants are ruined." She swears and touches one of the marks Abel left. "Yeah, this isn't going to come out."

I shrug. "Yeah, well, my kids are messy. Sorry if you don't like it." I don't know why I'm being such a jerk. I probably should have helped, but I'd also like to see how Lisa handles situations like this one. After all, this was nothing compared to some of Abel's best work. If she can't handle this, she can't handle *them*. And I'd like to know now, before I take things any further.

Her eyes widen a fraction, and she drops her sour tone. "No, of course. I get it. I'm a mom, too, remember?" She laughs, lightening the mood in the room.

But when I look at Addison, her eyes are swimming with emotion. Silently, she sets Abel down and heads for the backyard. I seem to be the only one who notices. Lisa apologizes to Abel for snapping, and Enzo remains content, thumb in mouth, while Izzy and Moxie tickle him.

I follow Addison outside.

She's pacing back and forth on the deck. She doesn't notice my presence until I close the sliding door. The noise makes her jump, and her gaze darts to mine.

There are tears streaming down her cheeks. I don't say anything, immediately pulling her into a hug. I stroke her back as she sobs, letting the sounds disappear into my shirt. "What's the matter?"

She sniffs a few times and shrugs.

"No, don't do that. Don't hide whatever it is from me. You can tell me anything."

She pulls her face back to look up at me. "I love your kids."

It's the last thing I was expecting to hear come out of her mouth, but I nod, urging her to continue.

She swallows. "I love them all so much and it's hard to watch Lisa get impatient with them. I know they can be a lot, but . . . I love every second of the chaos. I just wasn't expecting to feel so emotional at the idea of someone else becoming a parent figure to them and not loving it as much as I do."

My brows draw together. "Is that all that's upsetting you, bunny?"

"Doesn't it bother you?"

"Of course it does." I tuck a curly strand of her hair back into her bun. "But I want to make sure nothing else is making you cry."

She stares at me for what feels like eternity, before shaking her head and letting her face fall back against my chest. She makes an agitated noise. I don't speak, just continue stroking her back until she talks again. "I had a feeling I'd end up loving your kids. But I wasn't expecting to love you, too."

My hand stills, heart nearly thudding out of my chest. I still can't find comprehensible words to speak when she backs away from me, new tears on her face. "I'm in love with you. I admit it. And I can't watch this—" she motions toward the house, containing Lisa and the kids, "—go on a moment longer. I think I need to go."

I swallow hard, not expecting the sudden, unbearable emotion that's taken place inside me. "Please, don't go. I love you, too, Addison. So much." I reach for her, gripping her hand before she can take off again. "Stop running, for once. We can make this work."

"How?"

"Marry me." She starts to shake her head, but I hold up my hand, urging her to wait for me to finish. "Marry me after you become Miss Meadow. I'll wait for you. I'll call my dad right now and tell him how serious I am about you, that we're still engaged and planning a wedding for next year. By then, you'll be free and allowed to do whatever you want, right?"

"I think so. But—"

"Do you *want* to marry me? That's all that matters right now. I can handle the rest."

Her expression softens. "Yes, I want to. Of course I do."

My chest swells with emotion. I bring her face to mine and sweep my lips over hers. One soft kiss, two, and then the third is my tongue dancing with hers until I feel so dizzy I can hardly see straight.

I take her hand in mine, unable to keep the giant smile off my face. "Come on. Let's go break the news to Lisa before she convinces herself she actually likes me."

A laugh burst from her lips. The grin that lights up her face makes her look absolutely radiant. I can hardly keep my eyes off her.

"Let's do it."

❦

As it turns out, Lisa doesn't take rejection well. When I let the truth spill, she turns her heated gaze on Addison. By instinct, I position my body between them, and as a result, take the brunt of the metal pitcher she flings across the room at us. The rest goes crashing through the dining room window. The expletives Lisa rattles off ring in my ears as she packs her things, rushing around the house like an angry storm. I think the kids get scared, because Addison rounds them up and takes them all upstairs.

"Look, Lisa," I say when she's about to leave, all her bags packed and ready by the front door. "I'm sorry it had to go like this. You'll find the right person. It just wasn't me."

She doesn't even look at me as she mutters, "what a waste of time and money."

"Send me an invoice. I'll reimburse you."

She rolls her eyes. And then she's gone. It feels like a giant weight has been lifted off me.

Addison loves me. She wants to marry me.

I feel like I can fly.

A big, goofy grin is stuck on my face. "Bunny, get down here!" I shout up the stairs. A few seconds later, I hear the sound of her footsteps shuffling down. Thankfully, the kids' steps don't follow. As excited as I am to break the news to them, I want to make the phone call to my dad first, just to make sure everything goes well. There's no reason it shouldn't, but I know from experience not to promise anything to children prematurely, because the let down if it doesn't happen is too much for their little hearts to take.

Addison's eyes sweep the room, noting Lisa's absence, and then she jumps right into my arms from the third-to-last step on the stairs. She covers my face in soft kisses, and I spin us around.

"I've never felt this happy before," I say. "It doesn't seem real."

"That's how I feel, too. It seems too good to be true."

I grin against her lips. "Well, it's *not*. It's happening, and I promise I'm going to make you so happy."

"You already do." She bites her lip. "Let's call your dad."

I set her down, but don't release her just yet. "Okay." I make no move toward my phone.

She laughs. "Come on, let's just get it over with."

I let my arms fall to my sides and release a dramatic sigh. "Fine." I playfully tap her nose before retrieving my phone off the kitchen island. Before I tap my dad's contact photo, I tell her, "I'm going to be vague on this phone call with him and just invite him over, because this news seems too big to relay over the phone."

She nods, lacing her hands together in front of her and bouncing in place. I don't think she realizes how cute she looks.

I call my dad and he picks up on the fourth ring. "Perry? What's going on?"

"Hey, Dad. I have some exciting news. Do you think you could come over for dinner tomorrow night?"

Chapter Twenty-Five

ADDISON

THE NEXT MORNING IS THE KIDS' first day of preschool and daycare. I drop them all off in Perry's car because he already has the car seats installed, and when I get back, he's not working in the office like he's supposed to be. He's waiting in the foyer for me to get back.

As soon as I step inside, he pulls me against him and nuzzles his face in my neck. "Let's go ring shopping."

I melt into a giant puddle inside. "Really? But aren't you supposed to be working?"

"This is important, bunny. My dad is coming over tonight. He noticed you didn't have a ring last time. If there's any chance of him finding a loophole in the will or breaking the rules for us, we need to show him how serious I am about you and what says 'serious' more than an engagement ring?"

He has a point. "Fine. I'll let you pick out a ridiculously overpriced ring for me if you think it will help."

He presses a kiss to my temple. "Thank you."

Since he's already dressed and standing in the entry-way, we walk out the front door together. I still have his keys in my hand, so I toss them to him, and we get in his SUV.

Perry starts the car and takes my hand, holding it the entire drive. The way he strokes my hand with his thumb sends butterflies stirring in my stomach.

The ring shop Perry takes me to is in downtown Meadow Hills. I love coming here, especially in the summer. The prettiest, most picturesque scene comes into view as we arrive: narrow, cobbled walkways. A young girl riding her bike, tucking something into the basket hanging on the front. The sound of birds twittering a soft melody as we get out of the car and near the shops with hanging flower baskets outside their storefront windows.

We walk with hands intertwined, past two coffee carts with deliciously scented steam wafting through the air. Perry lifts my left hand to his lips and kisses it as we enter The Hidden Treasure Ring Shop. "I can't wait to mark my territory by putting a ring on this finger."

A laugh escapes me. "Are we not going to acknowledge how cheesy that was?"

His answering grin is blinding. "You bring out the cheese in me."

An elderly lady with a sleek, grey bun and kind eyes greets us from behind the ring counter. "Hello, I'm Edna. Are you two looking for anything particular?"

Perry lifts our joined hands again. "I'm looking for an engagement ring for my fiancée."

Fiancée. It's the first time he's said it in public and actually meant it. Nothing is fake anymore.

"She can pick out any ring she wants," Perry tells her.

Edna's face lights up. "Well, then allow me to show you these." She guides me to a display of massive, sparkling diamond rings on the top shelf.

"They're stunning." I study each of them, unable to imagine wearing any of them for more than an hour or two without getting annoyed and wanting to take it off. I duck down to see the shelf underneath. Most of these rings are understated. Simple. One of them catches my eye, so I point to it. "Can I try this one on?"

Edna blinks a few times. "Ah—of course." She removes it from the display stand and holds it over the glass counter for me to take.

I slide it onto my ring finger. Perry stares motionless at it, and so do I. The band is delicate, rose gold, and at first glance, the small center stone looks like a single round diamond. But when I look closer, I realize it's really five tiny stones clustered together. It looks so right on my hand, I already can't imagine my finger without it.

Something catches in my throat. "This is the one." I touch the ring ever so gently. "Five diamonds. One for you and each of the kids."

Perry's lips part, and his eyes turn glossy. "Wow." He turns back to Edna. "Can we take it home today?"

Edna also appears to be having trouble hiding her emotions. She dabs at the corner of her eye with the hem of her blazer. "Of course. Let me . . . let me get a box."

As soon as she disappears through the employee door, Perry wraps his arms around my waist from behind, kissing my neck. "What did I do to deserve you?"

"Don't get too optimistic. We're getting ahead of ourselves right now."

"True." He laughs. "Or you're wrong. And wishing on those dandelions work after all."

"I don't think it was the wishing," I say. "I think it was the prayers."

The rest of the afternoon passes in a blur. I can hardly believe there's a ring on my finger that Perry put there. But more than that, I can't believe I might get to marry him. I might get to stay with the kids!

We still haven't told them, so when I pick them up from daycare and Izzy sees the ring, I'll tell her I bought it from a store today, and nothing more. "Do you like it?" I ask, holding up my hand for her to see.

She beams. "Oh, yeah. It's really pretty, Addy. I think Daddy will like it, too."

I try to hide my smile and fail.

The kids spend a few hours playing outside while I make dinner for tonight. Apparently, Frank Whitmore's favorite meal is Perry's spaghetti and homemade meatballs, and I can't blame him. Perry makes phenomenal spaghetti. That's what we're having again, but this time, I'm making it because Perry has to work. I'm also having a meal plan-approved dinner before this one, so I'm not tempted to eat any of the delicious, saucy noodles this close to the pageant. As unsatisfying as my premade kale and chicken salad taste while my mouth waters over tonight's dinner, I get through it because the pageant is only getting closer.

Perry pours us each a glass of red wine. Before he can make a single joke about me spilling it again, I point my spatula at him. "Not. A. Word."

That earns me an amused grin. I sip a small fraction of the wine while I cook. Perry lingers in the kitchen with his laptop, telling me about his workload, and then drilling me on ideas for where we could get married. I haven't put much thought into it, considering up until recently, I still thought of marriage as something off the table or in the far future.

When dinner is ready, the table is set, and Frank finally pounds on the front door, nerves are swimming in my stomach. Perry and I served the kids an early dinner and put them to bed, so we'd have the chance to speak to Frank without them eavesdropping. Perry lets his dad inside, and Frank gives him a stiff hug. I can't stop looking at them, even though I've met Frank before, seen him from afar when he was still the owner of Rosemary Banquet. It looks like Perry from the present hugging Perry from the future, except his dad is a little bit shorter than Perry and has streaks of gray throughout his dark hair. It's still jarring to connect "old owner Frank" with "Perry's dad." I'm just glad he doesn't remember me from then because I'd really rather not experience *another* realization from an ex-boss about me slapping a customer.

When Frank sees me, he pulls me into a hug. "Good to see you, sweetheart." Then turning to Perry, "What's this dinner about?"

"Well, let's sit down first." Perry guides him toward the table where the spaghetti is waiting. "Shall we?"

"This looks delicious," says Frank when he sits down. "Who made it?"

"I did." I lift my hand in a small wave.

Frank twirls the noodles around his fork, then points it at me. "Let's see if it beats Perry's spaghetti."

I giggle. "It probably won't, but I won't be mad if you fib a little."

Frank winks and takes a bite. "It's settled. Yours is definitely better." It's clearly a lie, but I still appreciate it. "Now, will somebody please tell me what's going on?"

Perry takes my left hand from underneath the table and squeezes. Then he places my hand on the table so his dad can see my ring. "As you know, Dad, Addison is my fiancée." He turns his gaze to mine. "We *are* getting married." Hearing him say those words so proudly makes my stomach flip, but there's implication in his tone, as if what he's saying means something different to his dad than it does to the rest of the world.

Frank narrows his eyes at us. "You're trying to buy yourself more time, aren't you?"

"Dad. I don't want to rush things with her. I *am* going to marry her, but we want to have the wedding sometime next year."

Frank shakes his head slowly. "Perry. You know the terms. I'm not sure what you want me to do about it, or if this is because you're just trying to get the house and then back out at the last minute."

"This is because I love her." Perry's voice is hard. "I don't want to rush her."

Frank glances at me from the corner of his eye. "Look, from what I know so far, you're a nice gal. Don't take what

I'm about to say to my son personally." He turns back to Perry. "Your mother came up with this stipulation for a reason. Don't get mad at me." He holds up both hands. "You get married by the end of *this* year, and you get the house. Take the plunge. Say the vows in front of a priest. But I'm not going to find some nonexistent loophole for you if that's what you want. You could buy any woman a ring and tell me you love her. If I recall correctly, you did that with Jill for years. And look what happened."

I flinch at his words. Perry's face pales as he listens to his dad. "Dad, you don't understand— "

"No, it's you who doesn't understand." He points a finger at Perry. "Your mother and I loved each other. What we had was something deeper than you can imagine. And we . . . well, we wanted the same for you and Rebecca. And since your sister is already married, maybe it would just be best to let all this go, Perry. Why shouldn't she have this house when she's been so responsible with her decisions?"

Perry grips his fork in an iron-tight fist. "Hm, I don't know. Maybe because I've been showing you I'm responsible by running a successful business for months. And the house? This is your house with *my mom*." Perry's voice raises into a shout. I've never heard him yell before. It makes me jump. "You lived here with *my* mom, not Rebecca's. My kids are the ones growing up here. Why would you want to uproot them and let her take over? She doesn't care where she lives as long as she doesn't have to pay for it."

"Watch your tone with me. I refuse to let you try to find a way out of following the terms. This is one thing you're not going to have handed to you without some work,

Perry. In fact, I'm this close to taking the restaurant away just so you'd be forced to actually do some hard work for once in your life, something your lazy generation has never known the true meaning of."

"Dad, you think operating a business is *easy*? You know it's not. That's ridiculous."

Frank makes his way toward the door. He has his hand on the doorknob, ready to walk out. "How can you talk to me about what's ridiculous when you have Kiera running around doing half your work for you? You think white-collar work is hard? Try working on a farm from dawn till dusk like I did growing up. Getting your hands dirty, just hoping for your next meal. Owning a business is a privilege, son. A gift. And you've had plenty of handouts. For once, I'd like to see you just follow the rules."

Frank slams the door shut on his way out.

Perry hardly says a word after his dad leaves. He silently helps me put away the leftovers and clean up the dinner mess. We go upstairs without talking, but occasionally I see his body shudder. Whether it's because of rage or something else, I don't know. But I can't help but feel sorry for him, having such a strained relationship with his dad. Even worse, Frank's reaction tonight stung more than I wanted it to. I know he told me not to take it personally, but it still feels like such a rejection. Frank definitely wasn't impressed. I thought for sure he'd see how much I love Perry and it would be enough for him to bend the rules a little or wait another year to move. But he sees me as just another Jill.

It's one thing to be cast aside by my own family. But to be rejected by Perry's? It somehow just confirms everything I've feared all along. The words, "nothing special" and "not good enough" ring in my head, threatening to make me cry.

Perry takes me to his room. It's not until we're lying on his bed, bodies pressed together, that I start to sniffle back oncoming tears.

His eyes widen, his hands coming up to cup my cheeks as he searches my face. "What's wrong?"

I sniffle. "I'm just being ridiculous. I feel like maybe your dad doesn't like me, and it reminds me of my parents constantly brushing me off to take care of my brother. I know it's not the same thing, and it doesn't make any sense, but for some reason, it feels exactly the same." I close my eyes. "Like rejection."

"Bunny." Perry presses a kiss to my forehead. "My dad loves you. The way he acted is about me, I promise. Please, don't let him get to you. *Please.* You are amazing, and anyone who can't see that, including your parents, is truly missing out."

I smile faintly at him. "I love you."

"I love you more."

"That's not possible." I wind my fingers through his hair and pull his face to mine. The kiss is slow and gentle, and it ends much too quickly because Perry separates our faces and stares at me.

"What?" I blush, feeling suddenly self-conscious.

"You're so beautiful."

I take in his hazel eyes, his smooth olive skin, and messy, dark hair, knowing his stunning physical beauty is somehow the least beautiful part of him. It's his insides that melt my heart. "Right back at you." When I kiss him again, it's not gentle, but frantic and urgent as my tongue wildly tangles with his.

He groans, sliding his hands down my body and gripping my waist. He moves us so that I'm sitting on top of him, my legs straddling his torso. We're both a mess of harsh breaths and wild kisses, hands digging into each other's skin and not an inch of air between us.

And then it stops. Perry stops us. "Wait," he breathes. "We need to talk."

I had a feeling this was coming. Since the moment we admitted our feelings and Lisa left, I've been wondering about what would happen the next time we were completely alone. "Okay."

"Please don't take what I'm about to say as a rejection." Perry tilts my chin to his face so our gazes connect. "I know how important waiting till marriage was to you. And I just want you to know I'm okay with waiting—if you still want to."

That was so not what I was expecting him to say.

He laughs. "Why do you look surprised?"

I shrug. "I guess because you have four children. And you know I've done it before." I feel queasy with regret at the memory, especially since it was with Asher. "But if I could take it back, I would," I mutter.

His brows narrow as he strokes my face with his thumb. "Don't do that. Don't think about the past. It's just me and you now, and we have a whole future ahead of us. I remember what you said about Romilly inspiring you, and I want you to have that. And I know my dad thinks I do everything backwards, but this is something I'd like to try the traditional way." He taps my nose. "As hard as it will be . . . I can wait, bunny."

I lean forward and kiss him again. And again. And again. "I think I just fell even more in love with you."

He grins. "Too bad I still love you more."

He presses a final kiss against my lips. I breathe him in before I get up. As much as I want to remain intertwined, I force myself to go to my own room. Despite what happened with Frank tonight, I have to have faith that we'll find a way to work this out.

As he said, we'll have our whole lives to spend together. Tomorrow, we'll be one day closer to getting there.

Chapter Twenty-Six

PERRY

THE NEXT MORNING, I go with Addison to drop the kids off at school. As she's loading Enzo into his car seat, she smirks at me and asks, "It's kind of silly for you to come along, isn't it? This is what you're paying me for."

"About that . . ." I take her hand. All the kids are buckled in the car, waiting for us to get in, but I don't want to say this in front of them. "We need to talk about your job. Obviously, you're not really my nanny anymore, now that we're getting married."

Her mouth falls open. "You mean I'm your nanny *until* we get married. I still need a way to pay for things."

I laugh. "Addison, let's be real. Everyone except the kids knows we're together now. You're wearing my ring on your finger. And honestly, you stopped being my employee a long time ago."

She bites her lip. "But I don't mind working."

Of course she doesn't. My little bunny is an independent spirit. "That's fine. All I'm saying is that it doesn't sit right for me to pay you like you're still my employee. You're not going to be the kids' nanny anymore; you're going to be their stepmom. I'd rather just add you to my bank account so you can pay for whatever you need, and then you can get another job if you really want to." A flicker of happiness crosses her expression, but it's quickly replaced by more worry. She stares at the ground. I tip her face back up to meet mine. "What is it? Talk to me."

"If I get another job, who's going to help with the kids?"

"I can hire someone to help. It's no problem, really."

"But . . ." She winces. "I don't know. I know I said I wanted to work, but *I'd* rather be the one to take them places, make them food, and spend time with them, you know?"

I grin easily to show her that her worries aren't necessary. "Then you can stay home with them. Either way. Get a remote job if you really want to. I just want you to be happy." I squeeze her hand and nod toward the car. "Let's get these kids to school."

She smiles back at me, but I can't help but notice the trace of worry still visible in her big brown eyes.

The drive to Izzy and Moxie's elementary school isn't far from the house, and daycare for the boys is close to downtown. When they're all dropped off, I drive toward Pretzel Heart Bistro. "Let's get breakfast."

She bounces up and down a little, an adorable smile on her lips. "Okay. By the way, I told Romilly about us. I hope that's okay."

I meet her gaze. "Of course it is. How did she react?"

"She squealed so loud my hearing will never be the same on my right side."

With a chuckle, I kiss the back of her hand. We park on the street next to the white-brick cafe covered in ivy, and we stroll inside together. It feels so good to be able to take her out in public and not have to fight being attracted to her, being drawn toward her, being madly in love with her.

We take a seat in the middle of the restaurant. The inside is industrial, with furniture that looks like it came from repurposed materials. Obscure indie music plays from the speakers. A hand painted sign with the word "pretzel" hangs above the pastry counter. Addison quietly flips through her menu before setting it down and smiling faintly at me.

"What are you getting?" I ask.

"Poached eggs, half an avocado, and a slice of whole wheat toast. No butter."

I frown. "That doesn't seem like enough food."

"Preliminaries are next week." She scrunches her nose. "I have to stick to my meal plan. I've been a little too lenient lately."

It takes me a minute to realize she's talking about the Miss Meadow pageant. "There's a *weight limit?*"

"No, of course not. I'm doing this for me. I want to feel and look my best up there."

"The idea that you don't already look your best is crazy to me, bun." I take a bite of the freshly baked pretzel on the table. Around a mouthful, I continue, "In fact, if you somehow, impossibly, became more perfect than you already are, I'd spontaneously combust."

She covers her mouth and giggles. She looks like a Disney princess as she does it. Her shoulders relax a bit, and then she sighs. "There's a swimsuit portion, Perry. Not a part I'd like to fail."

I shake my head. "That's nuts. I've seen you in a swimsuit. You remember what happened after."

She blushes. "Yes, I do."

"There's no way you'd fail that portion," I grumble.

"I have before. Three of the years I've competed. I've worn every kind of swimsuit under the sun," she continues. "Bikini, tankini, whole piece. It doesn't matter. Romilly has beaten me three times, including last year."

I take her hand from across the table. "This is your year. You're going to win. And even if you don't, you're perfect the way you are. I don't care what some stuffy pageant lady has to say about it."

"Josephine Hayden isn't stuffy. She's very kind, and the whole purpose of the pageant is to donate to charity. To be honest, I'm much more worried about the final phase. The interview."

It's hard to argue with that.

We order our food when the waitress comes, and I watch Addison eat her bland looking breakfast with a twinge of pity. Reaching across the table, I offer her some of my egg, potato, and cheese burrito. "Take a bite. Please. I can't watch this go on a moment longer."

"There's no pineapple in it, right?"

"When have you ever heard of a breakfast burrito with pineapple in it? Besides, you know I don't go anywhere without my EpiPen."

She rolls her eyes, but I know I've won when she leans across the table to take a bite. Thank God.

I cut my burrito in half and place the uneaten portion on her plate. She downs it so fast that I can't help but wonder what her meal plan looks like for the rest of the day.

Work passes uneventfully. Kiera reports back to me that the restaurant is doing fine. I have her place an order for more utensils, mugs, and linen napkins in addition to other essentials. When I respond to her email with the news about me and Addison, I sit and wait patiently for her reply. It comes through, and I can't help but smile.

Mr. Whitmore,

Congratulations. I knew it the moment she walked in your house, and you couldn't take your eyes off her.

Sincerely,

Kiera Fang

I come downstairs at around five-thirty. The kids are home and Addison has them laughing, sitting in a circle as she pats their heads, saying, "Duck, duck, duck . . ." When she gets to Moxie's head, she shouts, "Goose!" and Moxie springs up to chase her as they run around the house, laughing.

My phone vibrates with a text. I fully expect it to be another work-related message from Kiera, but it's from Rebecca. My sister never texts me, not if she can avoid it.

REBECCA

Check it out, little brother. You're going to be an uncle.

Beneath her message is a photo of an ultrasound. According to my dad, Rebecca and her husband, Dale, have been trying for a baby all year.

ME

Congrats.

I know I should probably say more, but to be honest, I don't know much about Rebecca's life. She lives in Madison with Dale, about an hour away and I only see her on holidays. Sometimes.

I put my phone back in my pocket and look up to find Addison running at me, wearing an ear-to-ear grin. When she's an arm's length away, she crouches and jumps, so I catch her.

"Get Daddy!" She tells the kids.

The four of them come running, laughing, and reaching out to tickle me. I pretend to scream and try to escape, making them laugh harder.

It takes a few minutes to get the kids to wind down enough to eat dinner after that. But once we're all sitting at the table together, I look at each of their faces, and then I take Addison's hand.

"We have some news, kids," I say.

Addison stares with wide eyes. "We're telling them?"

I know I should probably figure out what to do about my dad first, but I already know that I'm marrying Addison, regardless. Whatever it takes. I might not be sure about the details yet, but I am sure about her. "I think it's time," I tell her. "Don't you?"

"Heck yes!"

I turn back to the curious faces of Moxie and Izzy. Abel and Enzo are pretending their forks are tusks as they make faces at each other. So, I tell the girls, "Addison and I are getting married."

They both gasp simultaneously.

"Really?" Moxie asks.

Izzy hops out of her chair and captures Addison in a hug. "Yes, yes, yes!"

Moxie gets up and joins her. "Wait, are you being serious? If you're being serious, then we are so lucky!"

As they squeeze her, Addison's stunned expression becomes glossy. "Trust me, you guys. I'm the lucky one here."

After the kids are tucked into bed, Addison begs me to watch a movie with her. I plop down on the couch, and she cuddles up next to me. I know we're both still trying to figure out what to do about my dad, but I haven't brought it up, and neither has she. A movie actually sounds like a nice distraction for now.

I gently brush her hair back. "What's your favorite movie, bunny?"

"Hmm." She nuzzles her face into my neck. "Probably *The Sound of Music*."

I reach for the remote. "Let's put it on."

She squeals and hops up from the couch.

"Hey, where are you going?" I reach for her and grab the empty air.

"Getting snacks." She opens the pantry and rustles around before returning with a bag of pretzels and a tub of cream cheese.

I arch an eyebrow. "Not that I'm complaining, but what happened to your meal plan?"

"That doesn't exist tonight." She crunches a pretzel into her mouth. "We're watching *The Sound of Music*."

An hour later, Addison's head falls forward a few times as she struggles to stay awake.

I nudge her. "Let's go to bed."

But she shakes her head. "We have to get to the part where they kiss."

I laugh and position her so she can lean her head against my shoulder better. I shift my gaze to the screen. It's actually a pretty good movie. The main character is a nun-slash-governess, and she's getting all these kids to sing and dance and have fun for once in their lives, all the while their dad is falling for her, even though he's engaged.

The dad is dancing with the nun girl, and when he spins her around, Addison whispers, "It's us."

She closes her eyes, so I scoop her up and carry her to her bed. She mumbles something as I tuck her into the thick comforter, but I ignore it because whatever she's saying is sleep-talk and doesn't make any sense, adorable as it is. I lie next to her, just for a minute, in case she wakes up.

Watching her sleep, I take comfort in the slow rise and fall of her chest. I think about what Addison was saying earlier, about wanting to work, but also wanting to stay home and take care of the kids. I try to imagine her in each scenario, and when I picture her staying home, a seed of dread sprouts in my stomach. Something about the vision makes me think of Jill, of how badly she wanted to be a stay-at-home mom. She grew to hate it so much, she ended up leaving.

I can't imagine Addison reacting the same way as Jill, but I don't know how she'd handle giving up work to stay home and take care of my crazy kids. I love them, and I know she does too, but they're a lot of work. I can't help but wonder how long Addison's patience with them will last. And when, or if, her patience does finally run out, what will happen?

For all I know, she'll come to her senses and realize I'm not as great as she thinks I am. She might regret taking on four kids that aren't her own, like their mom regretted having them in the first place. Even though I already can't imagine my life without Addison now that she's in it, I have to acknowledge that I've only known her for one summer. That's nothing in the grand scheme of things. I have no idea how she handles emotions like severe stress, depression, regret.

For all I know, she could leave us if things don't turn out how she hopes. Just like Jill did.

Something catches my eye on her bed, so I reach for it. I recognize her grandma's book as soon as my fingers meet the cover. I open it and read some of the hymns, trying to picture Addison carrying it to church as a little girl, maybe even as young as Izzy and Moxie. I wonder if she's read all of these hymns, or all of the Bible verses sprinkled throughout.

I stop at one in particular.

Cast all your anxiety on Him because He cares for you.
    –1 Peter 5:7

I look up at the ceiling. It's like He can read my mind. "Please," I whisper. "Don't let her regret choosing us like Jill did."

Chapter Twenty-Seven

I WALK through the front door, my arms laden with paper bags. The kids are dropped off at school and daycare—sad face—and the grocery shopping is done. This morning has felt like a possible sneak peek into my future being married to Perry, and I'm not going to lie, I'm loving every second of it. I also may or may not have picked up some goodies to throw a little birthday party for Romilly tonight. She's been so busy looking for a new grooming job, I haven't gotten to see her since she came over to help me get ready for the interview with Asher.

When I come in, the coffee table is covered with crayon drawings made by the kids, and a messy stack of bills and junk mail.

I sigh, a smile on my lips. This. This feels like home. Still, there's a trepidation in my gut I can't escape. The feeling that this could all end at any second, especially since we still haven't figured out how to get around the terms of the will.

I set the grocery bags on the kitchen counter and make my way upstairs to Perry's office. Through the cracked-open door, I see him hunched at his desk, typing on his laptop with intensity. My gaze lingers on his forearms, exposed from his pushed-up sleeves. He's already been at it for hours, and it's only nine in the morning.

I tiptoe in and slide my arms around his shoulders. "I vote that you take a mini-break."

Perry sighs and leans back into me. The tension in his muscles loosens a bit as I squeeze. "I wish I could. The manager and assistant manager for Rosemary Banquet are out sick all week. I have to schedule the employee shifts and update the print and digital menu because we added a new gluten-free pasta option."

My brows pinch together. "Lillian's sick?"

He nods. "Sometimes I forget you two know each other."

"We didn't just know each other. We were work besties." Even I can hear the longing in my voice. But as much as I miss working there, miss the regulars and keeping busy, I wouldn't trade that job for spending time with my four favorite kids in the world.

Before Perry can respond, a loud pounding at the front door makes us both flinch. Heavy, angry knocking. We exchange puzzled glances. "Are you expecting someone?"

"Nope."

I follow Perry to the foyer, hovering behind him as he swings open the door.

Frank Whitmore is standing on the doorstep, his handsome face pinched in concentration.

"Dad?" Perry says. "What are you doing here?"

"I'm here to talk to you, son." He crosses the entryway and makes for the living room, steady and determined. Perry and I have no choice but to follow. When we're sitting on the loveseat across from him, Frank points a rigid finger at Perry. "Have you spoken to Rebecca? I'm starting to think she might be right, and that the house should go to her."

"What are you talking about, Dad?"

"You have every right to this home if you get married. I'm well aware. And I can't change that. But I think it might be decent of you to back off and let your sister have this home."

"Wait, I'm confused." I cross my arms. "What's going on with Rebecca?"

They both ignore me. Perry sags, rubbing his temples. "Dad, stop. We've talked about this."

"Your sister feels it's unfair for you to have the restaurant and the house, and I can't help but feel like maybe she's right."

My voice rises an octave. "Did something happen with Rebecca?"

Perry looks exhausted by this conversation. "She texted me to tell me she's pregnant. That's all."

"That's all?" Frank booms. "That girl is doing it right. She's married, starting a family now. She needs a proper place to live, and she's asking for this house."

Perry's jaw flexes. "I'm sorry I'm not perfect enough for you, Dad. Sorry, I didn't live my life your way. But I wouldn't change anything I've done, because if I'd married Jill before having my kids, I wouldn't be here with the love of my life." Perry shifts in front of me protectively, but can't hide the anger in his voice when he speaks. "Besides, Rebecca doesn't *really* want this house. She wants to make my life miserable."

"Don't be immature," says Frank. "She's your sister. Think about her feelings in this situation."

Perry scoffs. "Her feelings? Why do you care about her feelings so much, but never mine?"

Frank seems stricken, unable to answer for a moment. "I know you think I'm disappointed in you, Perry. But the truth is that I'm more proud of you than I know how to put into words." His gaze flickers to my face before returning to Perry's. "You're a good man, and I know you'll make the right choice." With a final nod, Frank rises from the sofa and stalks off, shutting the door behind him.

Perry sighs harshly, his shoulders slumped.

"Don't worry," I say. "He'll come around, eventually." But there's a waver in my tone, one that tells me the same thing Perry's already thinking—he absolutely won't come around. Even if there is some sort of loophole in the will, there's no hope of Frank telling us about it now.

"I'll have my lawyer read over everything to look for a way around this," Perry says. "Hopefully, there will be enough time before the deadline to find a solution."

I wrap my arms around him, wishing I could erase the troubled look in his eyes. I know how much this house means to Perry. I don't want to be the one to mess this up for him just because of a stupid pageant rule. "I just wish your dad could see what I see when it comes to you."

"That's never going to happen."

"He did say he's proud of you."

"He said that to manipulate me into forfeiting the house."

I study his profile, the furrow between his brows, the tight set of his jaw. There's a weight on his shoulders I wish I could pluck right off and toss into the ocean. "Hey," I say, gently. "Look at me."

He turns, meeting my gaze.

"We're going to figure this out. And no matter what your dad says, you are kind and doing amazing. And you're more than enough for me."

Perry closes his eyes briefly. When he opens them again, some of the darkness has lifted. He leans in and kisses me softly. I can feel the tension in his body as he pulls me closer and murmurs against my lips, "I wish I could marry you tonight." His lips move hungrily against mine, exploring with an intensity that takes my breath away.

"So do I."

"If it weren't for the pageant," he whispers in between kisses, sending sparks of pleasure coursing through me, "I'd take you to a chapel right now and make you Mrs. Whitmore. But no matter how badly I want to do that, I'd never ruin your dream like that."

A seed of guilt plants itself in my stomach, because there's a chance I could very well be the one to ruin his dream. But I push it down and smile at him, wrapping my arms around his neck. "We should do something fun today, all six of us. Maybe take the kids to the park or the zoo."

If he knows I'm trying to distract him, he doesn't show it. A genuine smile finally appears. "That's a great idea. The kids would love that." His expression turns mischievous.

"Maybe we can stop for ice cream, too. I know a place that has the most delicious rocky road in the whole entire world."

I pop up instantly. "Kay. Let's go, like right now. We'll get the kids from school early." I shake him, earning a grunt followed by a laugh. "Come on. You know Rocky Road is my favorite flavor. It's one of the first things I told you about myself. I'm not messing around."

"Patience, bunny."

"No," I giggle.

Just when I think he's going to give in, my phone buzzes. It's a text from Asher.

ASHER

We need to finish your interview if you still plan on competing in the Miss Meadow pageant.

My shoulders pinch as I read it, ice cream plans forgotten. Perry searches my face and immediately sits up. "What is it?"

"It's Asher. I still need to finish my interview." I bite my lip. "Can you pick up the Rocky Road for the party tonight?"

Perry pulls away from me, getting up from the couch. "Yep. And while you're there, give Asher a big hug from me. Such an upstanding guy he is."

I roll my eyes. "Stop."

"And maybe throw in the fact that we're getting married as soon as the pageant is over. Feel free to send me a photo of his face when you tell him so I can frame it and hang it on the wall."

I try to hide my smile and fail. "You're terrible."

"Maybe." He waggles his eyebrows. "But at least I get you."

I'm all dolled up for the cameras again.

As many times as I've done this, it's still such a funny feeling, having everyone's attention directed at me, having Asher ask me prompts on-camera. And it's always even funnier seeing all my answers, remixed and spliced together to be inserted into whatever context the pageant sees fit.

We're at the lake near The Orchard Inn, where I'll be staying as soon as the pageant begins. There's a bench outside the building overlooking Gull Pond, and it's a common filming spot for the contestant interviews. I'm guessing Asher learned his lesson after the club incident when he chose this location.

He rattles off questions I've answered before, in past years, along with some new ones. He doesn't touch on the subject of me and Perry. Once we're done filming, Asher makes his way over to me. We haven't spoken since that night at the club with Perry, but he doesn't seem concerned as he approaches me.

"Great interview, Ad."

I hug my arms. "Thanks."

"Who's your sponsor this year?"

"Meadow Hills Children's Hospital. I finally just chose last week." As bad as I felt for not choosing Mrs. So, who Perry spoke so highly of, the children's hospital goes hand in hand with my chosen cause.

Asher's eyes round. "Last week? Talk about procrastination."

"I know." I shrug, laughing a little. "You know how I am."

"Yeah." He stops walking, which leads me to do the same. "I do. I know you, Ad. Which is why I've been wanting to talk to you about us again."

"Asher."

"I know you still care about me."

"Of course I do, but as a friend." I ready myself to continue. "I'm in love with Perry. And I'm marrying him as soon as the pageant is over."

"Wait." He exhales in a rush. "Okay, look. I owe you, an apology."

I frown, waiting.

"I've been pretty unfair to you. It's just that you're so beautiful, and I never thought you'd go for someone like me. But then you *did* and . . . I guess some of that insecurity came back when you told me you wanted to stop having sex."

"Asher." I shake my head. "It wasn't you. Not really."

"I get that, and I never should have told you that you're nothing special. It's not true."

His confession makes me feel lighter inside, like some of the weight I've been carrying around since our breakup is finally gone. "Thank you for that, Asher." I swallow. "It doesn't change anything between us romantically, but I forgive you."

"I accept your decision, I guess." He nods, but his face looks more resigned now. "Are we good?"

"Of course. Unless you have evil plans to make me look terrible during the pageant."

He laughs. "Don't worry, Ad. You're going to be great, as usual."

Romilly definitely knew about the party.

I can tell the moment she tries to act surprised. She's amazing at so many things, but faking it isn't one of them. "I can't believe you did this," she forces, gesturing to the flower garlands throughout the house, the appetizers, the balloons, and streamers. Finally, she sits on one of the island stools and pops a grape into her mouth.

I cross my arms. "How did you know?"

She covers her smile with her hand. "I didn't. What are you talking about?" Next to her, Cole shifts his weight impatiently, like he's waiting for her response, too.

"Tell me right now, Romilly Westfall."

"Well, for starters, it's September fourth, which happens to be my birthday. Not many people ask me to come by on this very special, very annual day unless it's to surprise me."

"But . . ." I scoff. "All I said was that I had a present for you! That doesn't mean a surprise party, necessarily."

"It does in your case."

Perry places a homemade pizza on the island, instantly silencing all of us. Cole moans around a mouthful of the

Italian herb pie. "Dude, this is *good*." His gray eyes roll back in his head.

I eye the pizza with suspicion. "This is from the restaurant menu, isn't it?"

Perry smiles proudly, dusting his hands on the apron around his waist. "A tried-and-true crowd pleaser. Came up with the recipe myself."

Romilly's eyes widen. "This. This right here is why you fell for him, isn't it?" She reaches for my hand. "Let me see the ring again."

As Romilly examines it, I notice Cole shift his attention back to the food. In fact, he barely says a word to her, but I do catch him firmly grabbing at her waist a couple of times.

"Have you picked a date yet?" Romilly asks.

I wince. Perry removes his apron and sits at the island with us. He pulls me onto his lap. "I'd love to marry her as soon as possible, but it's kind of against pageant rules."

Romilly melts at his answer, but only I can hear the worry in his tone. The weight. His dad's retirement timeline sucks big time. If I think about it too much, it's going to ruin my mood, so to change the subject, I round the kids up for present time. They've been enjoying the small bounce house in the backyard Perry ordered specifically for them, but they're more than happy to come in when I tell them it's time to give Romilly her gifts.

Izzy hands her a pink gift bag from the four of them. "Here's a prezzie," she says, remembering what Romilly called it last time.

Romilly beams as she takes the gift bag. "Thank you so much." She takes out the present I helped the kids make;

an acrylic crown with silk flowers decorating every inch of it. The card inside has an outline of each of their hands, and it's addressed to *The Real Miss Meadow*.

Romilly puts it on her head, somehow making the crafty DIY look elegant and regal. "This is the best gift ever," she tells the kids, earning a huge smile from each of them.

When the party's over, I put the boys to bed and Perry tucks the girls in. We come out of their bedrooms around the same time and tiptoe downstairs in hushed silence.

Neither of us speaks at first. I wonder if he feels it too, the pressure to find a loophole in the will. Romilly's comment about the wedding date was just a reminder, a little thorn against the happy bubble we've been hiding in all this time.

"We need to talk, bunny." Perry rubs his forehead.

"No."

He frowns. "No?"

I shake my head. "That phrase never means anything good. So, I'd really rather not."

He laughs softly. "Sorry, but I think we have to."

"I think I already know what you're going to say. You're going to keep trying to find a way around the terms of your mother's will. But I'm going to be honest. I don't think that's going to happen. You're going to end up losing the house, and Perry . . . I can't let that happen. I can't be the reason you lose your dream."

Perry studies my face for such a long time, I'm not sure if he's going to respond. Sitting here with him reminds me of the day we first started fake dating, when we sat here and peeled an onion together so we could get to know each other. That night seems like a lifetime ago, when in reality, it was only three months ago.

"I'm not going to lie," he murmurs, low and gravelly in a tone that goes straight to my knees. "I love this house. Officially owning it was my dream. I wanted it so bad that I associated that with my future happiness. I thought it was a safe dream, because ultimately, this house could never break my heart the way a person could. It couldn't abandon me and the kids the way Jill did. But when my dad told me the right thing to do would be giving it to Rebecca, it felt like Jill all over again."

I swallow hard. "See? I can't let that happen to you. I can't be the reason you lose your childhood home, or all those years of memories."

"Let me finish, bunny." He reaches for my hand and squeezes it, reassuringly. "The house was my dream for the longest time. But it's not anymore." He shakes his head. "Not since you gave the word dream a whole new meaning."

I'm speechless. My heart swells, even as my guilt claws at me.

Selfish, selfish, selfish.

I can't do this. I can't take this away from him.

He searches my face, his brows knitting in concern. "What is it?"

"I can't live with the guilt of letting you give up those things to be with me."

The corner of his mouth turns up. "There's no reason for you to feel guilty. This is my decision." He sounds so calm as he says it. Like we're discussing what to make for dinner tomorrow.

"But Perry," I say, voice cracking, "If I don't win that pageant, I will literally never forgive myself for letting you give up. You're giving up your dream so I can have mine."

"Addison, *you're* my dream."

"But . . . but . . ." I sputter, "it might not matter to you now, but it will someday. And I don't want to be the reason you couldn't have it. I wish I could make myself not care about the pageant, but I know I'd regret not trying one last time. I don't want to blame you, just like I don't want you to blame me." I inhale a shaky breath. "It's starting to feel like this has been nothing more than a summer of dandelions. A summer of wishes that can't possibly come true."

He threads his fingers through mine. "No one is giving up their dream here. I want to marry you because I love you, not because of what our marriage could gain me. You're going to be the next Miss Meadow. And me?" He laughs without humor. "I'm going to tell my dad I don't want the house anymore. I'm going to marry the heck out of you in a year and a half. And all of it will be better than my wildest dreams."

"Come here." I claw at his shirt as I pull him closer until he's flush against me on the couch. I press a delicate kiss against his forehead. One against each of his eyelids. One on his lips. "I don't know how I'm going to wait that long to do . . ."

An antagonistic smile pulls at his lips. "Other stuff?"

I roll my eyes. Nod.

"You mean have sex?" He says it loudly, teasingly.

I close my eyes, burying my face in his shoulder. "Yes."

"If there's one thing I promise, bunny . . ." He laughs softly. "It's that I'll make it worth the wait."

Chapter Twenty-Eight

PERRY

ON SATURDAY MORNING, I wake up to the smell of French toast wafting up from the kitchen. Addison must be up already, making breakfast for the kids. I stretch and hum contentedly. The past few days have been pure bliss. Since telling my dad I've decided to forfeit my house to Rebecca, it's felt like a huge weight has been lifted off my shoulders.

Now that there's no more pressure, no more rushing, Addison and I have actually started dreaming up what kind of wedding we want to have. She's found so many nice ideas online, and even printed a few photos out, pinning them onto the cork board in my office so I "have somewhere happy to look while I'm working."

I throw on a T-shirt and head downstairs, following the sweet scent of cinnamon. Addison is at the stove, wearing her lilac robe made from a silky, lightweight fabric that's fun to touch, hair still messy from sleep. Dressed like this, she's always so irresistible. I wrap my arms around her waist and kiss her neck. A little sigh escapes her.

"Morning, beautiful," I murmur.

She turns and gives me a dimpled smile. "Morning."

The sound of the doorbell echoes through the house. I move to get it, desperately hoping it's not my dad, here to give me grief for some new crisis, now that I'm finally feeling at peace. But when I open the door, I find Romilly on the doorstep, a wide grin on her face and holding an extravagant bouquet of pink and yellow wildflowers. The sweet fragrance from the bouquet hits my nose right away.

"I haven't had a chance to properly congratulate you guys," she announces without preamble, gliding inside and handing the flowers to Addison.

"Let me guess," Addison says, taking them. "You were in the area?"

Romilly ignores the question, imploring Addison with pleading eyes. "So, we didn't get to talk much about it on my birthday, but I'd love to throw you a bridal shower. We could do a whole flower, wine, and cheese theme, very classy and romantic."

Addison laughs. "That sounds perfect. I'd love that."

Romilly claps her hands together delicately and grins.

I tune out their wedding talk to finish up the French toast for the kids, but I can't help overhearing when Addison asks Romilly how things are going with Cole, and an uncomfortable silence follows.

"I don't think love is in the cards for me anymore," Romilly murmurs, leading me to wonder what is wrong with this Cole guy. Romilly is an attractive woman who seems great. I know it's nosy of me, but I try to hear more details.

"So, it's for sure over between you two?"

Romilly nods. "Let's just say he lied about being okay with waiting. And . . . he definitely does *not* want to get married. Which is fine, Adds. I really, truly think I'm just one of those people who will be perfectly happy alone for the rest of my life."

"Stop it." Addison reaches over and hugs her. "You're never going to be alone because you have me, silly."

Romilly seems grateful, but abruptly changes the subject. "So, you ready for the pageant?"

Addison chews her lip and plays with the threads on a throw blanket draped on the couch. "To be honest, I haven't had as much time as I'd like to get ready. You know, with taking care of the kids and all the wedding drama."

Uncertainty flashes across Romilly's face, but she says nothing.

A seed of guilt blossoms in my gut. I know my kids are a lot of work. On their own, they're distracting enough. And then there's me. She's said it before—I'm a distraction for her, one that could keep her from winning. And now, there's the wedding. The seed of guilt sprouts into a giant weed. I can't help but feel like our real engagement is the final thing that's going to take her mind away from where it needs to be.

I give the kids their breakfast and hustle them off to school, trying not to dwell on Addison not being ready for the pageant, but failing. I spend the entire car ride back worrying about her, in fact. If she loses the pageant, it's going to remind me way too much of Jill feeling like the kids and I stole her life away from her. Addison could easily blame us. I don't want that to happen. There's nothing I want to avoid more, in fact.

Romilly is already gone when I get back, and Addison is in the shower.

I go straight to my office and sit down at the computer, opening up a search engine. I type in 'pageant preparation' and look up tips for pageant contestants.

There are a few interesting articles about makeup techniques, physical fitness tips, practice interview questions, and more. I print out as much information as I can find and make a folder of all my research. Then I head into Addison's bedroom with the folder tucked under my arm.

The door to her bathroom is closed, but her bedroom is wide open, so I leave the folder on her dresser with a note that reads "For Your Pageant Preparation."

I go back to my office to get some work done, but that only lasts about thirty minutes before Addison peeks her head inside. When she sees me sitting at my desk, she plops the folder down on my work surface. "You did this for me?" Her eyes are practically glowing with gratitude.

"Of course." Some of my guilt melts away when her infectious smile appears.

"I don't know what to say, other than I love you." As if in a daze, she sits on the sofa next to my desk. Opening the folder, she flips through the first few pages, which turns into her pouring over the notes like they hold the answers to life.

Chapter Twenty-Nine

ADDISON

WITH PRELIMINARIES SO CLOSE, the Miss Meadow pageant should be the only thing on my mind.

This is it. My final chance to win the pageant Gran and I have put so much hope and time into together.

All those years she spent coaching me, teaching me how to walk like a lady, or to present my chosen cause with urgency and pertinence. All the laughter we shared as we looked over outfit ideas and ways to tweak common recipes to fit within the limits of my meal plan. All those memories are still as happy to me now as they were then, despite the bitter tang of not winning each year.

I know none of it was in vain, and I'll finally prove it when I win this for the both of us.

I shouldn't have a problem focusing, now that there's no pressure left for Perry to find a wife, or for us to plan a hasty wedding. I should be diving headfirst into the pageant.

I just didn't expect for Perry to have to give up his own dreams to make mine come true.

I try to push the looming guilt down over the next few days as I throw myself into preparations for the preliminaries, now only seven days away. On Monday morning, I'll have to move into the inn. The knots in my stomach are making me feel sick.

Over the past few months, I've tried typing my speech a few times, but each attempt has resulted in nothing but an empty screen, so I've decided to move on to pen and paper. I've been working on it for days, but this morning I had the urge to rewrite the entire thing.

I smooth out my crinkled paper. There are notes scattered across Perry's desk. The words I've scribbled read back to me like a foreign language; all my jumbled thoughts on housing for disabled adults spewed onto the page. I take a deep breath, trying to find the thread that ties it all together into a compelling narrative. This has to be perfect. I need to memorize these key points so they're second nature to me during the interview portion on the pageant. Otherwise, I'll just freeze up like I have in the past, every single time I've made it to this phase.

I move my papers to my bedroom, so Perry won't be tempted to distract me in the office. After spending the next half hour scribbling down a few more sentences, I give up. I stare at the patterns on the ceiling, trying not to cry. For a minute, I hear Gran's voice in my head. *Don't worry about all that. When the time comes, speak from the heart.* But then I remember the time I tried doing that and my tongue tripped on every word that tried to come out of my mouth.

I swallow down the knot forming in my throat. This is only my second season trying to do this without Gran, and last year was a complete train wreck. I didn't even make it past the first phase. I have no idea how I'm supposed to successfully do any of this without her, but I still have to try.

My eyes drift over to the gowns hanging on my closet door. Shimmering jeweled bodices and layers of tulle await me, each heavier than the last. I gently slip a lilac dress made of satin over my head, cinching and smoothing until it falls just right. It's an exquisite gown, hand-beaded and custom-designed just for me, but I've lost weight from stress and now it needs to be altered, which is fine. I turn and examine myself in the mirror, making mental notes. Take in the waist. Shorten the hem. The rhinestone brooch instead of the pearl one.

My gaze travels from the gown up to my face. I examine my hair, voluminous and curly. My eyes, bright and hungry for success. All of it looks right. Even the gown will fit me like a second skin once it's altered.

But no matter how tall I stand, I can't help but feel so small without Gran.

I shake my head, banishing the thoughts and take off the dress, carefully hanging it back up in the closet. I move to the bed where my open suitcase is, methodically packing some necessities—hair spray, bobby pins, makeup, stockings, heels. As I place each item in the suitcase, I go over my mental checklist. Hair styled just so, face painted to perfection, body cinched and smoothed. On the inside, I should feel the same as I look—polished, put together, composed.

Too bad my insides are currently a wreck.

I'm so focused, I don't hear Perry come in. He snakes his arms around my waist from behind, pulling me into him. I jolt at first and then relax. His scent overwhelms me, the teakwood and cologne making my brain drift to thoughts of us cuddling, kissing, folded into one another.

"I hate that you're packing." His stubble tickles my ear.

I turn in his arms to face him. "Perry . . ." I struggle to find my next words because I hate that I'm packing too, but at the same time, I'm itching to get through the pageant. "Please don't hate me for what I'm about to say next."

"Hate you?" He nuzzles his nose into the top of my head. "I could never hate you, bunny. What is it?"

I bite my lip. "It's just so hard to focus with you here, and the kids. I thought about asking Romilly if I could stay with her, but she's in the middle of moving back home with her parents. I could go to a hotel, but the one place I know won't be distracted is my old room. Would it be such a bad idea if I spent this week at Bronwyn's so I can focus?"

He stiffens. "You want to spend your chaotic, busy prep week with your extremely particular old roommate?"

"No. Not at all." I tighten my arms around him. "I want to spend every second of it with *you*. Which is exactly the problem. I'll have no issues staying in my room if talking to Bronwyn is the only other option."

He stares at me in dismay. One more second and I'm going to take it back. But then he drops his head. "You should go. You're right."

I hug him impossibly tight. "Thank you for under-standing. I just hope the kids take it well."

"I know it's only a month, but I'm still going to miss you like crazy," he says. His gaze is impossibly tender as he tucks a strand of my hair behind my ear. "I'll have to come visit you in your room at the inn."

"Oh, stop." I tap his nose. He's been joking about breaking all kinds of rules the past few days, including this one. "I swear, if you get me disqualified so I can come home sooner—"

I don't get to finish my sentence because he covers my lips with his own. I get lost in the feel of his mouth against mine, but quickly pull away because there's no time left for me to waste. "Perry, this is exactly why I have to go."

He chuckles. "Sorry, but if you don't want me to touch you, don't walk around in that." He gestures the sweatpants and T-shirt I'm currently wearing.

I snort. "I can't imagine what lingerie would do to you."

A wicked gleam appears in his eye, but then his voice turns serious. "Have you heard from your parents at all? Since you called them about us getting married?" He nods at my left hand where my engagement ring is glinting under the lights.

My face falls slightly. "Yeah." I avoid his gaze. "They texted me saying congratulations after I called and left that voicemail."

"Hmm." Perry sighs, his thumb rubbing small circles on my hip. "A *text?* I'm sorry, bunny."

I shake my head, willing the tears away. "It's okay. Honestly, I'm surprised they even thought to do that much."

He wraps me in his arms, kissing the top of my head. I close my eyes and exhale deeply, pushing all other thoughts aside. Tomorrow I'll be in pageant mode, every move choreographed and staged. But right now, I'm just me, here with him. And for now, that's enough.

After a long moment, we break apart. Perry sighs. "I should let you finish packing. I'm going to finish purging old boxes from the attic."

I nod, but the familiar pang of guilt strikes me. With him sacrificing his home so we can be together, I can't help but feel like he must harbor some resentment toward me for it. I never sacrificed competing in the pageant to be with him, after all. Instead, I'm just letting him give up everything so I can compete in another pageant.

I push the thought away as I gather my things.

This pageant means everything to me. It's my dream, and Perry wants me to follow it, no matter the cost to him.

Still, the guilt sits like a weight in my stomach as I drop off my dress at the tailor's and continue my errands. At the fingerprint center, I go through the motions, pressing my fingers to the ink pads and scanner. I've done this before each competition, which is silly, because I'm sure they keep everyone's prints on file.

The clerk hands me a wipe and I scrub the ink from my hands.

I imagine Perry going through all those boxes full of memories from his childhood. Condensing them, selling some of them so we'll fit into a smaller house or apartment together. I imagine him saying goodbye to the house he grew up in and couldn't wait for his kids to grow up in.

The house full of memories of his mother. The house he's letting Rebecca take, all for me.

With a deep breath, I climb into the car.

Eye on the prize, Addison. Your dream is literally within reach. Time to make Gran proud.

All I need to do is find a way to silence the guilt.

Chapter Thirty

ADDISON

ME

Please, Bronwyn. I'll literally sleep in my car if you say no.

BRONWYN

You're just trying to weasel your way back into my place.

ME

Omg, not true. I just told you I only need to stay for a week. Then I'm off to The Orchard Inn.

BRONWYN

And after that?

ME

Have you already found a new roommate or something?

BRONWYN

AHA! See. I knew you were trying to stay.

ME

> I promise I'm not. And I'm already on my way so it's too late to say no.

❧

EVERYTHING AT BRONWYN'S apartment looks exactly the same as the last time I was here. If the girl is good at one thing, it's consistency. I stare at my favorite thing I left here—my giant bed, covers still a rumpled mess. I bite my lip, memories of my life before Perry flooding back to me. Asher and I, cuddled on that bed together. Me crying into that pillow when he dumped me. Watching pageant videos on that bed, hopeful and dreaming of the future.

I was a different person then. I can't help but acknowledge how much I've changed since I left, and how coming back now feels like stuffing myself into a too-small box I've outgrown.

I'm about to plop down on my bed when I hear Bronwyn's voice from the kitchen.

"There's an extra enchilada out here for you," she calls.

I walk over to her. She's already scarfing hers down. On the counter, there's a steaming enchilada smothered in cheese and sauce. "This looks really good, Bronwyn. Thanks."

"I was . . . going to throw it out if you didn't want it. Like I said, it's extra."

"Sure."

"Or maybe I'm just trying to sabotage your meal plan."

With a smile, I roll my eyes. "As much as I hate to admit it, I kinda missed you, too."

She struggles for a response, ultimately settling on taking her food to her bedroom so she won't have to say anything back.

I take out my phone and check for new messages. My heart flutters as I open my text thread with Perry.

ME

Going to work on my speech in my old room. Love you.

PERRY

Love you more, bunny. Knock their socks off.

I fight the urge to cry, which is ridiculous. This was my decision, and I'm going to stand by it. Still, I sniffle a few times as I respond to his latest message.

ME

What if they're not wearing socks?

PERRY

No socks in Maine during fall? Come on.

ME

Does knocking their shoes off count as succeeding?

I stare at the sent message, awaiting a response but it never comes. I don't know why I expect it to. He's probably terribly busy trying to juggle work and the kids without me.

I take the plate to my old room and set it on the edge of the bed. Then I lower my face onto my pillow. Now that I'm here, the loneliness of not having Perry near me feels all consuming. A few more sniffles happen, so I cave and

let the silly, unnecessary tears out, so they'll knock it off
and leave me alone.

Chapter Thirty-One

PERRY

LIFE SUCKS without Addison in it. This is something I already knew, yet the realization still smacks into me with way too much force.

It's not the same, waking up in the morning without her sunshine face greeting everyone. I miss her wind-chime laughter, her bouncy footsteps skipping around. Her messy tendencies. Her kisses.

And how on earth does she get things done while the kids are home? It's like they just magically remember how to play independently when she's here. But when she's not here, chaos erupts.

I take several deep breaths to keep from exploding as I sweep Enzo's hair off the ground. Apparently, Izzy and Moxie thought it would be fun to play hairdresser. By the time I noticed, Enzo's new chop job was already complete. I'm just glad I came in time to save Abel from a similar fate.

"Sorry, Daddy." Izzy hangs her head as she apologizes for the fourth time.

"It's okay," I grind out.

How on earth am I going to survive a month of this? I think if this long, torturous week without her has taught me anything, it's how right I was about never wanting to be without her.

"Hey, Daddy," Moxie whispers from the doorway to her bedroom. "Abel flushed your phone down the toilet."

I slowly turn to face her. "What?"

"But it wouldn't go down, so I took it out, and we threw it away. It looks really yucky and wet now."

I drop the broom and follow her downstairs to the trash can in the kitchen. "Show me."

She opens the trash can under the cupboard and takes out a soaking electronic device that is definitely my phone.

I cringe and take it from her. It doesn't turn on. "Wonderful," I mutter. "This is just great. You know that, Mox?"

She shrugs, clearly unsure how to answer me.

The doorbell rings. Once. Twice. Three times.

With a deep sigh, I go to answer it. And the last person in the world I expect to see is standing on my doorstep.

"Hey, little brother," says Rebecca.

❀

It's not until she has a mug of tea in hand, sitting on the couch with Abel huddled next to her, that I get it out of her.

"Will you please tell me what you're doing here?" I ask for the third time.

"Can't a girl visit her brother without being questioned? Sheesh." Rebecca flips her black, straight hair behind her shoulder.

It's weird to see her. Weird is the only way to describe it. I still think of her as a child sometimes, probably because I saw her in spurts growing up instead of every day. But the fact that she's wearing eyeliner and is touching her lower stomach with her wedding-ringed finger is tripping me out.

"You never visit." I fold my arms. "And I'm gathering you didn't come to see the kids, since the last time you paid them a visit was the day they were born."

She rolls her eyes. "Don't be so dramatic."

"Why are you here, Rebecca?"

She sets her mug on the coffee table. Around us, the kids are jumping on the furniture, laughing and yelling, acting completely wild. I know it's mean, but I kinda hope it makes her afraid of her future.

"Dad called me the other day," she says. "Told me you don't want this house anymore and that it's all mine. I didn't believe him, so I figured I'd come hear it for myself."

"Seriously? That's why you're here? You could have just called." There's a bite to my tone I don't try to hide. If she came to rub this in my face like some sort of self-earned victory, she can just walk her snooty self out of here right now. It may be her house soon, but right now, it's still mine.

Rebecca shakes her head, frowning. "I don't get it. Why don't you want to live here anymore? Is there black mold in the walls or something? Because that would be dangerous to me and my baby, and also really messed up if you know something and refuse to fill me in."

"There's no black mold." It's so hard not to sound defeated as I continue. "And I do want to live here. Of course I do. I just wasn't about to force my fiancée to do something she didn't want to in order to keep this house."

She looks confused, so I quickly explain the situation with Addison and the pageant, skipping over any unnecessary details.

"Honestly, Periwinkle," another hair flip, "this never would have happened to you if you'd just listened to Dad and married Jill before you got yourself into this mess." Her haughty tone is one I'm used to, but it still ignites the same anger in me that it always has.

"You're the last person I want advice from. I think it's time for you to go."

She looks unimpressed. "You're forgetting I'm older than you. I don't have to listen to you."

That does it. All the anger and frustration inside me finally boils over. I stand up, raising my voice to a shout that hasn't happened in months. "Just shut up, okay? You already have it all, the house, Dad's approval, your *mom*. So just leave me with what little I have left and go! Leave, Rebecca!"

She stares up at me from the couch, mouth partly open in shock. I feel like a ticking time bomb as I glare down at her, chest heaving with the effort not to explode again.

"I—I didn't know you felt that way," she finally says in a hushed tone. "Dad's approval? Perry . . . you're the one who's his favorite."

I stare at her like she just spoke a different language. "You're joking, right?" I collapse into the seat behind me. *This will be good.*

"He obviously loves you more," she says. "I mean, he definitely loved your mother more. And it wasn't just because Marina was so beautiful. She was *perfect* for him."

Hearing her talk about my mom is suddenly too much. Tears start to cloud my eyes. Because it's one thing to cherish the delicate, breakable memories of a loved one you can hardly remember. It's another to have someone who knew that person confirm you were right. You didn't imagine any of it. The memories were real.

Rebecca reaches into her designer purse and hands me a tissue. "Here. Pregnancy hormones mean I cry all the time now. I have plenty of tissues on hand."

I take the tissue and swipe at my eyes. "Dad does not love me more." I mostly say it so she'll keep talking and take the attention off me.

"Yes, he does. That's why he gave you his restaurant business and let you live in this mansion. It would have been fair of him to give me one of those things, the business or the house. But nope. He wanted you to have both."

"They put it in my mom's will that I'd have to get married to get the house."

She rolls her eyes. "Oh, come on. The fact that you were the first option to have it meant he wanted you to inherit it more than me. It was the only thing I asked for, but still he gave you first dibs."

I exhale harshly. "This is the house I grew up in, Rebecca. It's sentimental for me. You have hardly any memories growing up here."

She makes a face. "Yeah, that's true. But it's not like it's easy to buy a house nowadays. Everything is expensive.

Not all of us have five-star restaurants to make us a ton of money."

"Oh, come on." I shake my head. "Dad would help you buy any old house. Don't give me that."

"Any old house. Not a mansion like this, though. He'd only do that for you."

I sigh. "Not true. This house is all yours now, remember?" I dab my eyes a few more times as she sits, watching me.

"Look," she continues. "For the longest time, I couldn't figure out why you hate me so much. But I think I finally get it now."

"You know how much the house matters to me. It's got my mom in every single corner, and it's been a home to my kids since they were born."

She nods. "I get that now. Which is why I'm giving it back to you, Periwinkle."

My head snaps up. "What?"

"All this time, I thought you just wanted to prove something. Wanted to prove what I already knew. That dad loves you more than he loves me. But it's deeper than that. This is about Marina for you, and she was a wonderful woman. You're lucky she was your mom."

"Rebecca, you're lucky to still have your mom."

"I know." She nods. "And if it's okay with you, moving forward, I'd like us to be closer. You know, in exchange for the house. I want to be a better big sister."

I'm at a complete loss for words. "You can't just give me the house, can you? Doesn't it automatically go to you if I'm not married?"

"If I want it. But if I don't, it goes to you whether you're married or not. Haven't you read the will?"

"Not in a while."

"Well, there you have it. You're the only sibling I've got. I want us to be close."

The angry knot in my gut untangles itself. Somehow, her words undo it all—the resentment, the hatred, the vengeance. All that's left inside me now is sadness and a little curiosity to see what could happen if I did give her a chance. If I forgave her.

"I'd like that," I finally murmur. "And I'm sorry about everything."

She gets up from the couch to hug me. And for the first time in my adult years, I hug her right back.

After Rebecca leaves, I ponder what to do next. I want to tell Addison the good news, that by the very grace of God, we get the house. We get the pageant. We get each other.

I know it will make her happy. It will ease the worries I've seen in her eyes when she talks about me holding the loss against her. There's a part of me that's worried showing up to see her would be a distraction she can't afford. But then again . . .

Maybe if she knew, it would help her focus on the pageant better.

Thanks to Abel, my phone isn't working anymore, so I can't call or text her. It's Sunday. She's moving into the inn tomorrow. I'm pretty sure it's her last free day, and that once preliminaries start, I won't be able to contact her until the pageant is over.

In a rush, I head to the office and e-mail Kiera from my laptop.

Kiera,

I need to see Addison. Please, please, will you come along to help me manage the kids? I'd bring them alone, but I don't want to get her in trouble. They tend to attract attention and I know they'd love to see her, so I don't want to leave them behind.

Regards,

Perry

Just like I knew she would, she responds immediately. I can practically hear the amusement in her response.

Mr. Whitmore,

Of course. I only ask that you hire a replacement nanny soon. I suspect you'll be needing the help with her gone, and I'm not sure I'm a great fit for the task. See you in the morning.

Best,

Kiera

Chapter Thirty-Two

ADDISON

PERRY DOESN'T ANSWER any of my calls or texts. I spend all morning sending him messages so long they take up multiple text bubbles, but I'm met with nothing but silence. As devastating as it is, I know I deserve it. After making such a big stink about needing no distractions, Perry has probably muted all incoming messages from me.

My spirits are low when I move into The Orchard Inn on Monday. It's a quaint, charming hotel run and owned by Mr. and Mrs. Gutierrez. I don't have a roommate this time, so there must be an odd number of candidates. Last year, my roommate was Romilly. I remember how grateful I was, too, because it was my first time competing without Gran, and Rom quite literally kept me from falling into a deep depression and dropping out.

I roll my suitcases into the well-decorated space. There's a full-size bed with a hand-painted nature-scape hanging in a frame on the wall above that reminds me of the spas Gran and I used to frequent. A comfy chair rests in the corner of the bright room, right next to a window with a breathtaking view of Gull Pond. A plush, pink rug sits beneath the bed frame, so soft it makes me want to rub my bare feet against it, and against the wall that leads to the closet there's a wooden dresser.

I take a deep breath and set down my bags. As I unpack, my mind is filled with thoughts of Perry. I miss him so much, it's like a physical ache in my chest. I try to push the thoughts away and focus on the task at hand. I have to finally finish my speech and I can't do that if I'm moping around, regretting my choice to come here every minute.

I pull out my notebook and start going over what I've written so far. I've already memorized most of it, but I want to make sure it's perfect, and it feels like something is missing.

After a few minutes, there's a knock on my door. When I get up and open it, I'm surprised to see a tall girl with a brown bob and an adorable spray of freckles across her milky brown face standing there.

She blinks a few times in confusion and then smiles. "Hey. I'm so sorry. I thought this was my room, but it's obviously not. Sorry."

I expect to feel a flash of annoyance, but she looks so sweet and lost that I can't help but forget my stupid speech for a minute. "No problem. What's your room number? I'll point you in the right direction."

Her lips part into a surprised smile. "Oh, sweet, thank you. I'm number sixteen B."

"That's just down this hall, around the corner." I point

her in the right direction. "My name's Addison. Come find me if you need any help."

"Thank you so much. I'm Paige. This is my first time competing." She lingers a little awkwardly, staring at her shuffling feet. "To be honest, pageants aren't really my thing. I'm a ballet dancer, and there's this cause I really want to raise money for, so I figured why not?"

She somehow looks so hopeful, but also so nervous and scared at the same time. I don't have it in me to tell her this probably isn't the best way to win money if she's never done a pageant before. So, I nod and say, "You got this, Paige. Good luck."

"Thanks." She grins at me before continuing down the hall where I showed her.

I shut the door to my room and wander to the other end to look out the window. I can see Gull Pond sprawling out beyond this building in a beautiful, glittering sheet of water. I want nothing more than to sit out on the dock and collect my thoughts, but the welcome breakfast will be starting any minute.

I change into a white sundress and add a denim jacket in case there's a cool breeze later. Then I head down the hall to find a table. Since Romilly was last year's winner, she'll be giving a speech at breakfast today. My stomach is filled with excitement, knowing I'll get to see her, but also dread because for the first time since we were eighteen, she isn't staying to compete.

First, I'll have to compete without Gran, and now her. It's going to be hard not to rip her from that podium and squeeze her into a hug so I can cry all over her shoulders.

I find a table near the front of the raised platform where the mic is waiting. A few other girls are starting to filter in, and I recognize most of them from last year. Normally I'd be excited to catch up and hear about their summers. I'd be eagerly waiting by the buffet trays, excited to fill my plate with eggs and sausage. I'd want to scope everyone out so I could mentally prepare for the competition. But none of this feels right.

I don't want to be here.

I want to be making Izzy's special breakfast just the way she likes it. I want to be brushing Moxie's hair into the princess twist that makes her smile every time. I want to help Abel find the socks that don't make his toes uncomfortable, so he has a good time at preschool. I want to tell Enzo the story about the prince who befriends the dragon because it really isn't very scary at all.

I want Perry.

All of him.

Every day.

Everything I've planned for, my *dream*, all of this feels completely meaningless without them.

I made a huge mistake, leaving them a week earlier than I had to. I should have been soaking them all in. Filling my time with them instead of thinking of them as distractions.

Tears spring to my eyes as my mind whirls like a chaotic black hole of regret. I cover my face with my hands. With every passing second, I debate whether to get up from this table and leave the inn altogether. I could leave right now. I could simply withdraw and let all this go. Drive back home and forget this whole thing. Without Gran, I'm only fooling myself, thinking I can actually win.

There's a tap on the microphone. "Attention please. Ladies, find your seats." The director, Josephine Hayden, grins around the room at us with her perfect white veneers. Her red hair is a curly pile on top of her head, and her gray skirt suit looks like it was ironed this morning; not a wrinkle in sight.

A bubbling chatter fills the room as the mingling groups of contestants disperse to find seats. The three empty chairs at my table scrape on the wood floor as they're filled up. I glance out the corner of my eye and see Paige in one of them, a shy smile on her lips. She slides a plate of eggs with a Danish over to me. "I brought you this. I noticed you didn't make it to the buffet before the line got long."

I force a wobbly smile onto my own mouth. "Thank you, that's so sweet." With my thoughts in a scramble, I pick up my fork and shove a cluster of eggs in my mouth. Eating will probably help with my nerves. I nibble on the Danish, too. It has a smooth, yellow custard inside that makes my stomach rumble.

Josephine taps the mic again to get our attention. "Welcome ladies. Today marks the first day of preliminary events for the sixty-seventh annual Miss Meadow pageant. For those of you who don't know me, my name is Josephine Hayden and I'll be the director for the duration of the pageant."

A few murmurs sound from around the room. Josephine tells everyone what they can expect as far as the competition and goes into some of the ways the panel of judges assesses each phase.

To be honest, I'm hardly listening.

Because I've already made up my mind.

I'm done.

I see Gran everywhere at this inn. This place brings back so many memories I've had with her over the years, like a home video I've watched too many times. But still, this place isn't Gran. She's not here at all. Gran is in the moments baking bread at her house. In the fluffy dandelions dancing in the wind. She's the hymn book stuffed between my mattress at Perry's. She's moments like this one where I realize I've had it all wrong, all this time.

Instead of Josephine talking, I hear the words Gran once told me, "Pageants are wonderful, my dear. They give us a platform, an opportunity to make a difference. But let us never forget about those right in front of us. Those who we already make the biggest difference to. It's easy to forget that we're the whole world to those loved ones we see every day and sometimes take for granted." It's like she's sitting here in the room with me; her voice is so easy to recall. And it's the final straw for me.

I care about Perry and the kids more than winning. All this time, I've been trying to prove to myself I'm good enough, and I've been trying to make Gran proud. But I have a feeling that letting the family I love sacrifice their beloved home for me wouldn't make her proud at all.

To Gran, and to Perry and the kids, I'm already good enough.

I always have been.

I pick my purse up from the handle of my chair. I'm about to get up and head back to my room to collect my bags when Romilly takes the stage. It's impossible to miss the way she captures the attention of everyone in the room without even trying. Her breathtaking beauty, along with her gentle but commanding demeanor, makes her the most perfect Miss Meadow, as much as I hate to admit it.

There's a delicate, rose-gold crown resting on top of her head. Her long, black hair is curled into waves that cascade down her back, and the plunge-neck gown she's wearing is made of silver beads that reflect the light every time she moves.

"Hello, everyone," she chirps into the mic. "My name is Romilly Westfall, last year's winner of the Miss Meadow pageant. It's my pleasure to pass the crown this year to one of you lovely ladies."

Romilly has given this speech several times now. I've heard it before, so I don't feel as bad for excusing myself down the hall to call Perry. I don't say a word as I slip out of my chair. If anyone asks where I'm going, I'll just tell them I need to use the restroom. But no one pays attention to me as I leave, not with Romilly front and center.

My heart is still racing in my chest, especially as I tap his contact photo.

The call goes straight to voicemail.

No, no, no.

My organs tie themselves in knots as I realize what's happening.

He's upset. He's mad that I called him a distraction and now he's ignoring me, and I totally deserve it.

I swallow back the devastation. *God. This is awful.*

But then a text comes through from Perry, and with shaky hands, I read it.

PERRY

Meet me outside, by the lake.

What? He's here? When? How?

My heart races in my chest. It feels difficult to breathe. *Don't get your hopes up, Addison. He probably took the kids to play by a different lake and meant to send that to Kiera, or something.*

I try not to trip on my dress as I speed-walk down the carpeted hall to the French doors at the back end of the inn that leads to Gull Pond.

And then my tongue starts swelling up.

I stop walking to catch my breath, coughing a few times.

Oh, no. What was in that Danish? Was there . . . pineapple in it?

Panic claws its way up my chest as I realize I never even checked. The room starts spinning around me. I think I might faint. This is one of those rare times I wish I listened to my mother and carried my EpiPen everywhere, no matter how ridiculous and unlikely it's seemed that I'd need it.

I need to get outside.

The ornately framed photos on the beige walls fly by as if I'm running, though I'm not. A maintenance worker glances at me curiously as I burst through the French doors, but I ignore him. My gaze darts around, searching desperately for Perry. I don't see him anywhere, but there's a small group of people walking by the dock near the bottom, so I make my way toward them. With every passing second, it's getting harder and harder to breathe. My tongue feels like it's the size of my arm.

"Helphhh!" I wave my arms in the air. No one hears me.

Black spots take over my vision. This is it. I'm going to die right here, without anyone knowing. I sit on the ground because my head swirls at a dangerous speed.

I take out my phone and send Perry a shaky, desperate text.

ME

I'm outside

Need EpiPen

Ate pineapple

Help

"Hey, you all right over there?" A girl calls from the dock.

I shake my head back and forth, motioning that I can't breathe by holding my throat with both hands. My breathing is loud and wheezy, desperate at this point. Tears spring to my eyes because now I'm really scared. This hasn't happened since I was in middle school and I forgot how terrifying it is, especially with no one else around who knows what's going on.

"Somebody call an ambulance! This girl is choking!"

I try to correct her, but it's impossible to speak when I can't even breathe. Can't even see anymore. My heart feels heavy and sluggish in my chest.

There are voices crowding around me. I can't make any of them out, but something sharp jams into my thigh, right through my dress. And it finally, finally becomes a little bit easier to breathe.

"Give her space. Back up."

The voice that's talking is familiar. I try to open my eyes, but the sun is so bright. Someone is making a really annoying sound over and over.

"Please," the voice whispers. "Wake up, Addison. *Breathe.*"

Some of the fogginess in my head clears. "Perry?" It doesn't sound like his name as it comes out. It sounds more like Pelly because of my swollen tongue.

"Shh. I'm here. It's me. Please be okay, bunny." He brushes my hair away from my face. It takes me a moment to realize I'm lying on the ground and he's cradling me. My vision clears, and I see a bunch of random strangers peering at me from over Perry's shoulders. They all look so concerned. That annoying noise I'm hearing gets clearer, and with a start, I realize it's my own wheezy breathing.

I sit up and vomit all over the front of my white dress. Everyone backs away, except Perry, and I hear a few gasps. I whimper. Perry shushes me and rubs my back. "It's all right. It's going to be fine. There's an ambulance on the way, okay?" The rest of the crowd disperses until it's just the two of us.

I lie back down and blink through the sunlight to look up at him. The sight of his familiar silhouette sends a jolt through me—of warmth, of longing, of sadness.

I swallow hard and take a deep breath. "Perry?" His name finally sounds normal coming out.

When our gazes connect, I feel it in my bones. I want to reach out and touch his face, but I feel too weak. "I've been trying to text you." I don't know why this is the first thing I say.

"Yeah. Sorry about that. Abel tried to flush my phone down the toilet, and it was all water damaged. I just got it replaced this morning."

Some of the tension in my stomach eases. *He wasn't mad at you.*

"I made a mistake." I take a deep breath. "I shouldn't have come. None of this means anything to me without you. You're not the distraction. *This* is."

I sit back up, feeling like my chest is wrapped in a vise grip. It's just now hitting me that I almost died of anaphylactic shock. I would have, if he hadn't been here.

Perry must sense that I'm struggling to remain calm because his arms come up to hug me, vomit and all. He rubs my back as I sob into his chest. "Shh, bunny, it's okay," he whispers into my hair.

"I...I almost died."

"Stop. I would never let that happen. That's why I carry an EpiPen everywhere, remember? Everything's going to be okay."

I lift my head from his chest. Perry's brows are knitted together in concern as he looks as me. He offers me a small smile. "Addison. Listen."

"Wait a minute. You're here. Why are you here?"

"Before you get mad—"

"You showed up here to tell me something important, didn't you?" My lips part. "Something bad happened, didn't it?"

"No." A giant grin appears on his face. "It's good news,

actually. But it can wait until you've been seen by a doctor."

"No. Please, just tell me now. I feel completely fine, I promise."

"I just feel like this is terrible timing."

"Please, Perry." I give him a puppy dog face I know he can't resist.

He sighs. "Well, this was supposed to be a romantic moment. I had it all planned out." He drapes his arm over my shoulder and spins us so we're facing the inn. "You were going to come out that door," he murmurs softly into my ear, "and I was going to be waiting over there for you." He points at the dock by the lake. "I was going to tell you my sister and I made amends, and that she wants me to keep the house."

I gasp. "Are you serious? Because this better not be a joke."

He presses his forehead to mine. "It's not a joke, I swear. That's why I came all the way here. To tell you that, and because I realized I still haven't had a chance to propose to you the way I wanted to."

"W-What?" My jaw wobbles as I struggle to think of a response.

And then he gets down on one knee.

Perry steadies himself with a deep breath and takes something out of his pocket. He holds out a single, white dandelion. "You once told me that you used to wish on these things with no luck. That our summer together was nothing more than wishes that couldn't come true." His throat bobs as he swallows hard. "Well, I refuse to believe that. According to your Gran, wishes might not come true, but prayers can, if your heart is right and you have faith. I've never blown out one of these things before, but I've also never wanted anything so badly until now. There's nothing I've prayed for harder than for you to marry me."

Perry pauses to gesture behind him, and from behind the topiary bushes lining the steps leading back to the inn, four little bodies walk out.

Izzy. Moxie. Enzo. Abel.

All four kids walk over to us, each holding a dandelion.

My chest heaves as I struggle not to cry. A little whimper comes out anyway.

Together, all five of them blow them out their dandelions. The fluffy, white dander flies into the air all around us.

Perry takes my shaky hands in his. "There's nothing all of us wish for more than for you to be my wife. I love you so much, and they love you, too. Please, say yes. Make our one and only wish—our prayer—come true."

The tears slide down my face. I nod so fast. "Yes. Of course." I'm in his arms within seconds, sprinkling kisses across his entire face. The sound of the approaching ambulance in the distance mixes with the kids' squeals and laughter. Their happy sounds penetrate me, making me feel so light inside, I could probably fly away with the flower dander if I wanted to.

"How on earth did you plan this?" I laugh in disbelief, gesturing to the kids.

Kiera comes out from behind a tree and smiles at me. "So glad you're okay, Addison."

My jaw drops. "Kiera is here, too?"

Perry nods. "She was here the whole time you were struggling to breathe."

"When I realized Perry was still going to propose, I went ahead with the plan and hid the kids, since it seemed like you hadn't noticed them yet," she tells me quietly.

I laugh. "Unbelievable."

The ambulance stops next to us, and the EMTs come pouring out, asking me questions, and offering me an oxygen mask.

But I'm grinning like a fool, gripping Perry's dandelion stem as I answer all the questions.

I get to keep them. Perry. Izzy. Moxie. Enzo. Abel.

For once, after all these years, it finally happened.

One of my dreams finally came true. And this one is the best of all.

Epilogue

ONE YEAR LATER

PERRY

I FIND Addison in the office when I come home from taking the kids to school. She's intently writing something, so I spin her chair around, just to watch her get all flustered with me.

"Perry!" Pink dots appear on her cheeks. "What the—"

I capture her mouth with mine to stop her from finishing her sentence. "Come back to bed with me. It's early."

Her mouth twitches with the effort not to smile. "This needs to get done. The wedding celebration is in less than a month."

I pick her up, ignoring her squeals. "Perfect. We have plenty of time."

Before she can start reasoning with me, I take her to our room and gently lay her on the bed.

"We're never going to get anything done if this keeps happening."

"Then I guess we're never going to get anything done, bunny. Get used to it. You're my wife now, which means I'm allowed to never take my hands off you." I kiss my way up her neck. "Or my mouth."

Her breathing gets more intense as I kiss slowly down her neck. She's wearing nothing but one of my oversized T-shirts, my new kryptonite as far as I'm concerned.

She giggles as my lips find the ticklish spot beneath her ear.

"Still want to get things done?"

She doesn't answer, so I continue, transferring my kisses to her mouth until her back arches off the bed.

I cradle her face in my arms. "I love you."

She starts to say it back, but I cut her off with another kiss.

Addison's next question comes quietly. "Do you ever want more kids?"

My entire body stiffens. "What?"

"I know you already have four, but would you ever want to have more?"

My first instinct is to tell her no. I don't want to make her a mom, and then have her hate it like Jill did. I don't want her to resent me someday for ruining her life, for changing it in ways she can never reverse.

And then I remember who I'm talking to.

She's nothing like Jill.

She's the most loving, caring, involved mom to my kids. She does it all with patience and enthusiasm. There's no way she'd ever resent being a mother to a child of ours.

"I would with you." Her gaze is imploring, her wild, fluffy curls half covering her face. "Why? Do you want a baby, Addison?"

She bites her lip. "Kind of. Maybe. I never considered it before, with the pageant and everything. But now that that's over and we're married . . . it sounds kind of nice."

I kiss her soft lips. "We can make a baby. I have no problem with that. We can start right now, in fact." I kiss my way down her stomach as she laughs, kicking and squirming at the places my mouth is tickling her.

"I have to finish what I was working on, first. So maybe after that."

"Fine." With a deep groan, I let her up from under me. Apparently, she's not going to be easily distracted by me this time. "Hop away, little bunny."

ADDISON

Sitting down to address these wedding invitations feels surreal. Part of me feels silly since Perry and I are technically already married. As soon as the pageant ended, we took off with the kids to the nearest chapel and made it official. Neither of us could wait any longer, even though our wedding wasn't for another six months. I'll never forget the way he looked at me as he slid the ring on my finger, and the way the kids hugged us after the ceremony made me feel more whole than ever before.

Kiera agreed to babysit for us that night, making us promise to hire a new nanny for those random times Perry and I wanted to be alone together. We've since taken her advice, and even though I love being the one to take care of the kids, it's nice to have alone time with Perry.

Like our wedding night. The, uh, *first* one.

After dropping the kids off with Kiera, we headed to the cozy lakeside bed-and-breakfast we'd be spending the next two days in. Drunk on happiness, the two of us remained entwined and kissing, pausing only to get into the room. Perry's tongue caressed mine as we moved toward the bed. The curtains were open inside our room, revealing the lake and the moon's reflection illuminated on the surface.

We both knew what would come next—this moment we'd been waiting so long for—so there was no need for words as Perry removed my clothes slowly, savoring every inch of my skin revealed to him. I did the same for him, marveling at how strong and beautiful he was in every way. My skin tingled with anticipation as his mouth found its way to mine again.

We melted into each other, our thighs hugging and even our toes connecting. My hands mapped out a journey along his frame, exploring everywhere new to me and savoring every moment. I was floating in the warmth and love emanating from him.

Perry's touch sent shivers down my spine as he caressed the curves of my body in just the right way. Every inch of me ached for more of his touch—more of him.

And as promised, it was very much worth the wait.

We stayed locked in embrace for what felt like hours, basking in the afterglow of our lovemaking as newlyweds. He smiled back before pulling me close and pressing a gentle kiss to my forehead. "I love you, Mrs. Whitmore," he murmured against my skin, sending a thrill through me all over again. I'm pretty sure we spent the entire two days in that bed together, because just once wasn't enough for either of us.

"That's Miss Meadow to you," I whispered back. I giggled at the way it sounded, remembering how much I missed him during the pageant. Spending the days with the other girls, talking about pageant stuff, and getting through each phase. I tried not to get too excited as I passed the first three—the evening gown, the swimsuit, and activewear.

Then it was time for the personal interview.

I shuddered as I made my way onto the stage. Sitting next to Asher on that red, leather loveseat as he held the mic out to me, I tried to think of all my notes. I tried to conjure up every line I memorized as he asked, "If you win, which cause will you be supporting and why is it important to you?"

And then I remembered Gran. Her words. Her urging me not to speak from memory, but rather, from within. I remembered what she said about having faith instead of trying to control everything myself.

So I took a deep breath, decided to trust God with this, and said, "I will be supporting long-term care and housing for adults with special needs." A pause as the audience murmured. Then I continued, "You see, Asher, this is a cause very close to my heart. It's affected my personal life. Growing up, I had to watch my parents sacrifice so much to care for my brother, Finn. They gave up friendships, time with their loved ones, including me, and time with each other. They used their savings to support my brother's quality of life. They had to live on one income, because no one could care for Finn, besides my mother." I took a shaky breath. "They even had to move states to find better care for my brother, leaving me behind. I wish things could have turned out differently for them here. I wish there was a place people could trust to care for their loved ones with any type of debilitating disability, all the way into adulthood, and that families who have to sacrifice working could afford to do so comfortably. I long for that to become the norm. But in order for that to happen, there needs to be more awareness and more funding."

I listened to myself as if from someone else's body, going on and on about the ways I wanted to support my cause and change things for the better. I had no idea if I sounded good or not, but at that moment, I didn't care. Because whether or not I won, I was doing what Gran would have wanted. I was speaking from the heart.

So, when, in the end, I was announced as the winner, and Romilly placed that crown on my head, I couldn't stop myself from sobbing. I thought of all those times Gran stood by my side, teaching and coaching me. Caring for me like the mother I deserved, the one I desperately needed as a young girl. I thought of all those dandelions we blew out together, from the very first one in her living room to the very last in the hospital, shaking grip and all. She stayed with me till the end. And now our wish, our dream, our prayer had finally come true.

Seeing Perry and the kids cheering for me in the audience was the part I didn't even know I needed. Having their support in a world where I felt mostly alone meant everything to me.

And now, as I address each wedding invitation to our friends, I know every struggle we went through was worth it. And for future struggles that come our way, I finally know the trick to getting those pesky dandelions to do their jobs.

In the famous words of Gran, "All it takes is a little faith."

Thank you for reading *A Summer of Dandelions*!

If you enjoyed this book, I hope you'll consider writing a small review. Each one helps indie authors like me so much.

Thank you from the bottom of my heart,
Whitney Amazeen

Acknowledgments

In a similar way that it takes a village to raise a child, it very much also takes a village to make a book come to life. I'd like to thank every member of my village.

God, always, first and foremost. Thank you, always and forever.

Michael, my husband—I literally could not write a single sentence without all your love, encouragement, and support. I'm so lucky to have a husband like you and after almost nine years, I still can't believe I get to keep you.

Mommy—Thank you for being my brain dump in the plotting phase of every one of my novels, including this one. You always help me work out the kinks, and make me so excited to start writing. Everyone needs a *you* in their life.

Haley Poezyn—thank you for answering all my endless, ridiculous questions about pageants, real estate, and SO much more. Thank you for the "Plot Talks" on the treadmill at the gym, the hyping up all my goals, and the ideas I never could have come up with on my own. I appreciate you letting me have a little slice of your genius mind every time we talk, and I love you so very much.

Cait-Elise—I never would have guessed that having you as a beta reader would turn into what it has: you being such an in-depth critique partner, a constant (virtual) shoulder to lean on, and a true friend. I'm so glad our paths crossed, and I can't wait to see the wonderful things you are destined to accomplish!

Ashley Seals—Thank you for always having your ears open to my nonsense, offering your amazing advice, and letting me unintentionally repeat myself while maintaining patience, and for all your love and encouragement. You've been here with me since the start, and I'm so grateful. I love you.

Thanks to my cover designer, Leni Kauffman, for bringing the characters in my head to life through your amazing talent and artistic ability. It's such an honor to work with you.

Thank you to my editor, Dr. Nicole Morin, and my lovely beta readers: Chelsea Higley, Nadia Sakkal, and the previously mentioned Cait-Elise, for helping this book become the best it can be.

Avid Readers of Christian Fiction group on Facebook, and also the Moms Who Write group. You all are my favorite, and such a supportive, uplifting, and helpful corner of the internet.

Thanks to my dad for teaching me the most important words I'll ever read, and to Arlee for helping me shape this book into what it needed to be.

Thanks to my siblings, Zach, Elijah, and Taylor, as usual, for always being so supportive and also for letting me tease you mercilessly. (And also my bonus siblings, Jordyn, Nikita, Kyle, Ember, and Matt).

My grandma Kathy, AKA Lala—You inspired so much

of this story. I wish you were still here to read it and I miss you so much.

Thank you to all my family and sweet, supportive friends in every season of life. I'm so grateful to have you all.

Awa—Thank you for teaching me about the amazing pageant women in our family.

And finally, you, dearest reader. More than anyone else, this story is for you, and I'm so grateful you took a chance on it. It means more to me than I'm capable of putting into words that you chose my little book to invest your time in. *Thank you.* I love you.

Keep in Touch with
Whitney Amazeen

Get all my book news, sneak peeks, bonus content, and
more exciting stuff by signing up for my newsletter at

WHITNEYAMAZEEN.COM/NEWSLETTER

About the Author

Whitney Amazeen writes cute, cozy love stories with a sprinkle of faith.

Her love for books grew into an obsession in third grade and has been going strong ever since. Before pursuing writing, she studied cosmetology, where she used to hide in the laundry room to read, and work on stories instead of clients.

When she's not writing, Whitney can often be found playing Sims, snuggling with her dogs, and obsessing over Jesus.

Whitney is a California native who now lives in Arizona with her family and expansive tea collection.

Please visit WhitneyAmazeen.com and find her on social media @WhitneyAmazeen!